BEDDING
rose

ANN

USA TODAY BESTSELLING AUTHOR

DENTON

Cover by *Book Brander Boutique*

Le Rue
Publishing

Le Rue Publishing
320 South Boston Avenue, Suite 1030
Tulsa, OK 74103
www.LeRuePublishing.com
ISBN: 978-1-951714-37-6

To you.

May you find someone who makes you feel seen.

AUTHOR'S NOTE

This book contains a dark, forbidden romance between a woman and her brother's best friend. It has some scenes that may make some readers uncomfortable. The following items appear in this book: violence, cutting, off-page rape, stalking, blackmail, sexual exhibitionism, explicit sex and language, and other content that may be triggering. There is no cheating or other woman drama in this book.

ANGELO

Two Weeks Ago

"Die, motherfucker! WHY. WON'T. YOU. DIEEEEE?!"

I glance over at my raging best friend in utter amusement. Enrique's cheeks are mottled red, his dark brows pulled down, arms flexing as he futilely swings his game controller and smashes the buttons harder, as if physical brutality is going to help him. He bites his lower lip as he perches on the edge of the couch and glares in frustration at the TV, and I can't help but turn and laugh in his face as I lean back against the cushions, nonchalantly holding my own controller—rubbing it in, just because I can. He is the brother I never had, in all ways—we love to one up each other.

"If you wanna kill me, you're gonna have to try harder than that." I release the cheat code buttons I've been holding down. Thank you, internet, for making me the *Call of Duty* king for the night.

Beer pong with Enrique Dalton—Quique to his family and to me—has transitioned into a marathon gaming session, the perfect release after a grueling week at work. I had no clue how much I needed to blow off steam with my boy until I got here, but I'm feeling more relaxed than I have in a long time. Now that I'm back home and doing the above-board work for my dad instead of all the things he had me do to prove my worth, the workdays can fill up and feel like wash, rinse, repeat. Build site after build site. Negotiation after negotiation. Subcontractor ass-chewing all day long. Blech.

But this? Pseudo-fucking-bloodshed, instead of the real thing, and yelling like maniacs? I feel like a kid again. This shit is fun.

"Suck on this!" I tell Quique, thumbs flying over my controller as I pummel his ass with bullets. I grin in smug satisfaction as I watch his avatar flop down and disappear.

"Dude! Unfair." Enrique slouches back on the leather couch in his living room before sulkily sinking his hand into a bag of barbecue potato chips on the seat between us.

"Unfair? You're such a noob! That was practically suicide on your part!" I quip as I toss my controller onto the coffee table and grab my bottle of beer. I swill down the rest, the bitter bubbles popping along my tongue and warming my throat.

"Motherfucker. Rematch?" Never one to hold a grudge—unlike me—Quique gives an easy grin as he ruffles his dark curls—he's always messing with them.

"Sure. Yeah. Let me hit the head first and re-up the beer." I toss my empty bottle up and catch it in the same hand as I stand and stroll around the couch into the adjacent kitchen area.

Quique's mom's place is one of those fancy, professionally-decorated houses where you don't really want to touch anything because it's all gray and white and shit. All uncomfortable and magazine-fake looking. Still—it's better than my apartment, which is roughly the size of a glue trap. I should upgrade, but I haven't found the motivation. When you spend all day building houses, all you see when you tour them are flaws.

Reaching underneath the marble counter tops, I yank open a cabinet door and slide out the hidden trash and recycling bins as I glance over at the clock above the stove. "Three a.m. and neither your mom or sister are home?" I ask.

"Not their keeper," he replies nonchalantly.

I sigh and shake my head. I can't be as casual about that shit as he can. I text my sister twice a day. And if my little sister looked like Rose … well, not my problem. I try to shake off the need to lecture Quique. He gets it enough from his mom for not following a "professional" career path. I toss my empty beer into the bin, listening to it clatter against the others we drank tonight.

"Touch my controller and I'll shank you!" I warn as I simultaneously shove the bin in and push the cabinet door closed with a thump.

"With what?" Quique calls out from the living room, which is glowing a dull blue in the light of the television. "You don't know how to make a shank, fool!"

"You don't know what I know!" I shout as I roam down the hallway, a grin stretching across my face. I'm joking, but I'm not. There are things about me Quique doesn't—and will never—know. But it feels good to be back home around someone who's only ever seen the good side of me, who doesn't side-eye me with suspicion or glance over their shoulder when they walk away. I'm glad I finally got the go-ahead from Dad to come back to Albuquerque.

Everything in life is almost perfect. Almost. There's one thing missing, but it's the kind of elusive thing that's hard to put a finger on. Just a discontent of sorts. It doesn't even make sense really, and it's definitely not something I have words for, so I shake off whatever bullshit is crowding into my head. Nope. I only have room in there for a piss and maybe enough to look up one more quick cheat code before I go back and shred Quique's self-esteem like pork, slather it in barbecue sauce and insults, and eat it right in front of him.

I pass a bunch of photographs of Quique and his sister, Rose, as they grew up. Photos of their parents are conspicuously absent since the divorce. I've seen those photos a million times, but have never really looked at them. I don't bother now, already jonesing to kill him again. I reach the bathroom and grab the knob. It doesn't turn, but the latch isn't fully engaged, so I shove the door open instinctively, not really thinking. I get two steps inside before I realize there's someone on the ground by the toilet and stop short.

Moonlight filters in through a lace curtain, leaving pale blue speckles of light all around the room. Rose sits on the tile, bare legs splayed out in front of her. When did they get so long? I try to shake off the errant realization that Rose has grown up as my eyes trace over the curves of her figure. Instead, I focus on her face. Her head is leaning against the cabinets, black curls wild and untamed, cheekbones sharp and feminine, green eyes glassy.

When did she get home?

My thought disintegrates into worry when I notice her cheeks are streaked black with eyeliner from teardrops that are still falling. A green sequined dress that is way too short for her to be wearing is hiked up around her hips, an edge of lacy black underwear on display. The way those panties cling to her skin ... my gaze roves over them even as my brain tells me I should look anywhere else until I spot a flash of metal in her grip. All my attention comes to a dead halt when I realize she has a razor blade in her hands and the beaded line of red on her thigh.

All the air leaves the room.

My heart stops beating—blood ceases to flow and my legs go numb with shock for a split second.

No.

Not Rose. Soft, sweet, shy Rose.

I force myself to shuffle forward and kneel on the tile in front of her, in the space between her feet and the tub. I'm uncertain what to expect, nerves spiking as my eyes flit over her pale face. The slight thrum of her pulse in her neck tells me she's here ... but her eyes, they're so far gone.

I glance down and swallow hard. There might only be a single red line on her body, but by her expression, I know her very soul is bleeding all over that bathroom floor. And somehow, that knowledge breaks me.

Fuck.

I can't breathe as I reach out and carefully pluck the razor from between her fingertips. As if it's a snake about to bite, I toss it away into the sink behind her before leaning down and cupping her face in my hands. Her skin is cold and clammy and so, so soft. But even my touch doesn't rouse her.

What could have hurt her so badly that this ... this was her outlet?

"Lil reina? What happened?" I use the nickname Quique and I used to tease her with, hoping it will draw her out. When she was fifteen, she used to screech like a banshee and throw pillows at us whenever we used it.

Her lips part and I hold my breath, waiting for her answer— for her to tell me how things have gotten so derailed. How the fuck the universe could let an innocent like her get trampled underfoot.

When she doesn't speak, I decide to give her time. Maybe she's in shock or something. I can't just stand and stare at her. I have to do something. Fix this. Make it better. The need grows in me and it's just as potent as hunger or exhaustion, a physical craving that can't be denied.

I retrieve a clean hand towel, surprised to find my fingers steady when my insides feel so jittery. I stand up, turn on the faucet, and let the water grow warm. Memories poke and prod at me: Rose peering around the corner of Quique's bedroom door. The way she'd grow silent and blush when she saw me. How she used to kick her brother under the table whenever he teased her for being a nerd. Fond memories, but now they cause an ache as I soak a corner of the towel. After I turn the faucet off and kneel in front of Rose, she finally makes eye contact.

Her expression is dull, so dull. It's like a vivid painting that's been toned down to pastels and I absolutely hate seeing her that way; she's not supposed to look like that. I've seen her real smile. I've seen her annoyed face when Quique and I push her too far and piss her off. I've seen her fight to stay mad when Quique cracks one of his goddamned jokes, lowering her temper to a reluctant simmer.

God—I wish I was in one of those moments right now. But I'm not. I'm here.

I'm here and she needs me. That realization makes something inside of me click, and all the discomfort I'm feeling fades, concentration taking over. She needs me and so I'll help.

"It's okay. I'm going to clean it up a little. Alright?" I don't know what the fuck I'm doing right now. I sound like a horse whisperer, but I'm just so worried about spooking Rose. She looks so delicate right now that a wrong word could snap her.

Crouched down, I lean forward and touch the rag to her cut, trying to dab, not wipe—to make my huge mitts for hands work for me instead of against me. I can't help but notice how dark my skin looks against her pale flesh, and I try to keep the rag between my calloused palms and her dainty skin so that my roughness doesn't scratch her. Of course, my hands are too big, and the side of my hand glides over her smooth thighs, but I focus on that red line and nothing else. Luckily, the cut doesn't appear too deep, though I can hear Rose sucking air in through her teeth as I work.

"Angelo, what the fuck?" Quique's voice comes from down the hall, playful and slightly drunk—his reality a million miles away from the one I just stumbled into here.

Rose gives a startled little gasp when she hears her brother and her eyes spark with the first real glimmer of emotion I've seen since I've walked in here. Fear contorts her brow and makes her teeth come out to worry her lower lip. "Please—"

she looks up at me, an entreating expression making her brow rise.

Whatever is going on, she doesn't want her brother to know.

Guilt and conflict swirl within me because if this was Tatiana, I'd want to know. But Quique and his family have always been different than my family, with my mother who hovered over us with all the love and protection of a mother hen and a father who provided.

In his family, each person has to fend for themselves. Maybe that's why he's never watched over Rose the way I do my sister. I've had to step in a few times over the years. But he's her brother. Maybe I should make him step up.

Why does the thought of handing her off to him make my heart thunder? I stand and turn to the sink on autopilot, running hot water over the rag, watching the pink evidence of Rose's pain swirl down the bowl. What do I do? I blink, staring at my face in the mirror, at the scar on my chin and I don't recognize the expression on my own face.

"Angelo—" Rose's voice interrupts my thoughts but she cuts herself off. Her broken tone has the intended effect, however. It sends a pang straight through my chest, setting off a chain reaction. It's as if there's a light bulb inside my skull and her panic tugs on the string, clicking it off—making me go dark. Reason snaps off and the only thing left is this burgeoning need to take care of her and erase whatever left her wilted on the ground.

I wring out the rag and toss it over the edge of the sink. Drying my hands roughly on my jeans, I reach out and touch her tiny shoulder, cupping it to reassure her as I tilt my head to the side and yell to her brother, "Start a one-player!"

"Really?" Quique's tone is skeptical.

"Really! I'm gonna be awhile."

She stares up at me, and I see colors in her eyes I've never seen before. Little gray flecks swam among the green stripes … if the entirety of space was green, it would look like a series of tiny universes floating in her eyes.

When we hear the sound of gunfire coming from the living room indicating that Quique's started up a new game, Rose finally relaxes underneath my grip. Something about her melting under my touch stirs up a tingling sensation in my chest.

I clear my throat. "I need to clean it out with alcohol next."

"No, it's fine—"

My tone comes out harsher than I intend, strained from the tension that's built in the air between us, when I say, "Sit on the toilet, Rose. I'm cleaning it."

She blinks up at me for a second, those thick, curled eyelashes of hers clumped together from crying. I'm struck by how intense her gaze is before I reach down, grabbing her waist to help her up to perch her ass on the closed toilet seat.

"I can—"

"Don't." I cut her off and give her my back as I yank open a drawer and paw through it, looking for disinfectant.

"Cabinet on the right," her voice comes out wobbly and a little froggy.

Heart thumping rapidly, I debate whether keeping this from Quique is the right thing to do I open the cabinet she's directed me to and find a little plastic container organized with anything I could ever need for cuts. In any other house, any other moment, I'd have thought the people were just crazy-organized. Right now, though? This discovery makes my stomach sink further.

I wonder if cutting is a regular occurrence and not a one-time thing. The idea that Rosie might do this to herself often stirs up a growling shadow inside of me.

I swallow the urge to ask.

My throat dries out and this uncomfortable, hollow feeling gnaws my ribs, whittling them down from the inside out as a million questions pummel me—a million questions that I don't speak because I know she's in no shape to answer anything right now. She needs to be coddled and cared for the way she deserves. Held close until that emptiness pours right out of her and light can filter back in.

But despite knowing what I should do, my brain is a hodge-podge of menial questions that flash in neon light: "Why?" and "How can I make you stop?" Not helpful.

I swallow those questions as I grab some cotton balls and pour alcohol over them before moving to where Rose is sitting, sniffling and swiping at her face, inadvertently smearing the makeup that melted with her tears.

Her skirt slid down and her cut is now partially obscured, so I lean forward and glide my palm over her thigh, edging it up just a little, her legs being revealed to me inch by inch. I ignore what that might mean in another context because that is—*that should be*—the farthest thing from my idiotic mind right now.

"Stop." The sensitive location of her cut is clearly not too far from Rose's thoughts either because she blushes and ducks her head.

"Just trying to reach your cut." I don't apologize or take my hand away because if I do, that skirt will fall right back down. Instead, I bunch it in my fist, maybe a little tighter than I have to because of the heaviness littering the air between us—the secrets that are simultaneously drawing us together and repelling us. We've now lied to Quique together, the secret of this moment a magnetic bond that makes the hairs on my arms rise. But there is still the giant looming question: What drove her to do this?

That secret has her pulling away from me. Or attempting to.

Thing is, I'm involved now. She might think pulling away is an option, but it's not.

My hand on her skirt holds her in place as I swipe the soaked cotton balls over the red stripe, noting that one or two other pale marks also reside on her tender thigh. Thankfully, they look faded and old. Apparently, this is a thing for Rose. Or was at some point. But whatever happened tonight brought her back to that point.

That knowledge makes me grit my teeth and I press down a little harder than I intended. Rose hisses, her hands shooting up to my arms and squeezing, nails digging hard into my skin, but her fingers are tiny—she can't even fully wrap her hands around my forearms. I lighten my touch and her grip softens, though she doesn't release me.

When I'm done, I throw the cotton into the trash can beside the toilet and then slowly pry her right hand from my arm, which she's pierced with her little claws. I carefully place her hand over mine on her lap so that she can hold her skirt bunched up in place.

"Keep your skirt up," I order.

She sucks in a breath, eyes growing wide.

Did I come across too harsh? I clench my jaw as I turn away. Tatiana's always complaining about how I'm so over-bearing.

"I'm good now," Rose whispers in a breathy voice. "You can go."

"I'll go when I know you're good. Not when you say you're good," I retort as I snag the box full of supplies and glance back over. Trying not to glare down at her is a challenge because that just pissed me off.

"You're not my keeper." A little fire comes into her eyes and the faintest bit of color touches her cheeks as she snarks back at me.

"Maybe I should be." The words just pop out, but I don't retract them. I don't even want to retract them. Quique clearly has no fucking clue what's going on here, and he's the man of the house now. Their mother—Ms. Dawson's so damn obsessed with her campaign I doubt she'd notice anything short of an earthquake. No one here is going to look after Rose the way she needs. And clearly, she fucking needs it.

Yes.

I think Rosie needs a keeper.

I just nominated myself for the job.

There is a long, slow moment where we stare at each other. I think it might be a battle of wills as she struggles to figure out how to resist me.

She doesn't know me well enough anymore to know that once I've made up my mind, that's that.

Her green eyes drop first, conceding, and then she whispers, "You don't have to do that."

"Maybe I want to."

Her free hand comes up to twist at her already-tangled hair, an expression of mystification crossing her face. "Why?"

The fact that she is asking that fucking question sends a flaming bolt of fury through me because it's as if she can't even conceive of being worth someone's time or protection.

God, my best friend deserves a punch to the mouth. And their mother—if I hit women, I'd fucking kick her where it hurts. Why is the idea that someone would take care of her a foreign concept? She's Rose! For fuck's sake, she's precious and fucking innocent as all get out. She's the silly girl who made Quique and me a three-tiered cake from scratch when we graduated high school. Best damn thing I've ever eaten, too. The girl I know loaned her brother the money he needed to get his car fixed on the down low after we wrecked it in a street race so their mom wouldn't blow her lid. She's selfless as fuck. A small, irrational part of me wants to scoop her up and carry her out of here and bring her to my house. I ignore it and answer her. "Because you deserve it."

Her brow furrows and her eyes narrow in suspicion. She doesn't trust or doesn't like my words. Fine by me. She doesn't have to. As long as she listens, we'll be fine.

ANN DENTON

I'm seething now, though. I want to punch something. I need to finish up and get out of here so I can spend some quality time with my speed bag back at my apartment. Fuck.

I turn to the counter and shove aside several bandages as I search for the antibiotic cream.

"You're scaring me," Rose whispers.

"You're scaring *me*. Why the hell would you do that?" I whirl back around and point at her leg. At the cut, and the scars that mar her beautiful skin.

It's the wrong thing to say. I watch her retreat into herself.

Fuck.

Fuck.

FUCK.

I reach up and yank at my hair in frustration, unsure what to say to make this better. The fury I feel—at her family, at the world, at whatever fucking reason she had to hurt herself—is whirling inside my ribs, revving like a chainsaw, cutting me up.

I clench my fists, struggling to get a hold of this sudden rage, because I don't mean to scare her.. But suddenly, there's an ardent need percolating underneath my skin, scalding me with the need to ensure that nothing like this ever happens to her again. "Promise me you won't do it again."

She stands, skirt still bunched in her hand. I'm about to grab her shoulder and tell her to sit back down when she whispers, "I won't. Okay? I won't do it because I won't ever see them again."

She bolts for the door, yanking it open, and darting across the hall into her own room. I hear the door slam shut and it startles me, making me jump inside my skin because the world stopped two seconds ago with her words.

Them.

Who *the fuck* is THEM?

ANGELO

THE NEXT MORNING

I don't sleep. Every time my eyes close, I keep seeing Rose's tear-glossed cheeks. Then suddenly, she'll transform into the face of my last assignment in Arizona and the memory will play out vividly in my half-asleep state.

"Mr. Walker. Mr. Walker, please! I've got kids! Please!" Dante Ambrose is a terrible beggar. He's so shrill that it's impossible to do anything other than curl my lips in disgust whenever he opens his mouth. Well, that might also have to do with the fact that he's a contemptible little thief who tried to underbid Walker Construction. He tried to weasel in on a deal that took me five months to secure.

But his bid is about to disappear—just like he is.

I lean over the chair he's tied to, studying the stripes I've already cut down his neck. They're shallow, not too deep. Just enough to make him panic.

"You want cash? I've got cash." he offers, chest heaving as he pants in terror and his eyes dart around looking for something he thinks I want. He's scrambling.

Some imbeciles think that money is the only driving factor on the planet. But it's not. Power trumps money any day. And power originates from love or fear. Love is something others have to freely give. But fear is a gift you can give yourself, the gift that keeps on giving--more influence, more contracts, more money. If I could wrap up the look in this bastard's eyes and give it to myself for Christmas, I would.

But ... no evidence.

I'll just have to remember it.

I step forward and lean down, watching the tip of my hunting knife as I dig it into his cheek, enjoying the drop of blood that forms on top of it before trailing down the blade, falling with a splat onto his polished shoes. I savor his expression as I blink at him and furrow my brow, as though his offer has me utterly confused.

"Dante, you've got me all wrong. No need for bribes. I just brought you here for a consultation." I like lying to their faces—watching the disbelief wash over them as they try to connect my ridiculous light-hearted conversation with the impending truth.

"What?" Ambrose blinks rapidly, trying to process. He doesn't get it.

"Yeah. There's a structural issue with one of the walls down here. I wanted to subcontract it out to you."

"You can't subcontract out the job. The bid rules didn't—"

I sigh because he's still slow to the draw. "You sure you own Ambrose Co.? Because right now, I don't think you're smart enough to fucking own a Guinea pig, much less a company." I snap my fingers and two hulking brutes come forward, Mint and Gary. Mint is a tall, bald man with a gold tooth and Gary looks like he could take out a sumo wrestler. Together, they lift Dante's snared form from the folding chair and drag him toward the freshly dug space for the wine cellar. The guys throw him into the pit and he lands with a loud thump. The three of us follow.

I land first and look up to see Dante trying to wriggle away through the dirt like an overweight little caterpillar. The ropes binding him mean he can't use his arms or legs, just his hips and feet.

It's pretty fucking funny so I hold up a hand and the guys and I just watch him for a second until I decide enough's enough.

I grab him by the collar and shove him up against one of the metal support beams as my flunkies grab a cinder block in each hand. I hold the foolish, pathetic lump of flesh in place as they slowly build up cinder blocks in front of him, pinning him into place. It's slow going, full of shrill begging.

But my father believes in the hands-on approach. If I'm going to take over Walker Construction, I have to prove I've got the cajones to handle it.

And so I stand there, holding Mr. Ambrose by the neck while Mint slathers cement onto cinder blocks that Gary carries over one by one. Normally, the guys are silent when they help me. I don't know if they like hearing a man beg the way that I do, or if they just want to hurry and get it over with. But tonight, Mint turns to me after troweling the last bit of wall to box Dane in.

"Yeah?" I ask, ignoring the muffled cries from behind the wall.

"Poe-etic justice. Get it?"

I scrunch a brow at him and his face immediately drops into a pretentious Chad expression as he quips, "Nah, brother. Don't tell me you haven't read Poe." He glances back and forth between me and Gary, who shrugs.

I've read Poe, and he knows it. Mint's pushed enough books at me over the years because I'm the only one he knows who seems to enjoy the habit he picked up on his first ten-year stint in the pen, but I know better than to engage with him. He and I have gone rounds about the classics before, like Poe and William Blake, but this is not the time for a literary debate.

"I have better things to do at night than read." Gary gives a salacious grin that looks completely and utterly fake. I've seen the guy. He doesn't get play. His 'better things to do' probably consists of drinking beer and yelling at whatever sports game is on that night.

I leave the two of them arguing over whether or not reading is a waste of time as they load up a cement mixing machine and prepare to pour it over our victim. I climb up the ramp we've built and stroll over to look down at Dante, who's futilely trying to free himself from his bindings.

"Thanks so much for the help, Mr. Ambrose. Don't think this wall would have held without your support." I emphasize that last word and wink at him before turning and strolling off into the night, whistling, while his screams become muffled by the whir and gloop of the cement mixer pouring sludge onto his face.

I lay in bed and stare out the window, watching dawn try to whitewash the pitch-black sky, knowing all the while that her efforts are useless. No matter how dawn hangs the sun and tries to blind us from reality, the light will recede each evening and show heaven's true face. The universe is vast and dark. Like me.

Like most of us.

Like nearly everyone.

Except Rose.

So why am I dreaming about her and then about that last job? She's innocent and pure and has nothing to do with the world I live in, the world her mother lives in. Shit, even Quique's not clean and crisp like her.

I think maybe … it's because she's the one good person I know.

And someone. No, multiple someones. *Them.* Somehow, they've tainted that. They've taken this girl and made her hurt so badly that she turned on herself.

God.

I. Can't. Fucking. Stand. It.

I need to know who they are and what they did. Have to. With that thought in mind, I shove up out of my bed. A glance at the clock says it's only five. It's too early to just show back up at Quique's even though my entire body is buzzing at the prospect. To burn off that restless energy, because I can't scare Rose ever again, I drop to the floor and start on some push-ups.

I show up bright and early with fast food, and Quique meets me at the door with a grin. "Fuck yeah. Hangover cure. Thanks, man."

"No problem," I say, handing him a paper bag that's already becoming translucent with grease.

"Mmm, nothing like the smell of breakfast burritos in the morning."

"Yup. Nothing like it," I respond blandly as I follow him inside, squinting as my eyes adjust from the early morning light to the dim interior of the house. "Rose up?" I try to keep my tone neutral, but the bags under my eyes can attest that I'm anything but.

"She's not even home yet, I don't think," Quique responds as he sets the bag on the counter and opens the fridge, pulling out a gallon of milk. "You want?"

"Yeah, just gonna wash my hands." I stride down the hallway, head thrumming from the fact that he doesn't even know or care where his sister is. Annoyance makes the air in my lungs feel as though it's been snagged on a hook, and I'm glad I'm walking away from him right now because there's no chance I'd be able to hide the look of disgust on my face right now.

Rose's door is closed. She's either still sleeping or out. Or ...

The final *or* makes me turn the knob without knocking, invading her privacy. "Lil reina?" I call out in a hushed tone. My eyes scan her bedroom, which is all done up in shades of pink and red—her mother's choices for what a girl named Rose should have. There's a lump amongst the floral bedding, and it moves at the sound of my voice.

I take a quick step inside and see a foot protruding from the covers. A foot, followed by a curved calf, and then a thigh.

My throat constricts—I didn't come in here to creep but damn if my eyes aren't plastered to the gap in the covers.

"Angelo? What are you doing here?" Rose's froggy voice is so deep that it startles me.

My gaze darts up guiltily and lands on her eyes. They're still rimmed in makeup, giving her the appearance of a rabid raccoon. Her hair is a wild swirl around her head, her black curls turned feral as she slept, and I realize I've never seen her like this before. She's always got her curls tamed. Herself tamed.

Strangely enough, I kind of enjoy seeing this side of her.

"I brought burritos." My excuse for waking her doesn't impress her at all. She raises one of those dark, arched brows of hers.

"Ever heard of a fridge? You could put mine in there."

"Ever heard of a thank you? You could give one."

She simply rolls her eyes and yanks the covers over her head. "Go away and let me sleep." Her dismissal is muffled by the comforter, which still hasn't covered up that very distracting length of leg.

I take a step closer, irritated now. I couldn't sleep all night because of this girl. I did something nice, brought breakfast, so we can have a civil conversation about all of this.

"You're forcing me to take drastic measures," I warn her, as my fingers dip down to her exposed foot. I slowly drag the pad of my index finger lightly over the sole.

Immediately, her leg contracts, and she kicks out. "Fucker!" Her entire torso pops up then, pissed as hell, those light green eyes narrowed on me as if she wishes she could shoot lasers out of them. "Get out."

"I want to talk."

"I don't."

"I want to know who made you do that—"

"It's none of your business," she growls defensively, wrapping her comforter around herself and standing. It's so huge that it swallows her up like a poofy winter cape, dragging on the floor behind her. One of her hands sneaks out and a flash of red bra appears before she shoves roughly at me. Her push is nothing, but I let her edge me out of her room because she clearly needs another hour or two of sleep before she tells me what I want to know. And she will, I'll make sure of that.

THREE HOURS AND SIX ROUNDS OF CALL OF DUTY LATER

SHE TOLD me to get fucked.

THE NEXT DAY

I FEEL LIKE A GODDAMNED MUMMY, dehydrated, dragging ass, and cursing every dick that crosses my path at work. I still can't sleep. I saw Rose crying in my dreams again and my mind keeps cycling back to that burning question about why she did this. Who made her hurt.

I'm so distracted, I nearly miss the fact that Dane has rigged his crane wrong and I have to run across the yard screaming and waving my arms like a maniac so the idiot doesn't drop a beam on someone.

My dad chews my ass for that.

"Where the fuck is your head?" He paces his office in the trailer we've hauled onsite, pulling his jeans over his paunchy belly and adjusting the bolo tie he wears. Paul Walker is a white guy who dresses like a stereotypical New Mexican cowboy, but it's all part of his ploy. He likes when people underestimate him. His gray brows furrow as he stops walking and turns to stare up at me. I've got at least four inches on him, but the man has a fury that can fill a room as quickly and brutally as any dirt devil. He speaks slowly and methodically when he says, "We need this job to go right. It's our ticket to the ski resort in Colorado—do you know what kind of pockets these people have?"

"I've got this."

"Do you?"

I nod.

His brown eyes narrow and he glares up at me. "You'd better." He doesn't threaten me. But he doesn't need to. I've seen what he's truly capable of.

Needless to say, when I pull up to the Dalton's house that evening, my mouth is set in a grim line. This ends now.

I'm getting answers, whether she likes it or not. I can't afford to keep letting her distract me like this.

❧

Two Days Later

Rose ran to her room, locked the door, and knocked out her screen, climbing out of the fucking window to get away from me. And that tied my hands—I couldn't run after her because her brother would see. I can only imagine the shit that would go down then. I'd detach his balls from his body with a red-hot spoon if he ever sniffed around Tatiana.

And I'm not doing the same thing—this thing with Rose is definitely not *that*. It's … concern. That's all. Just concern.

But if he asks, I can't explain myself without giving up her secret, which I promised not to do. Catch-22.

So she ran and I let her, biding my time.

But the girl hasn't been home since. I know because I keep dropping by. Quique's been asking if everything's alright—hinting I've been coming around too often—and I've barely been able to keep it under control.

I want to Hulk out and blow my goddamned lid because everything is not alright. I haven't slept in four mother-fucking days. Not one drop of sleep. Not a single grain of dirt from the sandman. Right now, I'm living off energy drinks and desperation.

I need to know she's okay.

I need to hear it from her lips.

And this running thing she's doing? The more I think about it, the more it just chafes my ass. I was checking on her, trying to do the fucking nice-guy shit.

God, I should just throw her over my shoulder and …

And what, idiot?

I scrub a hand over my soot-black hair in frustration, not allowing myself to untangle that thought.

I should have told Quique what was up that night. Should have let him handle this. But my entire body pulses with discomfort at the idea.

So here I am, all worked up, can't sleep, messing up at work—

Something's got to give, and it's not going to be me.

My phone buzzes in my pocket and I glance down to see a text from my sister, Tatiana.

Tatiana: I'm home.

Me: Ok. Thanks.

After my quick response to her check-in, I slide the phone back into my pocket but it almost immediately buzzes again. With a sigh, I pull it back out. I'm surprised to see my sister's calling me, not just texting me back. Did something happen?

My pulse picks up and I swipe to answer. "You okay?" I ask.

"Um, I think the question is are *you* okay?" My little sister's voice comes out a bit breathy but she just got home from Cross Country, so that's to be expected.

"What do you mean?" I ask, though I shift uncomfortably where I stand at my kitchen counter, a bowl of cereal unfinished in front of me.

"You never let me check in and just say okay. I always get the third degree." She drops her voice an octave as she openly mocks me. *"Who were you with? What did you do? What are you doing next?"*

I roll my eyes and turn, leaning back against the counter. "I don't do that." It's a lie. I do.

"Fuck off, you totally do! So what's going on, Dumbo?" She thinks she's clever calling out what she thinks are my big ears, but I'm over her nicknames at this point. Immune.

I hear her open the fridge and I can mentally picture everything she's doing. Tatiana and I are a decade apart—she was a surprise—but we're still tight. That annoying little pipsqueak has all of us—Mom, me, even Dad—wrapped around her little finger.

"I'm waiting."

I sigh. "I haven't been sleeping, okay?"

"Why?" The sound of juice pouring into a glass travels over the line. "Is it something to do with Dad?" She doesn't truly know the ins and outs of our business, but Tati isn't stupid. She's got an idea of what goes on.

"No. No. Not him."

"Who then?"

"Just someone."

"I need a name. I feel like I should send this person a fruit basket for incapacitating your growly papa bear tendencies."

If we were in the same room, I'd flip her annoying little freckled face off. But I have to settle for saying, "Just go drink your juice and watch your cartoons."

"It's anime, not cartoons thank you."

"Don't forget to take your blankie with you."

"Since we're bossing each other around, maybe you should fucking call this person you have beef with so you can yell it out and get your stubborn ass back to normal."

"Bye, Tati."

"Bye."

I toss my phone on the counter and spin around to my cereal, but it's gotten soggy and disgusting. Ugh. I go to dump the mess into the sink when I realize that Tati's right. The little shit is actually right about something. If I had Rose's number, I could just call her and check on her and get her to tell me who did this.

It would be over.

I'd be able to sleep.

I just need to get her number.

THAT NIGHT

I PULL up to the pool hall in a mood my grandmother would call a lemon. Her scraggly old voice drifts through my memories. "Get your lemon face out of here, mijo. I don't want to see it until it's lemonade." Sassy old lady. Rest in peace.

I blow out a deep breath and brace myself for what I'm about to do. I've done tons of fucked-up shit without blinking an eye. But deceiving my best friend isn't one of them.

I stride into the single-story, smoky pool hall with a purpose. Ignoring the looks my tattoos earn from a set of college hipsters to the left, I head straight to the bartender, who's polishing a glass that doesn't look the least bit clean. Quique's already found him, perched on a booth near the corner, and the two are joking like they're best friends. That guy can make friends with anyone. Me? I'm more of a loner, more likely to make someone piss themselves than befriend them. Normally, that's just fine by me.

Right now, I wish I wasn't, though. Maybe if I was ... I don't know, softer or something, maybe Rose wouldn't keep running from me. If I had a charm dial like Quique and could turn it up at will, wouldn't that be nice?

As it is, my best method for getting information out of someone is beating the fuck out of them or getting them drunk. In Quique's case, we're getting plastered.

Five rounds of pool and six shots are all it takes before Quique is sitting across from me in a booth and swiping through his phone, laughing and joking about old memories. "Damn. Remember the ass on Sarah Jayne? Girl had legs for days," he reminds me, holding up a senior year photograph of one of his old high school flames, the one he always laments *got away.*

"Hold on, lemme see tha-shit," I pretend to slur, grabbing his phone. I squint my eyes, as if I'm looking at her, but I really minimize the photo app and swipe over to his contacts. I find Rose easily and text her details to myself with a few quick taps before I delete the evidence.. Hopefully, he won't look at his phone history and see it.

"Hey! Hey! There are private pics in there!" Quique sets down his beer and clumsily reaches for the phone as I quickly maximize the photo app and swipe to one side as quick as I can. Sure enough, there's a girl getting a facial along with a close-up of my friend's dick I never needed to see.

I grimace. "I can see why you'd want to hide that picture. The shot has the neck of a beer bottle in there by your cock and the comparison is not flattering."

"Fuck you." His words are harsh but his expression is full of laughter. Quique gets my humor. Always has. "You're just jealous."

I shrug. "Guilty as charged."

"Hard not to be when you're working with a Q-tip." He makes a goofy face before laughing heartily at his own joke while I roll my eyes.

"Alright. I think it's time we call it. I'm getting us a car."

"I can get my own," he offers, but I'm quick to cut him off. There's no way I'm giving up a legitimate chance to go to their house and see if Rose is back.

"Nope. It's good. I asked you out, so I got this—"

"Dude. That sounds like a date."

"They call it a 'man' date."

"We are not dating. Just so we're clear. Even if you've seen my dick and liked it."

I chuckle as I swipe and see our driver is only two minutes out. I smack a bill onto the polished wooden table and stand, holding out my hand. "Come on."

He slides out, smacking my hand away and shuffling, slightly off balance. "Get off me."

"Dude, are you going to be good to work tomorrow?" I hate to ask and be that guy but he's looking worse for the wear.

He shrugs. "Worth it."

We get into the back seat of the ride-share and he immediately dives into his phone, probably trying to hit up a girl for some late-night Netflix and chill. I open my own texts and pull up my very new contact: Rose Dalton.

Me: Hey lil' reina.

Rose: Is this who I think it is?

Me: Depends who you think it is.

Rose: Stop. Just stop.

Me: Can't. Can't sleep.

Rose: They make meds for that. Also for being a psycho.

Me: And you know this because … you've taken them?

Rose: I know this because I know someone who needs to take them. AKA YOU.

Me: I'm a psycho for worrying about you?

Rose: Shut up and go away.

That one gets to me. It sends a little fire dancing underneath my skin because it's fucking rude and unwarranted. I swallow the burn of that statement in light of the bigger picture here. Trying to be magnanimous and all that.

Me: What have you been up to this week?

Rose: Do you really care?

Me: Am I the kind of guy who makes small talk to be polite?

Rose: Fine. Class. Studying. Ok?

A tiny thread of satisfaction weaves through me at the fact that I finally got some kind of straight answer out of her, minimal though it is. I find myself grinning as I type my next question.

Me: What's your major?

Rose: Undeclared.

Me: Undecided or undeclared?

There's a long pause and three dots appear in a text bubble to indicate she's typing. But then they disappear. Then reappear. Interesting. She's clearly trying to determine whether or not to tell me. She must have chosen a major that she doesn't want to talk about. Why?

Is it something her mother wouldn't approve of?

This girl is just full of secrets.

For a second, that makes me sad—because I know she's hiding her hurt and how she copes with it. Hiding the fuckers who hurt her. But if she's hiding her major, she's also hiding her hope for her future.

Does anyone actually know the real Rose?

I wait for her reply, but a message never comes through. She doesn't trust me enough to tell me. Unsurprising, though a little snarl of disappointment knots my gut. Didn't I prove myself by keeping this other secret? I try to ignore the feeling because there's more than one way to skin a cat. I lean back against the seat, staring out the window at the glowing balls of peach light cast by the streetlights as we drive toward the dark, looming mountains before I return to our chat. If she won't tell me her major, I'll have to find out another way.

Me: What if I guess?

Rose: Sure.

Me: Pre-med, since you know all about the psycho pills.

Rose: LOL. No.

Me: You sure?

Rose: Yes. Now, I gotta go.

Me: Wait. I want to know you're ok.

Rose: I'm ok. I'd be better if you'd just leave it alone.

Me: Can't do that. I'm involved now.

Rose: You don't need to be involved. I'm fine.

Me: I don't believe you. Prove it.

Rose: What?

Me: Send me a pic. Prove you're fine.

I almost type "of your legs" after "pic" but stop myself because that *would* be psycho. And the thought of having a photo of Rose's thighs on my phone makes my throat grow tight. Nope. I glance guiltily over at Quique, who's grinning down at his screen, oblivious.

A photo comes through of Rose's face, her eyes narrow, perfect bow lips frowning, middle finger saluting me.

Motherfucker.

Rose: Perv. Blocking you.

Me: Don't. (!)

I click the alert icon and it reads: Message not delivered.

Shit. I try again.

Me: Rose. (!)

Me: Rose, you better not push me. (!)

Fuck! Fuck.

THE NEXT DAY

I LIE and tell my dad I'm going to the doctor for a nonstop migraine. It's the only thing I can think of to get him off my back and get away from the job site for a few hours.

I feel like the fucking psycho she accused me of being when I park at the college campus. But I'm already in this deep. Screw it. I pull the parking brake on my truck and slam the door shut before strolling through the grounds, eyes peeled for Rose. I've reached a tipping point.

My father raised me to be a pit bull. To latch on and not give up. And last night, all I could picture as I laid in bed was some guy hurting Rose—shoving her, hitting her, calling her a piece of shit, making her believe she's unworthy … my imagination's gone off the deep end.

Perhaps Dad pulled me out of the underbelly of our work too soon. Maybe I'm more suited for that kind of shit than the respectable management position he wants me in now, because I'm itching, festering, needling to hurt someone. And that need is infecting me, turning me into this sick, twisted stalker.

Maybe I'm blowing this all out of proportion. Maybe nothing that traumatic happened to Rose. But I have to know for sure because these nightmares are burrowing into my brain and writhing around unchecked, taking over my thoughts and turning me into an insomniac. At this point, I don't just need to know, I crave it.

I grab a soda from inside the Student Union building before strolling outside into the crisp morning air, ignoring the looks I get. The tattoos sleeving my arms have earned me side-eyed glances since the day I got them. Or maybe it's the fact that I'm not wearing a winter coat like ninety percent of the nerdy short guys shuffling around here. But they wouldn't be wearing a coat if they'd been up since five, hauling wood and wallboard and climbing beams on an eighteen-story building. I shucked off my coat and my Walker Construction polo when I got here, so I'm walking around in a white tee that's on the thinner side. It probably shows off the work on my chest. Whatever. I don't care if I fit in with these preppy punks. I just want to find Rose and put an end to this idiotic worry winding me up tighter than a nun's twat.

Every girl who walks by with a set of black curls turns my head, but none of them is her. They don't have those red lips that keep popping up whenever I close my eyes or a sad, soulful green gaze. I grind my teeth back and forth in frustration as time wears on. I need to get back to the site, I've left Jorge in charge at the new hotel we're constructing, and he has a habit of skimping on safety.

Five more minutes. Just five more, I promise myself as I walk over to the Center of the Universe on the west side of the campus. It's this stupid concrete monstrosity some artist built with two intersecting tunnels that form a big X. There's a third tunnel that shoots up to the sky like a giant skylight and plummets into the ground. When you stand on a grate in the middle it's supposed to feel like you're in the center of a star. What it actually feels like is standing in the New York subway tunnels. It's ugly and drab and carries the faint stench of rot from all the dead leaves moldering under the grate.

Fucking artists.

It's not even great concrete work. Parts of it are pitted more than others—I could go on about the workmanship, but amongst all the students scurrying around like ants, I spot Lily, one of Rose's friends, walking to class.

"Lily!" I call out, raising a hand and striding forward. "Hey!"

She turns, flicking her light brown hair and smiling flirtatiously until she realizes I'm not smiling back. Lily's ... to say not my type is an understatement. She's one of those high-maintenance chicks who thinks the sun shines out her asshole.

It takes her a second to recognize me, so I decide to reintroduce myself and speed the process up.

"Angelo. Quique's friend. Rose's brother, Enrique." I give the quick rundown without mincing any words as I shove my hands into the pockets of my cargo pants.

"Hi …" she trails off, clearly waiting for me to explain myself.

But then, I find myself at a loss for words. Shit, what can I ask without it getting back to Quique that I'm sniffing around his sister? Does Lily know about Rose's cutting habit? Or am I wasting my time?

"Have you seen Rose? I was supposed to meet her." The lie slips out and it's as good as any, so I roll with it.

"Um, I think she's got an English class or something right now."

"Crap." Of course, she's in class. And never home. And avoiding me. "Has she seemed … off lately?"

Lily's eyes widen in this excited but almost predatory way that girls get when they scent gossip. "What do you mean?" She takes a step closer and her disgusting floral perfume invades my mouth.

I take a sip of soda to wash away the taste and also to buy myself time to think of something to say. I end up going the nonverbal route. I give a shrug, as if I don't care.

"Did something happen?" Yeah, she's practically frothing at the mouth. This could go either really well or really badly for me.

"She didn't tell you?" I try to twist it, to turn it on her, make her wonder if Rose trusts her.

Her face twists into a thoughtful expression as she purses her lips and tries to think. "Was it the Alpha Tau party? I told her she didn't have to come with me—One sec." I hear the quiet pulse of Lily's phone as she pulls it out of her back pocket. "Oh, look. She's texting me. She must be done with class."

Before I can stop her, Lily's texted Rose and I watch with a sinking feeling in my gut as Lily's phone vibrates in her hand. Her manicured nails curl around it as she lifts it to her ear. Her gaze turns steely as she glares at me before she turns, without a word, and strides away from me. I've been iced out.

GODDAMMIT.

THAT NIGHT

A FACELESS GUY in the shadows kicks Rose and when she stumbles, he knees her in the face.

No. Nope. I would have seen bruises. I tell my mind to take a hike, to go cool off, stop fanning the flames.

But it can't. Or it won't. I'm not sure.

Her mother comes up next, so uptight and proper. Ms. Dalton's Botoxed face appears inside my head. She leans down with an ugly expression I've only seen her use on me and Quique when we've done something she considers uncouth. *"Don't embarrass me, Rose. Or I'll have to tell people what a disappointment I have for a daughter."*

She only lasts a minute before a cocky jock, like the kind I saw on campus, materializes behind my eyelids. He grabs Rose and kisses her, one arm wrapping around her back and holding her to him as she tries to fight him off ...

Two Days Later

THAT'S IT. I'm giving in. After a week of sleepless nights, I'm officially the psycho that Rose believes I am. I've snuck over to see Quique on false pretenses and I'm here in the hall bathroom, perched on the granite countertop, hiding a battery-powered miniature camera at the bottom of the light fixture like a pervert so I can make sure that Rose doesn't cut herself ever again.

The Alpha Tau party that Lily mentioned ... goddamn her. That's set off an entirely different string of nightmarish possibilities for me to deal with, ones that have led me to punch my speed bag until my knuckles bleed.

But ... one thing at a time.

First, I'm going to make sure Rose is safe.

Then, I'm going to get her to confess everything to me.

ROSE

*T*he desert's January night air creeps around me, cruelly cold and scratching at my skin so it peels, chapping my lips and drying my eyes.

I hate the eerie way the wind blusters through the canyon in the distance, the same way I hate everything that just happened. I can't believe I just burst out like that and yelled. I never do that! Ever.

But what I saw at Daisy's house shocked me to my core and hit on the very thing I'd been agonizing over in silence for days.

I wrap my arms around my torso, the chill seeping into me and mingling with the fire raging within, as I stomp down the hill at top speed, determined to leave Daisy's house behind. The neighborhood is dark and silent, except for the occasional golden glow of a streetlight.

Bile singes the back of my tongue and I have to breathe steadily so that I don't puke onto the nearest Spanish broom's feathery green stalks.

I can't believe Daisy was okay with her stepfather setting up secret cameras in their house to watch her. More than okay! It didn't even fucking bother her that Gunnar violated her privacy, watching her get out of the shower without her knowledge.

Insanity.

She's blinded by the fact that he's a hot fucking surgeon and she's pined after him for so long, not as secretly as she thought. She thinks it's okay because they're together now? Because he's not *technically* her stepfather anymore? Because he only pity-married her mother so Darla could get cancer treatment, swooping in like some hero?

Bullshit. None of those things erase what he just did. What I caught him doing.

He watched her *without her consent*!

Videotaped her just like that bastard recorded my mom—

Rage curdles the pizza I ate earlier and my fingers curl into fists where they're tucked close by my sides as I duck my head, winding with the sidewalk around a stunted tree someone didn't have the heart to chop down, heading for the park at the end of the road.

I pretend I didn't just blow my top in front of my three best friends since elementary school, the Wild Flowers. Just like I pretend I can't hear one of them—Lily—calling out behind me.

"Rose! Come back! Please. It's cold. Come on. We don't have to stay at Daisy's. You can come to my place or I'll drive you home. Rose!" Her heels click against the sidewalk, because even for a girls' night in at Daisy's, Lily is always done up. That's just who she is. Wake up and makeup.

She's also trying to help me, which is more than she did a few weeks ago after the nightmare that shall not be discussed or even thought about ever again.

No, don't blame her, I remind myself. *It's not her fault. She was drunk. You were drunk ...*

But even just the most minor reminder about that night throws me off balance. Vertigo hits me and I feel like I'm falling—just like I did the one, solitary Saturday night I tried to go out and not be myself for a minute. Not be the shy good girl who does as she's told. That backfired royally, quickly jettisoning from free-spirited into haunting.

A flash of a dark room and three men hits me and panic flashes through my system as if they're still here.

Nope. It's over. It's over and you're fine, I try to tell my screaming nerves. I would be fine, if I could just put it behind me and forget it. If my brother's idiotic friend would stop bugging me about it.

Except that right now ... triggered by that stupid video playing on the screen in Gunnar's office, the plunge into the darkness feels even worse than it did that night because this fall is accompanied by betrayal, the slice of a huge knife stabbing me right in the back.

What those strangers did to me is nothing ... nothing compared to what Angelo's done with *his* stupid video.

Bastard.

I walk faster, hissing as the frigid air presses against my ears, which feel as if someone is holding ice cubes against them, trying to burn the skin away.

But I embrace the cold because the physical sensation is a distraction from the way my stomach keeps tumbling and my mind keeps reliving things I never want to think about again.

"Rosalinda Lee Dalton! You stop right now and tell me what the hell is going on!" Lily shouts.

God, she's going to wake up the neighbors. I start to jog, the need to get away pulsing through me faster. I can't deal with Lily right now—she's a low-key drama queen at the best of times. There's no way she'd just let me be. No, she'll insist on talking. The auburn-haired beauty will want me to slice open my insides, hari-kari my secrets.

I won't.

Not for her. And definitely not for Angelo. Doesn't matter how many times he's fucking asked, demanded, called, cornered me—

I grab my phone out of my pocket. Swiping up with a finger that feels colder than a grave, I find my brother's number. He owes me, so I shoot off a quick text.

Come pick me up at the park by D's. Hurry. Bring me a coat.

Enrique better be quick. I know he's not working tonight, and our house isn't far. My brother's in his mid-twenties, five years older than me, and should probably be living on his own by now but isn't.

I don't know if he and his greasy hair stick around to help Mom with the house because she needs it or if he's lazy. In fact, I don't really know much of what's going on with him, other than the fact he hates her campaign trail events.

Though Quique and I see each other a lot, we don't really talk. Not about anything beyond who ate the last of the left-over enchiladas or whose night it is to take out the garbage. Whatever the case may be, tonight, I'm glad he's close enough to pick me up. I'm also glad we don't talk, so he won't ask questions. I don't want to deal with an inter-rogation.

"I am not dressed for running! Come on, Rosie! I'll take you to the store and then we can T.P. Gunnar's place, okay? Just stop!" Her middle-school-style offer of vengeance softens me a little, and my tennies slow—the clack of her heels growing louder as I let her catch up.

I shouldn't punish or ignore her. She's done nothing wrong. God, she was just a bystander too. It's not her fault that whole secret video thing triggered me. I make myself inhale and exhale slowly, trying to get my raging nervous system to calm down.

We carpooled tonight, so Lily feels obligated as well as concerned. I'll just tell her Quique's coming for me and then she can turn back and go inside where it's warm. I scrub at my cheeks, brushing away the tear tracks that feel like they've frozen on my face.

Turning on my heel, I face her as she totters forward the last few steps before grabbing me and crushing me into a painful hug. "I'm so sorry about whatever's going on, but I'm also shamelessly going to use you to warm my nipples because they feel like they're about to fall off!"

I burst into thick laughter, my throat swollen. "I'll put that on my resume. Nipple warmer."

"You should. I hear it's in high demand."

I wrap my arms around her waist as my chest vibrates and we both fill the night with slightly manic laughter that is completely at odds with everything else in my life. I shouldn't be laughing, I really shouldn't, but God, it feels so good to let go of *something*. I've been keeping things bottled up and fighting the urge to release the tension the best way I know how because I don't want him invading my space *again*. I'm so close to cracking, teetering on the edge. But laughter lightens the load, fills my lungs with helium or something, so that I float, light-headed, for just a moment.

Of course, the moment ends and sadness tugs me back to earth, her grip so much stronger than joy's.

I dig my fingers into Lily's ribs, crushing her closer as mirth flees.

Concern colors her tone when she softly asks, "Rose, what is it?"

I consider lying. I do. It would be so much easier to just brush this all off. But I just had a massive freak out in Daisy's house about that video I caught Gunnar taking of Daisy, so whatever excuse I come up with, I'm not sure it will be enough.

Lily's gray eyes are trying to cut right through me. I glance around, wishing Quique was here already to rescue me from the uncomfortable conversation about to unfold, but he's not. So, I take a deep breath, an inhale that makes the inside of my lungs tingle as if I'm strung with little bells that jangle along with my nerves. Then I whisper, "Someone took a video of my mom and a married guy screwing in our bathroom. They're threatening to release it."

"WHAT?!" Lily's outrage is instantaneous and so damn loud I think she might have injured my eardrum. Her hands come up to my shoulders and she cups them, a vicious expression on her face. "Those low-down motherfuckers. Who? We can set Violet's family on—"

"No." The word comes out sharp and fierce, exploding right from my chest and out my lips, as fast and sudden as a grenade. I'm not even sure where it comes from. But as soon as it's out there, I realize that I don't want to tell Lily the whole story. I don't want to tell her who took the video or why.

Fuck.

Why not?

Violet's family has Irish mob ties. They could easily wipe this away.

But Angelo took that video. He set up that camera to spy on me … and ended up with something more than he bargained for. And then he decided to use it to find out what he wants from me.

God, he sets my blood boiling.

But why does the idea of throwing him to the wolves make my throat feel filled with wood chips?

Is it because I know the video isn't really about my mother or her campaign for senator? A sharp twinge in my chest tells me that's not the only reason.

I don't have time to psychoanalyze myself when Lily's staring at me like I'm crazy.

"I don't want to get more people involved. If it gets out—her campaign is over."

"Rose, we'd never let anyone—"

"Quique's coming to pick me up." I change the topic instead of arguing. "He's going to meet me at the park. Might already be there." I start backing up the sidewalk before turning and briskly setting off again. Part of me wants to have Lily relay an apology to Daisy but another part of me is still so pissed at Gunnar that I can't bring myself to do it.

I just need space.

Yes.

Space and quiet. Time for this roiling mess to cool down to a simmer. Meanwhile, I am not going to say another word about why I'm festering. I put enough out there for the girls to have some idea about what's going on so that they can draw their own conclusions.

But the rest of it? The fact that the video isn't really about Mom at all?

No one needs to know that.

I'm a vault.

I'm a statue.

I'm one of the soldiers in the terra cotta army.

My chest feels as hollow as one of those unearthed soldier statues, a creation whose sole purpose was protecting an emperor in the afterlife.

Sometimes, I feel like my sole purpose is protection too.

But I'm the only one in my stupid family bothering to try to protect us.

The press are absolute vultures.

If that video Angelo took of my mom gets out … her campaign is over.

Goodbye Senate. Goodbye to everything she's worked for over the past decade. Goodbye to rebuilding her life and proving herself to my lush of a father who deserves to rot in Hell.

That motherfucker who recorded her is trying to ruin all of it. And for what? To find out my secrets? Fuck him.

He's a bastard … just like Gunnar.

But I used to be blind, just like Daisy is right now.

Hell, even just a few weeks ago, I was dumb enough to think that my blackmailer was perfection personified.

I recall the first time I ever saw Angelo—six years ago—when I was just fourteen and foolishly believed heroes actually existed.

Mom's talking with the mayor and a bunch of construction guys about the site of the new Balloon Fiesta facility they are putting up. Every October, nearly a thousand hot air balloons blot the sky, a rainbow of thumbprint shapes, dragging in thousands of visitors to ooh *and* ahh *over them while sipping overpriced hot chocolate.*

Of course, everyone's hoping a new venue will bring even more cash in.

"This project is long overdue …" The mayor gives a toothy grin as the other grown-ups chatter among each other.

Blah, blah, blah …

Their words fade as I meander away around dormant construction vehicles. I'm bored, annoyed mom's dragged me to one of these things yet again.

Where the hell is Quique? At nineteen, he should hate this shit even more than I do, especially since Mom's making him play chauffeur. But he hopped out of the car all excited, like this wasn't going to be another mind-numbing experience.

"Walker Construction is doing this project? Is Angelo here?" He'd darted over to a cluster of guys in hard hats and now, I'm going to suffer through this meeting—which will no doubt last a couple hours (they always do)—alone. There goes my hope of bribing him to take me for ice cream if I pay.

I squint at the harsh afternoon sun as I retrieve a hair tie from my jeans pocket. I toss my annoying black curls up into a ponytail to get them out of my face. Wishing I had sunglasses to protect my light green eyes does me no good, so I turn my face back down to the piles of gravel and dirt.

There are entire miniature mountains of the stuff here, piled and waiting to be moved around, perhaps to make a gravel parking lot. With nothing else to do, I begin to climb one of the piles of dirt, but it slides under my feet, packed too loosely—so I quickly give that up. Instead, I use a two-by-four lying on the ground as a balance beam, humming and singing bits of "Heathens" by Twenty One Pilots as I walk across it, debating a cartwheel but deciding against it.

Maybe I could get out of here.

That thought spurs me to shoot off a text to the Wild Flowers, hoping Daisy or maybe Violet will answer. Lily's at cheer, and probably has a date tonight, too—but maybe one of the other girls could swing by with their parents and take me away from this misery. Violet usually has eighty-thousand family events with her huge Irish family ... but Daisy just has her mom. She's usually able to hang. And her mother, unlike mine, actually enjoys doing fun shit. Like bowling.

I think Mom posed with the mayor once for a bowling picture, but that's about it. Ever since the divorce, she's been all work, work, work.

I sigh when no text bubbles appear on my phone. The Wild Flowers must all be busy.

I glance back over at the adults, but they're animatedly speaking. I give myself a twenty percent chance of getting out of this place before the sun goes down.

Waiting. Life's nothing but waiting around with Mom. It's always one more meeting. One more phone call. One more minute.

I get she's trying to make a name for herself. Set a good example. But ... I sigh. Daisy says I'm just sensitive, that I take things as slights when I shouldn't. Maybe she's right.

I spy a trench off at the edge of the property near some trees. Trying to ignore the brutal heat of the afternoon sun, I meander near the edge, peering over to see how deep it is. It can't be more than six feet. Hmm ... I kick a little pebble over the edge and watch it smack the other side and tumble down.

"Metaphor for my life," I mutter. Freshman year sucks. It doesn't matter that I got my braces off or finally got boobs ... I still wander the halls and I'm fucking invisible. No one sees me.

"HEY!" A deep male voice startles me and I spin around to see a man barreling toward me, a tall guy with long black hair and a neon yellow construction vest, running faster than anyone I've ever seen. "Get the fuck away from—"

The end of his sentence is cut off because the earth shifts underneath my feet and my knees buckle. My heart flies up and smashes into the roof of my mouth. The dirt beneath me collapses, and the entire ridge lining the trench appears to liquefy, rushing like a waterfall into the gap. A cloud of dust chokes me as my body tumbles backward.

Holy shit. Holy shit.

A scream doesn't even have time to rip from my throat as the weight of all that soil starts to cover my feet. It feels like a car is driving right over them—so heavy. Who knew that dirt weighed so much? I kick out, trying to avoid it as I fall, not to let it cover me but I can see it gliding like a wave, coming for me.

SMASH.

The stranger's shoulder smacks into my solar plexus and I go flying backward through the air. My back slams into the ground hard and weight presses down on me—the air compressed from my lungs. When my head hits, my vision blinks red and then black.

Blind, unable to make out a single shape or color, I feel fingers dig roughly into my shoulders, and then I'm rolled roughly across the ground again and again—under and over this stranger—rocks biting and scratching at me as I drag in shallow, painful breaths.

Finally, we stop with my body pinned beneath his.

After a frantic moment of blinking, my sight flickers back, silver flecks speckling the edges of my vision for a moment before they clear away.

Shock dulls my pain as I lay there for a second, unmoving, just taking in my surroundings

I'm on my back in the empty field where hot-air balloons take off, staring up at the construction worker who yelled at me. Who tackled me across a collapsing trench. Who leans over me on muscled, tanned arms. He doesn't look that much older than me, to be honest. Maybe just out of high school? Mid-college?

His deep brown eyes blaze with fury, black hair plastered to his forehead as he scans my body up and down, jaw twitching. "What were you thinking?"

I don't have enough air to answer. I wheeze as he climbs off of me to kneel at my side. Painful breaths finally start to circulate through my lungs. Once my oxygen levels improve enough for thoughts to re-emerge, I realize dazedly that this guy is the most handsome guy I've ever seen in my life.

Wavy black hair, deep brown eyes glinting in harsh beams of afternoon sun, the hint of a dimple in his cheek even though he's unsmilingly serious right now—he's got the trifecta of all the best male facial features. And he's also got the sort of thick, luscious lips that have always drawn my attention. I don't know what it is about a guy with big lips ... maybe it's because I'm a smile girl or because their pouts are so much more adorable and pronounced.

This guy has the best pouty lips on the planet. And right now, he's giving me one hell of a delicious frown.

Shit. I'm a little loopy.

"Did anything break?" The question comes out tight, each syllable fighting to get out from between his clenched teeth as his eyes scan my body. "Dirt weighs over a hundred pounds a cubic foot ..." he trails off.

I shake my head, struck dumb—unable to speak as I feel my brain metaphorically leak out my ears. I'm not sure why—if I'm in shock or there's something else—until he touches me. Then the why becomes alarmingly clear.

It's an innocent touch. He simply cups my shoulder and drags his hand along my arm to search for any pain points.

But my stomach tumbles like I just fell into that trench all over again. Sensation swoops through me, dazzling and flickering like glitter, coalescing into the world's most potent, most naive crush.

The memory fades as I stomp up the sidewalk, rubbing my hands up and down my frozen arms to try to chafe some warmth into them and shaking my head at how utterly idiotic I've been.

Just like Daisy sees Gunnar as some shining testament to what a man should be, I've always viewed Angelo through rose-colored glasses because of that moment—there in the dirt, with aching ribs and a broken ankle, I developed a schoolgirl infatuation, not just a crush, but a low-key obsession that made my eyes trail after him every time he visited my brother. It was a painful, pathetic, one-sided exercise in futility. And not because I was too young for him to ever look at me the same way. Because apparently, at their core, all men are corrupt.

Daisy's a fool.

But no more than I've been.

Fucking Angelo Walker.

Already friends with my brother, Angelo's big heroic moment secured his place in the family. Mom invited him over weekly for dinner and I'd sat through countless family gatherings with him seated right beside me, his perfection making the very air vibrate so that I couldn't breathe properly.

I put him on a pedestal. Thought of him as a god. Wrote down all his favorite things in my diary, from hot Cheetos to The Red Hot Chili Peppers.

When he'd left Albuquerque two years ago for some job, it had nearly crushed me as badly as falling into that trench would have. I spent months digging myself out of that fixation.

But when Angelo returned, about a month ago, I'd been shocked to find his effect on me hadn't dimmed in the slightest. I'd fallen right back into hero worship and secret, silent longing.

But he's changed. He's not the same guy I knew. Now, at twenty-five, his arms are thicker, muscles massive, and skin sleeved in tattoos that weren't there before. His black hair is cropped short, and he has an earring these days. There's a dull scar on his tanned chin, the jagged little streak a slightly lighter shade than the rest of him. His straight lashes bracket eyes that no longer look like sparkling umber stones. Now, there's something darker in his gaze. He's harder than he was before he left. More somber. I haven't seen his dimple emerge once. Those lips though? They're the one thing about him that hasn't changed. His lips are still as magnetic as I remember.

Of course, devils are meant to tempt aren't they? A beautiful face can hide ugly truths. And Angelo's hiding the ugliest of them all—the fact that he's a controlling, blackmailing fuck.

I reach the swing set at the park. It's right next to the parking lot and so I turn, tapping my boot impatiently on the concrete and staring at a pair of approaching headlights.

Lily finally catches up to me, winded. Her gray eyes latch on and tug at my heart. "Hey! You can't just drop a bomb that big and then jet off. You are talking about something really frickin' serious, Rose," she scolds me breathlessly.

I press my lips together but don't answer, because the head-lights turn into the parking lot and I recognize the shape of Quique's Jeep gliding to stop in front of us.

"Look, I'll tell you more later," I lie to her as I dart through the shadows toward the warmth and silence of my brother's car.

"Rose!" she screeches.

But I just want to get away. I need to get away from all of this. I need to relieve the pressure steaming inside my chest and building up until my head feels like it might explode.

I'm yanking open the door even as I look at her and mouth, "Sorry."

Sliding into the passenger seat, I gasp at the temperature difference—with the heater blasting, my brother's car feels like a sauna compared to the air outside.

Sweet relief.

A leather jacket plops onto my lap.

"Whoa, thank you." I turn to look at Quique as I pull my door shut. Only, I discover my brother isn't in the car.

The rat-bastard blackmailer is.

ANGELO

*W*hen Quique got that text from Rose and was too drunk to drive to get her, I jumped at the chance. This ends tonight.

I'm going to drag the truth out of her no matter what it takes.

I pull up and see Rose huddled in the dark, her bare arms wrapped around herself as she shivers. She's wearing black leggings that outline every curve and an off-the-shoulder purple t-shirt. Who wears that shit outside in the middle of winter? What's she playing at?

Taking in her outfit makes me furious, but taking in her surroundings amps me up to absolutely livid. She's standing in front of some playground equipment and right behind the slide is a set of tall bushes that cast a shadow so black the devil himself couldn't see through it. Fucking junkies or psychopaths could leap out of there at any moment.

My chest tightens. Doesn't she know how goddamned dangerous this is? Where is her common sense?

Why the hell is she outside in the middle of the night? What the hell is going on here?

Does this have anything to do with that night?

The image of her huddled on the floor of the hall bathroom, silently sobbing, slams into me with all the force of a steel beam dropped by a crane. The memory alone has the power to crush my skull—and it has been, on repeat, every night since I saw her there.

The fact that she's been avoiding me ever since and nothing I've fucking done has gotten through to her ... that makes me want to crush someone else's skull.

My hands tighten on the steering wheel as I roll to a stop, the Jeep's headlights outlining her hourglass figure perfectly.

Fury thrums through me as she hurries to the Jeep. I force my eyes up to her face, to those glossy red lips and the dark curls spilling over her shoulders, trying to tell myself I did not just see her hard nipples or breasts bouncing underneath her shirt when she ran over.

Nope. She doesn't even have breasts.

As she climbs in, bringing in a juniper-scented gust of cold with her, I accidentally take in how long her legs are and every hair on my arms stands up, my body very aware that she's not young at all anymore.

Fuck. *Quique's sister. Quique's sister,* I tell myself as I grab my jacket off the center console and throw it in her lap, relieved that she's going to cover up, because I cannot be having these thoughts.

Anger and sex don't mix well for me. They become this potent cocktail that topples my good sense.

I quickly pull up a mental image of Rose as a scrawny four-teen-year-old. It doesn't quite erase the vision of the woman before me so I have to pull out the big mental guns: football, and the easy pass my QB missed last game that pissed me off.

Rose grabs the jacket and turns to see me in Quique's seat. She freezes. And the gratitude in those huge, gorgeous green eyes of hers withers, turning them into cold, hard peridots.

"FUCKER!" She grabs the door handle, about to push the car door open.

Oh no. She is not running off into those bushes. We are fucking talking and that's the end of it.

I do the only logical thing possible to keep her inside the vehicle. I jam on the gas and do a donut in the parking lot.

"What the hell!" she screeches as she reaches up and clings to the oh-shit handle as we circle.

"Buckle up, lil reina."

"Fuck off! I'm not going anywhere with you! And don't call me that!" she spits, all fierce fire. She's always hated being called a queen, though when she was younger, she used to just flip me off for doing it. While I've been away, it seems she's developed a little more fire.

"You're not getting out of this car," I reply, in as calm and even a tone as I can manage. "There could be crazy people out there."

"Out there! Try in here!" Her hand is on the door handle, ready to pull it open as soon as I slow.

"Don't you dare!" God, does she have no sense at all? I'm about to lose my shit. I shove down even harder on the gas, cranking the wheel, and tightening our loops.

59

"Are you trying to kill Lily? Stop! Right fucking now!" she screeches pointing out the windshield.

My gaze follows her finger and I realize that another girl is leaping off the sidewalk and running toward us like a lunatic, waving her arms. One of Rose's little friends, the one I talked to on campus.

When the hell did she get here? God, I knew it would be horrendously easy for people to hide in this damn park. Point proven.

My eyes scan the park and I see a third girl charging up the sidewalk, arms full of coats. Okay, good. Rose's friend isn't alone. She'll be safe.

Time to deal with the girl who refuses to tell me the truth, no matter what I do to wring it from her.

I brake hard and reverse out of the parking lot, ignoring the effect Rose's squeal has on me or how my jeans have suddenly become uncomfortably tight in response to that high-pitched, breathy little noise. My dick is an inappropriate bastard who deserves the cold shoulder I give him.

I focus on getting her out of here. She's still shivering hard enough between curses that her teeth are chattering.

Coffee. She needs to drink something warm after stupidly wandering around in the dark.

"Put your seatbelt on. And the jacket," I demand, as I make a left to exit the neighborhood.

"Where the fuck is Quique?"

"Passed out drunk in his room," I reply as I check the rearview mirror and switch lanes.

"We're going the wrong way. Did you forget where my house is? Probably so. You probably have amnesia or some kinda brain parasite—maybe that explains why you've lost your goddamned mind recently!" Rose grits out through her teeth. I can feel her anger pulsing through the air, just as hot as the vents I have directed toward her.

That's fine. She can be as pissed at me as she wants. What she can't be is unsafe.

I breathe deeply, ignoring her outburst, focused on driving for the moment. Maybe if I wait long enough, she'll calm down.

But my silence only seems to amp her up further.

"So, you're adding kidnapping to your list of crimes? Blackmailing wasn't enough?" Her snark makes my fingers clench the wheel even tighter. I'm surprised the metal doesn't warp underneath my grip.

"It's not kidnapping."

"You sure? Because I don't want to be here. You wouldn't let me get out."

"And it's not blackmail—" That's a lie.

"It sure as fuck is blackmailing when you threaten to release a video of my mother and a married donor screwing if I don't tell you what you want to know!"

I snap. Even though I know I'm not in the right, the need to know what happened to her still overpowers common sense. "I was trying to make sure you were safe!"

"You had *no right* to set that camera up."

61

"It wouldn't have fucking happened if you'd just told me what the hell was going on!" I growl and I swear, there's an earthquake brewing underneath my skin when I glance over and see that defiance on her face.

Her cheeks become a mottled red as she scoots toward the door, as far from me as she can get. She still hasn't put on her seatbelt. The urge to pull the car over, shove her into place, and buckle it myself comes on so strong I can practically taste it. The air between us grows thin and it becomes hard to breathe as we stare at one another until a bend in the road forces me to pull my eyes away.

The second eye contact is broken, she finds her voice—the shrill version of it. "I. DON'T. OWE. YOU. ANY—"

"Yes, you sure as fuck do!" I yell, rationality flying out the window as I yank the wheel to the side and stop at the curb. Some feral part of me takes over and I have to spend a minute breathing deeply, fighting it back because her words made me see red.

She must sense the lava bubbling just beneath my skin because the girl is smart enough not to make me blow my lid. She presses her lips together, eyes narrowing, but keeps her mouth shut while I get myself under control.

Part of me wonders if she's right.

Maybe I am going a little crazy.

I did set up a video in her bathroom.

Only to make sure she didn't ever do that shit again.

And I just tried to check on her.

When Rose stonewalled me and then her mother made use of the room ... I saw an opportunity. I took it.

Evil?

Yeah. Maybe.

But she didn't see herself that night. She didn't see how broken she looked. Who could leave someone looking like that?

Especially her?

Rose has always been innocent. Delicate. Naïve in this endearing and adorable way that makes her walk with a skip in her step and smile at strangers, not recognizing their leers. Someone shattered that.

I'll be damned if I let them get away with it.

Her hatred is the price I'm willing to pay in order to get a name. So if I have to hold this video over her head, that's what I'll do.

I press down on the gas again and keep navigating through the neighborhood until I get out onto a main drag. There's a fast food place with a drive-through and I pull in, ignoring how the silence has become as thick as cotton.

Rolling down my window, I place an order for two coffees and a large French fry.

Turning to Rose, I ask, "Milk or sugar?"

She's sitting with her back against the passenger door, her head tilted, gaze dangerous, no doubt measuring me for my coffin. "You care what I want? Since when? Since you dropped that blackmail note on my bedspread—"

I roll up the window so the fast food people don't get an earful too.

"I tried talking to you first. You blocked my number and avoided me."

"I didn't want to fucking talk!" She throws out an arm and ends up clenching her fist at me.

"What you want and what you need are on entirely different planets, little girl," I snarl, pulling forward to the drive-through window.

A smiling teenager with a zit-scarred face and a greasy blue streak in his hair greets us.

"That'll be six ninety-five," he says.

"Can you please call the police, sir?" Rose leans toward me for the first time since she realized I was driving. "I've been kidnapped." I roll my eyes and hand the guy a twenty. "Keep the change. And please excuse my little sister. She's got her phone hidden, doing some dumb TikTok challenge."

The guy rolls his eyes and just points at the next window. I doubt we're the first TikTok prank to roll through.

But I'm seething. I turn and breathe fire. "What the hell?"

"Your sister!"

"You trying to get me arrested?"

"You deserve to be arrested!"

"Do I? Do I? If I'm getting locked up, then so are you, lil reina. Padded fucking cell." Goddammit. I've devolved to threats. I didn't want to get here. I told myself I'd stay calm and cool and get names out of her. "I didn't mean—"

I can't even get my full apology out before she screams a full-on banshee screech that shreds my eardrums. "You are ruining my life!"

"Ruining! I'm trying to fucking save it!" I yell as I pound on the side of the steering wheel, frustrated as shit at her, myself, the goddamned universe. Why does it always have to go this way?

When she speaks next, her voice is tiny, minuscule, as soft as a single note from a piano. "Why? Why do you even care?"

My jaw works as I turn to look at her. How can she even ask that question? Why do I care? Why?

Those light green eyes of hers grow twice as glossy as her lips tighten into a bud. She swallows hard and I can see her neck strain as she stiffens. "Fuck you," she curses before yanking open her door and jumping out of the Jeep.

No. Not again. Not motherfucking happening.

I yank the parking brake up, turning off the car before kicking open my door and leaving it gaping as I stride after her into the dark parking lot next to the building.

My pulse booms underneath my skin, explosive and loud in my ears as this need that's been driving me, the fear and worry that have been eating at me, shove me forward. The soles of my shoes crunch over the blacktop as I chase her down, the inability to let go, to let *her* go claiming me.

I reach out, grabbing Rose by the elbow and she spins, immediately shoving me as hard as she can. Her tiny hands aren't strong enough to move me, but I take a step back in surprise and throw my hands up to show her I'm not actually a threat.

"No! This is enough! This is—" Her face is streaked with tears, mascara running just like it did that night. The sight makes my ribs crack open and words come pouring out of me.

"I can't sleep thinking about what happened. I can't sleep because it makes me angry—furious—that someone or something hurt you. Nothing should ever hurt you, Rose. Ever."

"But why do you give a shit?"

Her eyes bounce between mine and I experience something I've only ever felt before when I was in the middle of a fight —my brain short circuits. It fritzes and sparks, sending a desperate beam of energy right down the core of my spine. My body's screaming as if this is a life-or-death moment. Fight or flight. It makes absolutely no sense but every instinct tells me I'm poised on the edge of a cliff, and one wrong word will topple me off.

For some reason, this feels like it's the most important moment of my life and I'm not completely certain why.

My mouth opens and closes as I stare at her, at my best friend's little sister, who's so beautiful even in her anger, who's gut-wrenchingly lovely even in her sadness. Words fail me, and not only because there's something about this moment that has my stomach coiling into complicated Celtic knots. My eyes trace the sharp lines of her cheekbones, the soft curve of her lips, before trailing back up to those spring-green eyes. I find myself breathless as I whisper, "Rose, I need you—"

Her body slams into me and her kiss rips away any other words I might have said, obliterates any other thoughts I might have had. Her tiny arms twine around me, and all of a sudden, all this wild energy, this obsessive fury sheds the shell of "protective older brother" I've been trying to force onto it.

That excuse cracks wide open and an animalistic fervor, a desire to claim her, rears up.

No one should ever hurt Rose because she's mine.

The realization hits me with a force that nearly buckles my knees.

My tongue darts out to trace her lips, but she eschews gentleness and sucks my tongue right into her mouth before stroking the underside with her own. I immediately fall into her frantic rhythm, getting caught up in this giddy, wild moment as the energy between us transforms from a one-sided obsession into something else.

Our teeth gnash and fight as our naked lips skim over one another, tongues tangling as my hands seek out her hair and I wrench her head back so that I can get a better angle, seal my lips more fully to hers, and suck out her soul.

We kiss.

And kiss.

And kiss.

The moon could explode overhead and I wouldn't know it.

I don't know anything beyond the yearning in my chest, one that isn't sated by kissing, one that wants more. Not just Rose's body. But something else ... something I can't define.

My hands fly down to her sides, skimming her perfect figure which is barely covered by the t-shirt she's wearing. Those leggings I hated when I first picked her up? God, I love them now as I get a handful of ass in either hand, adoring how—even though she's tiny in comparison to me—her ass over-flows around my fingertips. I dig in, getting a good grip on her as her teeth bite down on my lower lip.

Grinning at her frenzy, caught up in the maelstrom with her, I whirl her around and push her up against the window of this fast food joint, uncaring about the show we're giving the few patrons inside.

I shove my leg between those soft thighs of hers, those precious thighs that are now mine to protect—

"Um. You can't do that." An awkward voice makes Rose freeze and my head swivels to the side.

I stare daggers at the fucker who's interrupted us—a gangly, pimple-pocked teenage boy who can't weigh over a buck twenty soaking wet. He's got on a stupidly bright polo and a name tag that reads Miguel. He holds our coffees in a cardboard carrier in one hand, while his other hand scratches awkwardly at his flushed skin.

"Oh my God. Oh my God." Rose immediately slides down my body to my knee, her arms detaching and pushing at me as a blush covers her cheeks. I step away, reaching for her hand, but her arms sweep up and she digs her fingers into her hair, a distressed expression overtaking her features.

It's almost as if someone tied up my hope, handcuffed it to a beam, and poured cement all over it.

Fuck.

She regrets it.

She acted impulsively and now she regrets it.

No, don't go there. She just needs a minute to process. And this fucker embarrassed her. She's shy. Well, except with me. It's probably just that.

Stoically, I go over to the teenager and pluck our coffees and fries from his grip.

"Your sister, huh?" His smirk makes me want to smack him, but I resist, until his eyes drift salaciously over to Rose. Then, I grab him by the collar and lift him up until his feet dangle an inch from the ground. I don't say a single word. I don't have to. His bug eyes and frantic apologies do all the work for me.

When I release the kid, I walk over to Rose, who's turned her back on me and didn't see that little exchange. I hand her coffee to her, careful not to touch her trembling fingers when she reaches out to take it because I'm going to give her a little time to process the line we just crossed. Can't say I don't need one myself. I swing my arm wide and gesture toward the Jeep.

We ride home in silence. I keep replaying the way she threw herself bodily at me, how good she felt in my arms. The things I want to do to her now …

I park in the driveway of her mom's house, noting all the lights are off. Quique must still be asleep. I turn in my seat so that Rose and I can talk, but I'm surprised to find her simultaneously unbuckling and shoving open the passenger door.

"This never happened," she mutters. The words burst apart the silence and send shrapnel right into my chest.

So she *is* going to try to act like our kiss doesn't exist—sweep it under the rug. Just like she has been about the night I found her in the bathroom and whatever set her off then. Well, I'm not going to let her get away with it.

"Yes, it did." My annoyance and anger are clear in my sharp tone.

"No, it didn't," she growls forcefully as she hops out and then slams the door.

I debate climbing out after her, but I don't. We need to deal with what's going on between us ourselves before she starts screeching and bringing Quique into it. I stay in my seat and let myself enjoy the sight of her ass in the moonlight as she stomps up to the front door.

When she glances back, I just grin at her, delighting in the way her cheeks blotch red in either embarrassment or fury. Her lips can deny it all they want, but her body can't. This shit definitely happened. And it's going to happen again, I guarantee it.

ROSE

I stare at the ceiling fan spinning slowly, the stained wooden blades cutting across the white ceiling in a soothing rhythm, circling just like my thoughts.

I'm tucked under my covers, laying in bed. I'm supposed to be asleep already, but every time I try to close my eyes all I can see is that desperately intense, obsessive look on Angelo's face.

My throat and my nipples both grow tight at the memory of the way he stared at me in that parking lot, of the heady sensations that swept over me almost like a spell. A look like that is dangerously intoxicating. Bewitching. Addicting.

It's more tempting than anything I've ever encountered.

Why haven't I been warned about that look?

Schools shouldn't just campaign against drugs—they should campaign against overbearing assholes who can't stand to let you make your own mistakes, who stalk you, call you relentlessly, and then sear you with a gaze that leaves your skin branded, permanently marked and painfully sizzling. That type of man is perilous. Bad for your mental health. He'll strip away your ability to make good decisions and leave you lust-starved, craving him.

But *why him*? Why couldn't that look have come from anyone else, dammit?

Brutish blackmailers are apparently my drug of choice.

My fingers drift over my lips, which still feel swollen from his kisses. They might even be bruised.

I can't believe I did that. Why? Why would I kiss him?

I never should have judged Daisy so harshly for forgiving Gunnar. Hot men should come with warning signs. Caution: Brain will short-circuit within a five-foot radius.

My logic had certainly failed me when I'd stared up into Angelo's deep brown gaze and seen, not just the bossy caveman glare I'd grown used to, but actual vulnerability shining in it.

He'd said he needed me.

Not I like you. Not I want you.

I need you.

Fuck. I'd swooned right into kissing the bastard.

Even now, my core clenches at the memory of that kiss. Then he'd pinned me up against the wall and owned me. I'd been on the brink of an orgasm just from making out with him.

Me.

Me!

It takes me almost forty minutes with a dirty book and my vibrator to eke out an O. But he had nearly wrung one from me with nothing more than a kiss. Off-kilter—and completely at odds with the part of my mind still pacing and swearing and calling Angelo a blackmailer—my pussy pulses gently, begging for a touch. A release after the tease of that kiss.

But can I really touch myself to thoughts of him? Yes, his muscles and his tattoos, those lips—his body was made for naughty thoughts. But what about everything else?

He set up that camera in the bathroom to spy on me!

Yes, it was after I blocked his texts and avoided him for nearly a week, but still. He didn't have any right to invade my privacy or to try to force me to confess who drove me to cut myself by blackmailing me with the most mind-bleachingly disgusting video of my mother imaginable.

Even as I think about the thumb drive he'd left on my bed with a note that read: *Tell me who THEY are or this gets out*, my face heats up in anger. But it's not all directed at him. There's also a bitter, burnt-tasting edge of the anger that's reserved solely for my mom.

How many times have I gotten lectures about my life choices? About how we're under a microscope? How we have to be paper-doll perfect?

How many times did she pull me aside when I was younger, my crush on Angelo so painfully obvious, and tell me that a girl like me is too good for the likes of him?

"Please, Rosalinda. Mija. He's in construction and his father hires criminals. Criminals! They're little more than thugs. He's a sweet boy but you're going to be a doctor. There's no future there."

"Quique's friends with him."

"Friends are one thing. This," she'd pointed a finger and gestured at the expression on my face, *"this cannot happen."*

All those lectures about how I should dress, act, speak. And she's fucking around with a married man?

And with her campaign, her little plans for me have gotten even more involved than they used to be. They've included dates with guys who have cardboard cutout personalities but fathers sporting thick pocketbooks. I never slept with them but still … she's been essentially whoring me out.

And I let her.

I let her because I believed. In her.

I've jumped through every hoop she's ever asked of me, thrown my back into all this campaign crap, getting signatures, putting up signs all over Timbuktu, and asking how high whenever she told me to jump.

I'm not just a bad judge of character, I'm a horrible one. I couldn't see the truth about my mother and now I've kissed my own blackmailer. Well, if I suck at it, I blame my mother; I obviously inherited my broken judge-o-meter from her. She married a drunkard, after all.

I grind my teeth as my fingers twine in the sheets and squeeze, frustration and resentment pitting tiny little holes all over me. It's a special sort of ire, the kind that a girl can only feel toward her mother.

But just as quickly as I grow angry at her for being a goddamned hypocrite, for dictating my life while she's out there ruining other people's marriages, I shift my thoughts back over to Angelo.

He deserves some of this vitriol too. He unmasked her and turned my own mother into a villain. He amped up my resentment toward her and he did it by violating my privacy. God, I wish I could choke him. But, for some reason, the idea of wrapping my fingers around his throat isn't just about the violence for me. Anger and lust intermingle when I think of him. They don't separate like oil and water, but swirl and mix with all the sugar-sweet memories I have from years of carrying a torch for him.

Yeah, this stalking is overboard. Wrong to the nth degree. But I still remember the time my swimsuit tie ripped during an intense game of pool volleyball. Angelo stood in front of me, back to me, walking sideways and hiding me so I could climb out of the pool and grab a towel without people seeing everything. He's always been so protective. It's just now … he's taken it to an extreme. It's an utter mindfuck to hate him after I've wanted him for so long and the two emotions combine into something decidedly bad for me.

He's evil yet delicious.

Deliciously evil.

Angelo Walker is like a … a giant cake—the kind you eat to compensate for all the horridly confusing feelings you have about this bullshit thing called life.

The problem with eating cake is I can't ever stop myself from having a second slice even though I know I shouldn't and will end up with a stomachache the next day. Just like with that kiss. I'm going to regret it, even though it was by far the sweetest one to ever touch my lips.

I shove aside the softer feelings that keep tripping me up and focus on the cold hard facts. He crossed a line and it's unfor-givable.

My mind shouts those words but my stomach is still so flut-tery at the thought of his stare that I know they aren't true. *Why* aren't they true though? They should be true. I should loathe the sight of him instead of feeling like this.

Even if I don't completely hate him …

He's my brother's best friend. We couldn't. My mother would kill us. We shouldn't.

But …

Those eyes. Those gorgeous eyes surrounded by straight, soot-black lashes. That expression when he'd stared at me in the parking lot and the way his lips had pursed as he'd searched for the words to explain why he couldn't just let me go on my merry way. Couldn't ignore me.

Couldn't just use me for his own purposes and then forget about me like my very own mother.

Yeah, his attention is infuriating and wrong on a level that I can't simply absolve him from. But when he stared at me like I was the center of his entire fucking universe, all that right versus wrong seemed to dissolve.

No one's ever looked at me that way before.

And the fact that it was him?

And that kiss? The hair on the back of my neck rises as the memory floods me once more, still just as potent as the first time I recalled it.

Coupled with the way he kneaded my ass … It's wrong, but I wanted him to pull my cheeks apart and squeeze them tight as he forced me up and down on that massive, muscular thigh of his, making me ride him.

God.

I bite my lip, my canines needling the still-sensitive flesh as a current of giddiness darts through me. I'm so fucked.

Against my better judgment, I grab my phone and scroll into my contacts. I unblock Bastard, the nickname I gave him.

But then my fingers freeze over the screen. What do I say? How do I say it? I'm not forgiving him. Not by a long shot. He had no right to invade my life even if he thinks he had reason to. Ugh … I'm starting not to believe my own argument. What the hell do I send?

Hi, I want to use your body for my own personal porn is not going to cut it.

I start to type but pause before sending the message.

Me: Thank you for the ride.

No. Nope. Forget it. Unblocking him was stupid. I erase the message and stare at my screen in frustration. I glance over to my window and watch the curtains sway because I have the window cracked open to fill the room with fresh, frigid air while I sleep.

In the distance, a coyote calls out to the moon.

I should just block him again. Avoid him like I have been. That's the sensible solution. I turn back to stare at my phone and when I swipe to turn it on, I'm shocked to see a new text staring me right in the face.

Bastard: Thank fuck you'll never see this. But I'm warning you now. Some day soon I'll come for you. And on you. And then I'm going to pin you down and come deep inside you.

Oh God.

Oh my fucking God.

I don't think I've ever heard or seen anything hotter in my entire life.

Holy hell. Angelo fucking Walker wants to fuck me.

My free hand is down inside my panties before I've even finished gasping in surprise. All thoughts about how I should deal with him become tomorrow's problem because right now, the only problem I can handle is the lust pouring from my skin in palpable waves.

He could pin me down right here in this bed, those massive biceps of his flexing as he hovers over me, my hands scratching down his thick, muscled chest as I stare at the tattoos I've only seen glimpses of while he slides inside me. Would he be rough like when he shoved me against the wall or gentle like the night he cleaned me up? Why does the need to know that feel so urgent? So important?

My eyes flutter closed as my fingers tease up and down the length of my slit, which is already plump and swollen.

Is he touching himself right now? Is he jerking off, thinking about that kiss the same way I am? Fantasizing about me the way I'm thinking about him?

All my life I wished for something like this, never *ever* expecting it to happen. Now, that kiss and that text make secret wishes seem like they might be reality. I'm a bit starstruck by that fact and more than a little lust-drunk as I wonder how thick his cock is. Would it hurt … stretch me wide? I hope so.

Regret that I didn't rub up against him more earlier surges through me, though I do have to admit that years of staring at him makes me think his package won't disappoint. Back when I was still a virgin, years ago, I remember one summer night in particular when he wore board shorts, no t-shirt, and a few gold necklaces that overlapped. My teenage brain had seared the image of his bare chest, dark nipples, and rock-solid abs into my skull even though the outline of his dick in those blue shorts had intimidated me. Of course, that was back when the idea of a guy coming on me would have made me pull a face.

Now?

Now the idea of him marking me with his cum only turns me on more. I kind of hope he's the type to pull my hair and hold me in place while he defiles me. Even better if he whispers dirty words in a smattering of English and Spanish.

I drop my phone to my side and pull my hand off my slit so that I can shove my panties down. Fingers aren't going to be enough right now. I'm already panting and soaked, my body needy and worked up from earlier, almost aching at this point. I roll onto my side and yank open my nightstand drawer, grabbing my lipstick vibrator.

I don't even need lube. That dirty text Angelo sent, and the fact that he sent it thinking I couldn't see it, that's all the foreplay I need.

I flick on my buzzing little friend and press it to my clit as my other hand snakes underneath my bra and plucks at my nipple.

Desire rushes up through me faster and more potent than any other I've ever felt. Angelo's dark eyes invade my mind and I imagine his plush lips on my ear as I whisper his words aloud. "I'm going to pin you down ..." I don't even make it all the way through his sentence before I'm whimpering, my thighs trembling, my pussy clenching harder than it ever has in my life. Fuck! Sparks fly through my body until nothing matters but the mindless, blissful hum that fills my mind. Yes. I crank up the intensity of the vibrations and draw out my pleasure again and again until I can't take it any longer and my hips collapse back down against the mattress.

Fastest. Longest. Orgasm. Ever.

I toss the toy aside and reach for my phone, only to find three more texts.

Bastard: Did you unblock me?

Aw shit!

How could he tell? My face heats up and I slide underneath my covers, tenting them in my embarrassment. But that's no good, because it smells like sex under there, a stark reminder of the crazily stupid things Angelo can get me to do with just a look or a hot line. Fuck me. I shove the sheets back off my face and read the next texts.

Bastard: Lil reina?

Bastard: I'm not taking back what I said. But I'll add that I'm going to spread your thighs and go to town like I'm in a watermelon-eating contest. I'm going to eat you until you beg me for mercy. But you should know I'm mean, baby. I won't stop until you're sobbing.

Damn. Is he always a dirty talker? Because that last one gives me a very intense visual and it's nasty but I also kind of like the idea of his cheeks soaked from eating me out and the indirect promise of multiple orgasms. Shit. My clit flares weakly back to life for just a moment before waving the white flag. Not yet.

A new text pings.

Bastard: It's going to happen.

Yeah, we'll see about that.

Part of me loves his confidence and dominance and wants to sass back, engage in whatever game he's playing.

I chew on my thumbnail as I debate what to do.

But, honestly? I haven't forgiven him and I'm not sure he deserves to be absolved after what he's done. Yeah, I might be a little bit of an idiot around him. But texting isn't the same as him standing in front of me with bedroom eyes, and I find the strength to resist his lure. So, I swipe back over and block him again, but not before I screenshot those texts he sent.

Because I at least deserve some hot spank bank material out of this mess.

PINK STREAKS of morning light halo Daisy shivering on our stoop in a puffy white coat. Her brown hair is in a French braid and her pale cheeks are flushed. The bright, clear sky gives the impression that the day should be warm instead of cold. It's not—the second I open the glass-paned front door at her knock, my breath mists in the frigid cold. The sun and the temperature are clearly at odds.

Just like my best friend and me.

But as she stares at me with her gray eyes and droops her lips to give me a begging puppy face, I can't help but want to erase the awkward, distant feeling between us. So I lean forward and give her a giant hug.

Tears choke me up when her arms encircle me and she squeezes me back.

"I'm sorry," I whisper.

"No. I'm sorry."

A chorus of *I'm sorry*s volleys back and forth between the two of us becoming louder and louder each time—a remnant of the fact that Daisy's been my very best friend since elementary school and we haven't been able to let go of some of our more ridiculous traditions. Like our sorry-offs.

A door cracks open down the hall behind me and my mother's head emerges, her lips stretched into a thin line. "Keep it down, girls. I'm on a conference call." Her smooth black hair is pulled up in a French braid, slim figure tucked into a perfectly pressed black suit. My mother doesn't even say good morning or acknowledge the fact that I didn't know she was home. She just shuts the door to her office and gets back to work. It thumps closed as Daisy and I exchange a look that's become more and more common over the past six months.

A look I call, *Yup, that's my mother.*

Daisy just gives a what-can-you-do shrug before saying, "Anyway, you don't need to be sorry at all. You were trying to protect me." Her words are soft and kind and so utterly Daisy-like. It's why I love her. She can't hold a grudge to save her life. Me? I can grudge with the best of them, though most people would never know it because I'm just not brave enough to say something. Angelo seems to be the exception in that arena, though I don't quite know why.

Daisy reaches out and squeezes my hand. "I actually love that you got mad on my behalf. You couldn't know that I gave Gunnar permission to do anything he wanted to watch me. He's got … a couple kinks."

What? Uptight Gunnar? Color me intrigued but definitely planning not to ask. I'll wait for her to tell me what those are when she's comfortable. I'm kind of surprised she's even okay with that word, given the fact that she was a virgin mere days ago. But it just slid off her tongue easily and she appears utterly unembarrassed about it. Isn't it strange how we can change in an instant?

Of course, the moment Daisy starts to study me, an eyebrow quirking as her eyes scan me up and down, I grow awkward, because I know what's coming.

Her voice doesn't hold an ounce of judgment, only concern, as she asks, "But what happened? That was … unusual for you."

I press my lips together in a morose sort of grin because even though I don't really want to explain everything, I feel like I should. Actually, maybe explaining it all to someone would help me make sense of it, help me quash the stupid attraction that's still intermingling with my anger. "Want to come in?"

"Yes, please."

We end up making steaming mugs of tea in the kitchen in silence before I jerk my head toward my room, indicating we should go there to talk. Daisy keeps her cup in one hand and weaves her other arm around mine, all the tension and discomfort from last night evaporated as if it never even happened. And I haven't said a single word yet.

That's how best friends are.

They're just there when you need them. Patient. Unswervingly loyal and forgiving when you've accidentally made an ass of yourself in front of them and their new significant other.

God, I'm lucky to have her. And she'll set me straight. She'll help me get my head on right and come up with a plan to avoid Angelo, I just know it. But once we're settled on my comforter, sitting cross-legged and facing each other, I find my heart thumping faster and my throat closing up.

I take a quick sip of tea and awkwardly ask, "Um, do you want to tell me about you first? How's everything with Gunnar? Did I make it worse?" It feels awkward to ask that. But, if I'm not quite ready to let it all out, then the least I can do is try to be supportive.

Daisy immediately blushes and ducks her head. "Oh gosh no. It's good. So, so good. Like more amazing than I ever could have imagined. He's perfect for me in ways I didn't even know I wanted."

"Yeah?"

She nods and plays with the end of her braid, plucking at individual strands of hair. "I know it's fast, or we got together quickly, but he's been there for everything, Rose, you know."

"Yeah. I know." I know she also cried her eyes out to me after he proposed to her mother when she had been so certain he was going to ask her out. Oh, crap, there I go with my judgmental grudginess instead of being supportive. I find a positive and throw it out there. "He has always spoiled you rotten."

"Yeah. He's planning a getaway for us."

I blink. "Already? How long have you actually been together?" I'm a little taken aback.

"We've known each other almost two years, Rosie-Dosie. He's *the one*." Her eyes shine as she says it, and she wears this ethereal expression I've never seen before, almost like one of those old religious paintings where someone's staring up at an angel in awe.

I'm thunderstruck. And I have to admit, I'm the tiniest bit jealous that her dream guy didn't turn out to be some kind of creep like I assumed he was. Like my dream guy has turned out to be.

"Yeah?"

She presses her lips together as she meets my eyes once more and nods emphatically. "Yeah. Gory details?"

"Definitely."

She chews her lip for a second before she blurts out, "He's a total dom in the bedroom. And it's so frustrating but so hot because he won't just let me come. He makes me wait."

"What!?" Mental gymnastics ensue in my head as I try not to visualize Gunnar naked but simultaneously process the fact that my best friend just basically admitted to being a submissive in the bedroom. "But he's not a jerk, right? He does get you there?"

Her giggles are absolutely giddy. "Oh, he gets me there. Don't worry. God. I didn't know it could feel like this!"

She's on cloud nine but watching her makes me sink down deeper and deeper, slowly sucked under like the Titanic or Atlantis—drowning—not just in jealousy, but in self-loathing. Because I can't imagine something like that ever happening to me.

Even the kiss last night. That epic kiss … it's tainted. It could have been perfect, if Angelo wasn't such a fucking prick.

A hand covers mine and I glance up only to realize my eyes have grown blurry. Daisy flips my hand over and holds it while I fight against the way my throat cinches closed and my tears threaten to spill out.

"Sorry. I'm happy for you. I am."

"Tell me." Her tone is so soft that it's really more of a coax than a command.

I need to tell her. I need to get it out there so that I can just move on. So I force my lips apart and I spill my secrets, laying it all at her feet, exposing everything. Tears interrupt me twice. I have to gloss over what happened at the frat house because I just can't get the words out. And when I admit to cutting after it, I choke up again. But I make it through, and after I'm done, my soul feels lighter.

But I fully expect my best friend to dole out my penance, to lay into me for being so dumb. As I swipe away the last tear and stare at her expectantly, she chews her lip, deciding what to say first.

Nerves dig a hole in my stomach and burrow into it as I await her judgment.

"Was he a good kisser?" Daisy, still holding my hand, cocks her head to one side as she nestles her mug between her legs so she can reach up and tuck a strand of hair that's fallen out of her braid behind her ear.

What? I gape at her in silence for a moment before I unwind our hands and punch her lightly on the shoulder. "Are you fucking serious right now? *That's* what you want to know?"

She gives me a look that says, "obviously."

"He's *blackmailing* me," I remind her, in case she's forgotten that very salient point. That sword point. That point of no return.

"Yeah, to get you to tell the truth about what happened the night you reverted to old habits *you'd promised me* you'd never use again." Daisy gets a little pedantic on me and I grind my teeth. "He's blackmailing you because he knows you'll sweep it under the rug and go on with a smile, while you're seething inside. He knows you won't do anything about it because you're Rose."

"It's fucking wrong!"

"Newsflash: he gave you that video like a week ago. And you haven't given him the names of those frat fuckers he wants. You should by the way. But he still hasn't released the video." She points a finger at me, as if her logic puts an entirely new spin on things.

But the fact that he hasn't released the video yet doesn't mean he won't. He had the gall to threaten me with it in the first place.

I cross my arms and lean back, jaw ticking. "So, you support his illegal behavior?"

"I do. Because he's not actually going to do it. He's just trying to play your hero like he always has." My best friend leans back against the wooden frame of my bed, looking smugly superior at my aghast expression.

"You are zero fucking help," I curse, frowning at Daisy even as hope flutters inside my ribs. I try to capture it, shove that little bird down before she flies off, out of my control. But with a sarcastic twitter in my direction, she's taking flight.

The idea that Angelo just wants to play my hero is too potent a fantasy to ignore.

No. NO.

"You want me to help you hate Angelo?" My best friend furrows her brow.

"*Yes!* That's exactly what I want." That's what he deserves. Isn't it? My chest grows tight as the words I'm saying contradict everything I feel.

She shakes her head. "No. You hate him already. That's obvious. But you love him more."

Fuck.

Fuck me.

My arms uncross and come up to cover my face in despair. That right there might be my problem, because underneath it all, I think Daisy might be right.

ROSE

*S*ince I don't have class on Fridays, I spent all of yesterday out hiking alone in the mountains. Well, some hiking and a lot of hot chocolate drinking at a little hole-in-the-wall restaurant I found. I should have done some homework or reading, but I needed to escape after Daisy's truths scraped me raw. I needed time away from my family too because I knew today was going to be a shit show.

Fundraisers are the modern equivalent of the ton attending a ball in a historical romance. They're a requirement in order to court donors while being a lovely reminder that you're utterly tied to and indebted to horrible people who look down their noses at you. I can't wait for tonight's shindig.

I finish applying my ruby red lipstick and check my reflection in the mirror, giving myself a fake smile so that I can ensure that none smeared onto my teeth. Then I smooth down the backless black midi dress I'm wearing and plump my dark curls one last time. I left them loose tonight, to help keep myself a smidgen warmer than I'd be with it up. It's probably futile, though. Most likely, I'll end up ducking inside eighty times to avoid getting the shivers because tonight's fundraiser is in the courtyard of The Piñon Hotel in Santa Fe. My mother's event coordinator, Ricardo, planned it, and he's an idiot with the same tactical precision as Napoleon marching on Russia in midwinter. We're going to freeze.

I check the time on my phone as I slide on a thick silver and turquoise bracelet I inherited from my grandmother. We need to leave soon. "Quique! Get a move on!" I shout, because my easy-going brother can't be on time to save his life. He's coming tonight because this is a big enough deal that it will probably make the papers and Mom wants a photo of the three of us all together, smiling happily for the press.

I briefly wonder if that guy she's screwing is going to be there tonight. Will he bring his wife? Disgust and anger zigzag through me like little lightning bolts and I have to breathe deeply to regain my sense of calm. It doesn't matter. I can't stop other people from making shitty life choices—not even my own mother. And family … even when you resent them the way I do right now … they're still all you have at the end of the day.

I blow out a deep breath as I pack my beaded red clutch. I just need to do my job, keep my head down, and make it out of there as quickly as I can. Instead of focusing on my mother's secrets, I try to think about the night and mentally lay out how it's going to unfold.

The drive to the hotel will take an hour, then we have to check the set up before the guests arrive and Mom has to practice her speech. I've got placard duty, checking that the names match our little layout map. Mom doesn't want to foist such a boring job on anyone else.

I sigh as I slip on my red heels and tuck my clutch under my arm. I toss a black velvet coat on top, a coat I'd wear all night if Mom wouldn't verbally elbow me with snide comments every two seconds.

About to step into the hallway, Mom opens my door just as I reach for the handle.

"Oh, good. You're ready. This is a big one, tonight, Rosa."

I nod, though she says the same thing for every event. Each one is always essential, big, important. She hardly ever shows up at my room like this though, so I'm curious about this display of nerves.

"Well, how do I look?" she asks, holding her arms up for inspection as a professional hair and makeup crew file out of her room and through the front door behind her. In a deep red suit that offsets her tan skin perfectly, her dark hair is teased and fluffed like a news anchor's. Though she left a few crow's feet around the corners of her eyes for authenticity, she's gotten a few touch-ups elsewhere and there isn't a line to be seen on her forehead. She looks like an older, less pale version of me, sans the green eyes—hers are a rich brown.

"You look great, Mom." I give the requisite, expected answer with a smile. She really does look good. Seeing her look so professional used to make me swell inside with pride, but right now, I just feel queasy. I'm not certain if it's due to the fact that I really don't want to go to this event tonight or the secret knowledge I have that knocks her off the pedestal she used to stand on.

"Thank you. You do too, honey. Now, look. There's going to be a big donor there tonight. The Garcia family. But there's been a little bit of a complication. I know you can handle it for me."

My fingers dig into the beaded purse as I study her eyes and the serious expression on her face. Her lips thin in displeasure before she says, "Your brother doesn't take this seriously enough. He's treating this like a party. He's invited a date and … Angelo."

I nearly drop my purse. "What?!" Immediately, I can feel my cheeks heat as if I just touched them to a piping hot griddle. I'm not ready to see Angelo yet. I'm not ready to deal with him, especially not in front of my family or in a situation where I have to be on my absolute best behavior. I want to cover my face with my hands, but then I'll ruin the makeup that I spent over an hour applying. So my purse takes the brunt of my aggravation, dimpling under the press of my fingertips.

Mom mistakes my dismay for outrage on her part. "I know. I've had a chat with him, but the damage is done because they're both already here."

Angelo is already inside my house? My throat goes dry and though I lock up my knees, they tremble slightly.

"Maybe I should stay behind—that's too much for your entourage—"

"Absolutely not! I need you to help me minimize this disaster. The Garcias hate the Walkers."

"They do?"

"Yes. Apparently, some deal went south about twenty years ago. I don't know all the details. But I know they hold a grudge as deep as the Capulets and Montagues. In any case, you know I hate to ask this, but I need you to keep Angelo away from them."

My mouth opens in dismay and a nervous sweat immediately breaks out along the back of my neck. "Mom—"

"I know I can trust you to keep it professional, mija." Her hands come up to clasp my shoulders. "I need your help. Your crush is long gone, yes?"

I press my lips together as she stares at me, the weight of her expectations draping over me like heavy chains. I find myself nodding automatically, an ingrained response, to give her the answer she wants.

"Good. Good. I knew when he came back looking like a criminal with those tattoos and things, you'd start to see him for what he really is."

She's such a snob. I don't know that I ever realized it before. Or maybe I glossed over that knowledge, just like I ignored a million other little things—her late-night meetings with donors, the trips she's always on, the fact that I don't think she's checked in once with me about how classes are going now that the spring semester has started.

"Thank you, mija." She gives me a loose hug, careful not to muss my hair or her outfit. It's a fake hug, a hug more concerned with our appearances than anything else, and I derive absolutely zero comfort from it.

When she pulls away and turns to open my door, I want to cry like a stupid little girl. Even though Angelo's video lifted the veil from my eyes, seeing my mother's machinations in person cuts a whole new wound into my heart. She's not evil.

She just sees other people as a means to her end. Or ... is that the definition of evil?

I blink rapidly, trying to contain the burning behind my eyes. Even though my mascara is waterproof, I don't have time to fix everything else. The inside of my chest compresses, pressure building, and I wish more than anything that I had a tiny razor in my hand—just a quick and easy way to bleed off some of the chaos tainting my thoughts.

"Okay!" Mom claps her hands loudly as she steps into the hall. "Let's get this show on the road! Guys, I have boxes for you."

I move out into the hallway and I'm surprised to see Quique's door already open. He's dressed? This is a first. Mom must have spoken with him already. That, or he's actually excited about this date he's got. I didn't even know he was seeing someone.

I take a deep calming breath and force my fingers to relax their death grip on my bag. They ache as they release and I switch the clutch to my other palm so I can shake my hand out as I follow my mother to our open-concept kitchen.

I stop dead when I see Quique in a suit, carrying a big cardboard box full of pamphlets. Not because I've never seen him in a suit, but because he's walking straight toward the one man I don't ever want to see again but also dream endlessly about.

Holding open the door to the garage, wearing a black suit that fits him like a glove, his neck tattoos just stretching above his starched white collar, is Angelo. He looks like a fucking mob boss with his dark hair and thick brow. But his face is relaxed and smiling as he says something to my brother that I can't hear because the blood has suddenly fled from my head and all rushed south.

Those lips hold me entranced for a moment as I remember the way they felt, how they molded to mine so perfectly.

Fuck!

No.

I'm not ready to see him. My stomach drops out and my palms instantly grow sweaty even though they're cold. Despite my discussion with Daisy and my massive hike to clear my head, I'm not ready to deal with him in the flesh. He's too much. Too overwhelming.

My eyes dart to my mother as my breathing grows shallow in panic. Her gaze flicks over to mine and I think I might pass out from dread, certain that Angelo's effect on me is as subtle as a strobe light.

How am I supposed to get through tonight fulfilling all of my mother's expectations, smiling and making small talk, and staying focused on being prim and proper? How am I supposed to do that while staying near Angelo and keeping him away from the Garcias?

This is an impossible task. I'm doomed to failure.

I bring my eyes back to Angelo's only to find his gaze is absolutely molten as it traces down my figure and ignites a fire between my thighs. I quickly drop my eyes and call out, "Shotgun."

"Not happening!" Quique yells from the garage. "You know I get carsick!"

Mom chimes in to support his claim as she swishes past me, a faux fur coat in her hand. "Quique's driving. I'll be in the passenger seat going through my speech. You two will have to take the back."

"Us? What about Quique's date?" I ask desperately. I really need a buffer to sit right between the two of us, even if she's as vapid as a balloon animal.

"Candace is meeting us there," Quique calls out before I hear the trunk slam shut.

My nose scrunches and I glare up at Angelo as if he's orchestrated all of this. It's illogical, but my annoyance has to funnel somewhere so I direct all of it at him. He has the audacity to simply look amused.

He gestures toward the garage, still holding open the door under the pretense of being a gentleman. I almost snort at the fake picture he presents. There's nothing gentlemanly about blackmail. Or the way he slammed me up against a restaurant window and grabbed my ass in public.

No. Crap. Now I'm thinking about that and it looks like he can tell, if his smirk is anything to go by.

I try to scurry past him but he's quick and I feel his big palm sliding over my lower back. The jacket is not nearly enough barrier to stop my skin from pebbling at his touch. Panic grips me. My mom's already in the car, and the garage door is up. I just have to dart around the back to the other side and I'll get away from him.

But Angelo's hand hooks onto my hip and stops me. He steps up close behind me and leans down. In a low voice, he whispers, "How are your thighs doing today?"

I stiffen. That bastard! I want to retort that what I do with my body is none of his fucking business. Actually, I want to smack him with my purse. I do neither, deciding that saying nothing is the smarter move right now if I don't want to endure the verbal equivalent of World War III this evening.

But then, Angelo takes the conversation in a direction I don't expect, one that dries out my throat and leaves me trembling.

He leans even closer to my ear as he whispers, "I plan to check on them later. And kiss them all better."

ANGELO

*R*ose is wearing a perfume that weaves together citrus and floral scents and is driving me mad; it's so mouthwateringly good that I want to inhale it directly from her skin. In fact, I'm noticing a million tiny details about her as we ride next to each other that I hadn't before the kiss—before the moment I decided she was mine.

Tonight, I see it all. The delicate way the bones of her neck swoop down and form a hollow at the base of her throat that I want to lick. The thick, unruly black curls she's tamed enough to be presentable that I want to muss with my fingers and see spread out over a pillow. The way her dress drapes over her legs but leaves her shapely calves exposed. My fingers twitch as the desire to drag my hands along her legs, to slowly lift that skirt, turns into an ache that's hard to ignore.

Rose isn't openly studying me the way I am her—but that's to be expected. She's nothing if not the good girl, as Quique always bemoans. The proper daughter. I can't wait to unravel all that sweet innocence she covers herself in and find that naughty little hellcat I know is waiting underneath … the lusty, wild version of her that I know exists behind the facade because I saw it for the first time last night.

A secret version of her that belongs only to me.

She pretends nonchalance and disinterest, gazing out the window, edging away from me on the bench seat. But I can tell from her shallow breathing and the quick glances that keep darting in my direction that Rose is affected by our proximity—and that fills me with a smug sort of contentment. My eyes drift down to see if those nipples of hers are pebbled, but she must be wearing a bra that hides them.

I press my lips together and decide that bra will be the first thing to go. I'm going to ensure I rip it or lose it later, because I want to see how her body reacts to mine. I'm going to buy her an entire slew of lace bras that are so thin I can see everything.

I glance back up from her delectable breasts, to find her eyes attempting to burn a hole right through me.

Busted.

I don't really care. I've already told her how this night is going to end because I want her worked up and thinking about it as much as I am.

I've fucked my own hand at least five times to the thought of that kiss, the feel of her ass under my fingertips, her perky breasts pushed up flush against my chest. I've spent a ridiculous number of hours fantasizing about her pussy. Clean-shaven or groomed neatly? I'm guessing groomed because she seems too shy to stare at herself spread-eagled in front of a mirror and shave. That thought process led me into a whole new fantasy where she's splayed out on a bathroom towel in front of me while I shave her myself, revealing that precious pink pussy inch by inch.

God—I'm fucked up. I even jerked off again in the bathroom next to her room when I got here, just to take the edge off so I'm not walking around unable to think with anything beyond a caveman brain all night.

I probably shouldn't even have come. It's probably a terrible idea, thinking I can restrain myself around her when every other thought I have is of spearing her cunt with my cock. But I've officially given into this obsession, the realization that she's mine only energizing it further. Rose belongs to me and the need to claim her in every way possible, the need to get her to acknowledge and then embrace that claim pumps through me as surely and steadily as my own blood.

I had to tell her brother that I'm going through some shit and don't want to be home thinking about it to score an invitation to tag along tonight. I'm going to ensure this opportunity doesn't go to waste.

I give my little queen a salacious grin as I spread my knees wide so that my left knee knocks into her leg, and then I drape my arm across the top of the bench seat, walking my fingers slowly toward her.

She gasps and her eyes widen, staring down at where my knee deliberately rubs against hers before she turns her head up to glare at me and spies the hand that's crawling closer.

My little Rose's eyebrows arch in a challenge as she leans her elbow on the side door and tries to prop her head casually on it as she scoots her torso away, but we both know exactly what she's trying to do. Resist me.

"Resistance is futile." I quote, winking at her as my fingers descend. She pulls back but the window blocks her. She has nowhere left to go.

The sight of her eyes dilated, her chest rising and falling rapidly, makes me want nothing more than to unclip her seatbelt and drag her down across the seat before leaning over her and caging her beneath my body.

I dip my hand under her gorgeous curls, diving through the wild mass until I reach the back of her neck, where I trace a tiny circle on skin as soft as satin. God, just touching that tiny patch of her skin makes my dick thicken in my pants.

Her breathing becomes even more shallow than it was in the garage and her lips part, drawing my eyes to them.

I'd give anything to know what she's thinking right now.

"What's that?" her mother asks distractedly in response to my statement, not even glancing back at us. Still, Rose stiffens under my fingertips, nervous.

"Just encouragement. You're going to kill it tonight, Ms. Dalton," I lie, eyes firmly on her daughter.

Rose looks absolutely edible in that dress. It's classy instead of revealing, but I love the red heels that hint at the spark she hides underneath her propriety. I wonder if she matched her panties to the shoes. The hope that she did sends a band of heat up my spine and I lick my lips in anticipation.

I'll find out later. I meant what I said to her. I'm going to drag my thumbs along Rose's thighs and kiss those scars until she's begging me to kiss other places.

My expression must telegraph my intentions because Rose's eyes widen in alarm.

She leans forward, escaping my fingers, and curls over her purse, digging out her phone. I watch her glare at the screen as she swipes it on. Seconds later, my phone buzzes.

I pull it out of my pocket to find a new text.

Rose: Stop it!

It's a challenge to respond one-handed, but I refuse to give up the patch of skin I've claimed on her neck, so I type slowly.

Me: Stop what?

Rose: Behave.

Me: Or what?

Rose: You are infuriating.

Me: Well, you were pissed the other night before you attacked me with your lips. Maybe I want the same thing to happen tonight.

I hear her huff out a breath and glance up to see her click on my contact information. Dammit! She's going to try to block me again. That's not acceptable. I reach across the seat and pluck her phone from her fingertips.

"Hey! Give that back!" she whispers furiously.

"Trade." I wink at her and slide my phone across the middle of the seat, keeping my hand over it so that she'll be forced to touch me.

"Keep it down, please, I'm trying to memorize this," Ms. Dalton says from the front, waving some note cards in the air. Rose's mother is in her own world—as always.

"Yeah, if I don't get to have fun, you guys don't either," Quique glances in the rearview mirror with mock severity before returning his eyes to the road and changing lanes.

Rose turns a delicious shade of pink that I think is a combination of fury and embarrassment. She won't say anything, because that's just not who she is. She gives in. Unless she's with me. Then she turns into a bold little vixen who'll turn around and jump me in a parking lot.

That better only be with me.

Her fingers scrabble at my hand, roughly shoving it away as she takes my phone, quickly texting her own from it.

Rose from my phone: I hate you.

Me from her phone: Oops. I see you have me mislabeled in here. Bastard, huh? Fixing that for you. Boyfriend sounds better.

Rose from my phone: Don't you dare!

Me from her phone: Want me to skip right to husband?

Rose: We are not dating.

Me: We are now.

Rose: NO. WE. AREN'T!!!!!!!!!!!!!!!

Me: Shouty capitals make you hot, babe? Because they're getting me hot.

Rose: Stop it. Change the subject. Why are you even here?

I decide to take pity on her and give her a little reprieve, though I've only laid out the facts. It's still going to take her a little bit to get used to them. But she's mine and I just told her as much.

Letting out a sigh, I give her a softball text that's nowhere near my real reason for accompanying her tonight.

Me: I have a burning need to know. Are you majoring in ... chemistry?

Rose: If you're about to turn that into a lame pickup line, I'll hate you even more.

Me: Glad you're picking up what I was putting down.

Rose: Lol.

Me: Ok, not pre-med and not chemistry. Religious studies?

Rose actually gives a tiny, adorable little snort when she reads that text and I find myself grinning, edging closer to her. Her fire is tempting, but her amusement is absolutely irresistible. I want to make this girl laugh again and again. I want to swallow that sound with my mouth.

I have to restrain myself so I don't just lean over and kiss her right this second in front of her family. I know better than to do that. Ms. Dalton ... she liked me in the beginning, but it wasn't long until she found out who my father was. Now, she tolerates me because she has no choice. But I've heard her go rounds with Quique about me and my thuggish connections while I was in the next room. Her fancy-ass open-concept house lets sound carry.

It's never bothered me before that she disapproves of me. Thinks of my family as glorified gang bangers. As if she's any better. The fuckers she takes money from have more blood on their hands than I do.

But Ms. Dalton's disdain bothers me now, grates on my nerves. I want to call her out on it just like I used to want to call her out on the fact that she kept her ex-husband's last name—not to stay connected to her children but because his family is well-known throughout the state. That woman in the front seat is the epitome of double standards. I don't know how Rose has retained her innocence growing up being raised by a shark like that, but I'm fucking glad she has.

And Quique … as much as he says he isn't Rose's keeper, I know if she protested against my advances, he'd batten down the hatches in two seconds flat. He's actually the one person in the world besides Rose that I'd never want to hurt. I'm closer to him than even my father, and the knowledge that I'm going to have to figure out how to do something delicately, for the first time in my life, holds me back.

So I don't give in to the urge to kiss her in front of them. Instead, I drag my finger up and down the back of her neck along her spine. But, oddly, I don't feel the collar of Rose's dress. I let my hand drift lower, sweeping from side to side underneath her coat. Nothing. Not even when my fingertips reach her shoulder blades.

Is she wearing a backless dress?

Does that mean she's not wearing a bra? That just the dress and coat are hiding those cherry nipples from me?

I get even harder at that thought. The idea that I could sneak her into some hallway at this party, push her back against a wall and peel the dress down to suck those delicious tits fills my head. God, I want to shove my hand down further and find out if I'm right, but I can't. Any more and I'll start dragging her coat down.

But if I can't touch her …

I take my hand from her neck and drop it to the seat. Watching her expression flicker with disappointment only amps me up even further. I love that she likes my touch. And I know exactly why she likes it. Because she belongs to me.

I type one last text.

Me: Want your phone back? Come and get it.

Then I set the phone down right on top of the very obvious tent in my pants.

Rose gives me the most exasperated look I've ever seen from her.

She gives a little *hmph* and turns away to stare out the window, clutching my phone so tightly that her fingers grow white. Clearly, she's not quite ready to play stroke the snake.

I sigh and pick her phone back up. Guess I'd better find something else to do with my time.

I swipe open her photos instead.

When my phone buzzes in her hand a second later, she looks down. The screen has locked, but my clever girl whispers, "Angelo," and holds up the screen. I turn my head to glance at her, and my face unlocks the device.

I just smile as I send myself yet another text from her phone.

She opens the messages only to find photo after photo of herself popping up on the screen.

"What are you doing?" she hisses.

"Picking a new background for my phone," I respond nonchalantly.

I watch her tongue dig at the back of her lips, making them bulge out with all the savage retorts I know she's just dying to say right now. Riling her up has always amused me but now it turns me on.

Rose stays silent, but her fingers fiercely jab at the screen as she deletes photos just as quickly as I text them. It becomes a game. I try to send photos twice as fast as she can delete them.

That's how we spend the remainder of the ride to Santa Fe, ferociously and immaturely competing with one another. It ramps up my giddiness to a level I haven't experienced since I was twelve and got to touch my first boob. I chuckle quietly and I hear a tiny giggle escape from her before she swipes her foot sideways and kicks me. I retaliate with an embarrassing photo of her making a stupid face. She gives a low gasp. This is more fun than a coaster at Six Flags. By the end of the ride, I've looked at every single one of her photos from the past five years.

I've learned that she loves to hike, screenshots all kinds of dirty lines from romance books, takes pictures of her desserts which seem to veer towards lemon-flavored anything, and that she has very few selfies. Almost all of her photos are group pictures. My Rose is not nearly vain enough given how beautiful she is. She needs eight thousand more pictures of herself on here.

I raise her phone as Quique pulls into a parking space, and her eyes narrow into dangerous slits that I ignore. I snap a photo of her just as the engine cuts out.

She immediately leans forward, trying to snatch her phone away but I hold it out of reach and grab my own back, pulling it easily from her tiny hands. I airdrop her entire photo album to myself before handing her back her own phone.

Her nails dig into my hands as she grabs them. "You bastard," she seethes under her breath as her mother and Quique climb out of the car, none the wiser. Though her eyes are hostile, her mouth keeps fighting the urge to curve upward.

That's right, Rosie. You loved this just as much as I did.

I wink as I unbuckle and open my door, glee tap dancing along my ribs at the way her fury and lust are filling up the backseat, as potent as her perfume. "Not bastard. Boyfriend, remember?"

I snap another photo of her resulting glare with my own phone.

Tonight's going to be the most fun I've had in a very long time.

ROSE

*M*y mother has asked the impossible of me. There is absolutely zero way I can stand to be within five feet of Angelo, much less corral him all night. He can't even be appropriate for five minutes!

God.

He's so... so ... I don't even have words for what he is.

My heels click on the concrete as I shove open the door leading from the hotel lobby to the courtyard in the middle of it. I leave behind the warmth of the indoors and the coat Mom insisted I check at the counter. I try to abandon all my infuriated thoughts about Angelo as well.

At least he's off with Quique, checking on the audio equipment and carrying heavy boxes for the next half an hour. I get a reprieve.

I take a deep, intentional breath, emptying my mind of the confusing hodgepodge my thoughts become when he's nearby. Right now, my task is simple: Ensure the seating arrangements match my mother's little master map so that everyone has a good time.

I pull out the sheet of paper her campaign manager, Debbie, handed me upon arrival and start walking past the portico that's lined with round, polished wooden beams as I reflect on the opulence of tonight's event, which is just as ridiculous as Angelo's behavior.

Boyfriend? Please. I scoff even as my thighs clench.

No. I'm not thinking about him or how utterly soaked my panties are right now. That shit in the car was just foolish. I shouldn't have engaged with him, because now he thinks he's off scot-free and he hasn't even apologized! Not once. I even fucking cackled at his stupid photo game. I hate that guys think they're forgiven because they can make you laugh. My father used to pull that stuff with me all the time and then go off whistling, thinking we were right as rain, while underneath, I was still hurting. Seething. Frothing. But I would always swallow it all down.

God, sometimes I hate the fact that I hate confrontation. I wish I had more of a spine. I wish … a lot of things.

I force myself to focus on my surroundings before my thought processes go cliff-diving. I can't have that happen;I have to fake-smile and pretend to be happy for hours. I look around and soak in the opulence.

It's a sad truth of life that money can buy nearly anything. It's the middle of January, and I'm in a very traditional pueblo-revival courtyard. Turquoise doors set into brown stucco walls showcase all the entrances and exits to the upscale hotel.

I stare for a minute at a running fountain in the middle, which fills the air with the soft, soothing burble of running water. Normally, it wouldn't be running in January, but for people with deep pockets, normal rules don't apply. It makes me want to roll my eyes as I turn toward the hundred round tables covered in white tablecloths with centerpieces featuring fake white candles glowing with electric flames and gleaming red chili wreaths.

Music wafts across the courtyard from hidden speakers, and I weave around caterers setting out hors d'oeuvres, trying to double-check and move placards for the seating arrangements. Debbie was very specific about who should sit with who because part of this fundraiser is an auction for some donated paintings.

"The Garcias and the Jimenez family like to show one another up. Be sure they can see each other. Direct line of sight to drive up the bids. Make it happen, kid," she'd said before tapping the list and handing it over. A short, Hispanic woman with a square build, Debbie is the smartest person I've ever met, and I think she's even more ruthless than my mother.

I do exactly as she ordered, shifting around the Jimenez placards so that he and his wife have an unobstructed view of the Garcia table. They'll have to twist a little to see my mother's speech, but that's clearly less important.

I sigh.

Money.

Money and status.

That's all my mother wants to be happy. And after everything with Dad, I want her to be happy.

But her brand of happiness and mine aren't the same. Telling her that, though? It would be impossible. She'd dismiss me as naive, the way she was when she married Dad. And maybe she's right. Maybe what I'm thinking about is stupid. Maybe the plan I toy with when I think about my major is just some big, foolish pipe dream. It probably is—

"See the game last weekend?" Angelo's voice drags me from my thoughts and I turn around to find Quique and the fucker himself standing casually behind me. Dammit. Has it been thirty minutes already? My frozen toes say it has.

Quique's tapping away at his phone, but Angelo's smirking at me, his weight on one hip, one hand in his pants pocket, his suit jacket undone, tie coming loose—he looks like an Instagram model. Messy in a deliberately perfect way designed to drive you mad and make you want to fix every little thing and run your hands all over his massive chest in the process.

His deep brown eyes draw lines over my body, like he's playing connect the dots. Nipple. Nipple. Crotch. Face.

I want to slap him but I annoyingly also want to jump his bones as he blatantly checks me out and licks his lips. Fuck. Who was it that said divide and conquer? Because my mind and my body are definitely divided right now. My thighs are physically tensed; they're primed and ready to send me hurling through space into his arms. I internally shout *No!* and that's still not enough. I have to wrap my arms tightly around myself, which only makes me all the more aware of how sensitive and ready for his touch my breasts are right now. Damn him.

"Well, did you see the game?" he asks again, staring straight at me.

I'd thought he'd been addressing Quique, but I'm not that lucky. Angelo apparently wants to have a civil conversation with me in public. I breathe out a sigh that's half relief and half exasperation because it would be easier if we just didn't talk at all.

"Yeah, I saw it." I assume he's talking about his team.

The downside of having an older brother is that he hogs the TV. The upside of having a brother who hogs the TV is that you become well-versed in football and sports metaphors and can easily impress guys at parties with stupid tricks, like rattling off stats. Their eyes go wide and men get half-hard, thinking that maybe, just maybe they've found a unicorn—a girl who would encourage their Sunday football habit and not mind them crumbing up the couch with snacks as they use their warrior bellows to cheer on men in tight pants.

Little do they know, I typically zone out after ten minutes at the start of each half and turn to reading historical romance. Sports Center is the real source of all my knowledge, and only because one of the announcers has a voice that really should be narrating my naughty audiobooks.

"What did you think? Did they do a good job protecting *the pocket*?" His tone drips with innuendo.

That fucker. So he isn't trying to have a decent conversation. He's trying to continue what he started in the car.

I won't let him.

I decide that this evening's upside to my sports knowledge is that it's also very useful for having a discreet argument with a certain hulking, overbearing brute. He's been breathing down my neck, trying to crowd my personal space for weeks. And despite the fact I may or may not have feelings for him, he hasn't apologized. That's unacceptable. The spine I was lamenting not having hardens the tiniest bit and gives me the courage to spout out my next words.

"You mean did I see the disgusting, cheap trick your team tried to pull—the one that was totally *illegal*?" I shoot daggers from my eyes at him, because yeah—I'm not talking about football.

"You're still upset about that? The Saints had to try something new. Their normal plays weren't working against the defense."

My fingers clamp around the map I hold and the paper dimples under my grip.

"Saints?" That arrogant bastard. Yeah, he definitely knows we're not talking football. His team is the Ravens, which makes no sense for a kid from New Mexico, but that sort of twisted logic also clearly applies to his real life, where he makes batshit choices with eerie casualness.

"Yeah, you know. The good guys." He gives me a shit-eating grin.

The most caustic laugh spills from my lips and I'm surprised it doesn't corrode his ears, the very sound eating through him like acid. "Good guys? I don't think so. I think they're nothing more than a pathetic, no-talent team—"

"Sorry, what game are we talking about?" Quique finally looks up from his phone to join the conversation.

I roll my eyes and move away, back to checking placards. "Nothing. A crappy one. We didn't watch it. I just saw the highlight reel. The team's manager owes the entire league an apology." I flash a vicious gaze at Angelo before I walk off.

Behind me, I hear Quique exclaim, "Dude, I don't think I've ever seen Rose get so pissed. I didn't even think she liked football."

"You know, I've found that women like a lot of things they pretend they don't," Angelo replies in a tone that does *not* sound repentant but pompous. He better not be talking about himself.

"Think that applies to ass sex?" My idiotic brother forgets to ask the question quietly and I overhear it even from twenty feet away.

"Quique, my ears are burning!" I call out. Gross.

"Least it's not your ass," Angelo replies with a chuckle.

My face heats. I'm going to kill him. Murder him. Take that tie from around his neck and yank on it until he can't breathe. I'm not a violent person normally. Other than the outburst at Daisy's, I haven't yelled at anyone in years. Normally, I fold rage inward until it resembles some kind of sharp origami star that cuts me internally. No one has ever driven me to blazing fury like this before and it's both worrying and strangely liberating to turn that wrath elsewhere.

Except, Angelo keeps poking at me, stoking that rage, and we're in public—at an event where I absolutely cannot burst into screams and verbally whip him the way he deserves.

I stand there, staring blindly at the map in my hand without seeing it, trying to control my breathing, when I hear the chatter of a crowd start to drift in our direction. Fuck. Fuck my life. People are arriving early.

I suck in a deep breath full of chill January air and try to ignore the fact that my fingertips are getting icy. I need to go discard this seating layout so I can 'shake hands and kiss babies.'

The lobby's warm air envelopes me in a hug as soon as I step inside. I paste on a smile as I dart to the side and put the map away in a small meeting room that we reserved for Mom to practice her speech and for all our stuff. The auction paintings line the wall and I nod toward Debbie as I toss her map onto the closest table, then vigorously rub my hands together because now that I'm inside, the true extent of the chill that invaded my system is somewhat painful.

Emerging from that meeting room, my eyebrows shoot up in surprise when I spot Violet and Lily walking in through the massive glass front doors, Violet's parents behind them. I completely forgot they were coming, even though we texted one another outfits this afternoon. Apparently, everything else flew out of my head the second I heard that Angelo was coming.

Violet's blonde hair is a glossy waterfall down her back, and she wears a pale lavender gown that offsets her blue eyes. She's dressed conservatively, like me, for similar reasons. Her family is Irish mafia and they fully intend to keep her pure and clean until they marry her off to the mob boss of their choosing. Her parent's approval drags invisibly behind her, chaining and weighing down every step she takes—rather like Jacob Marley, the ghost who haunted Scrooge.

Lily, on the other hand, looks like she's dressed for a night at a club rather than a fundraiser full of stuffy blue-hairs. She's wearing a cream-colored silk dress that ends mid-thigh and cream-colored velvet high-heeled boots to match. A long string of pearls dangles nearly to her waist and her hair is pinned halfway up, spiral curls still spilling around her shoulders. Every eye in the lobby, male and female, turns to look at her. Santa Fe does get its share of movie stars, and she has the looks that could easily vault her into that category. She's also got the gossipy, dramatic tendencies. But Lily's always said she'd rather model than act and always half-joked that she's too old for a modeling gig now anyway.

I rush over and hug the two of them, nodding politely at Violet's parents as they walk on by, uninterested in our chatter, the same sort of thing they've heard almost weekly at their house for over a decade.

"You look so good! Sexy but subtle," Violet gushes.

"Love that it's backless. What'd you do for a bra? Did you use those pasties I gave you for your birthday?" Lily asks, reaching out and dragging a manicured finger down my spine. She's never had much of a sense of personal space.

"Lily!" I gasp, wanting to smack her for using that word in public at my mother's function.

"What? I told you they're the best. They are, aren't they? I think I can see the flower shape under your dress. You're wearing them aren't you?" She's completely oblivious to the fact that my stomach just liquefied and sank in between the wooden floorboards in a puddle of embarrassment.

Violet notices and grabs Lily's arm. "Shh. Geez, we talked about this shit, Lil." Lily wasn't raised the way Violet and I were, with expectations looming over her every moment.

"Sorry," Lily gives a shrug and then taps her purse. She leans in quietly and tries to be more subtle when she whispers, "I brought us a flask to share."

"Thanks," I tell her stiffly, though I have absolutely zero intentions of drinking tonight. I'm 'on duty.' Besides, the last time I drank with her ... Nope. Not thinking about it. I quickly shove aside the image of the frat house that pops up in my head, blaring with loud music, colored lights, and my own sobbing pleas. "I've got to go mingle for a little, but I'm so glad you're here. It would suck without you."

"I'm glad to get out of Albuquerque for a night," Lily confesses. "Every single noise I hear around the apartment wakes me up. I keep thinking it's *him*." She chews on her glossy lip as she shakes her head, a far-off look in her gaze. Her stalker just got out of jail and it's keeping her up at night.

Guilt invades my system. "Hey, if you ever need to stay over …"

She shakes her head. "No. No. I'm good. Just being paranoid, I'm sure. Like, I thought I saw a guy following me yesterday when I went to the coffee shop." She rolls her eyes. "It was a delivery guy. So embarrassing."

I put a hand on her arm and squeeze. "It's okay to be paranoid after what happened."

She swallows and nods, before shaking her flask discreetly. "I'm going to go freshen up. Anybody want to join?"

I shake my head. "No. I really do have to mingle or Mom will freak out."

Violet's lips thin. "Can't."

Lily saunters off with a tiny wave, smiling at a few older men who pause in mid-conversation to gape at her.

I used to envy that about her. But ever since her psycho-stalker, I can see the downside. Now, I only want one guy looking at me that way. Shit. No. Don't even think it. My cheeks heat up as my thoughts betray me.

A hand grips my arm and saves me from the awful revelation going on inside my head. I turn to see Violet has stepped closer. She whispers in a low voice, hardly moving her lips. "My parents have invited a potential match tonight." She rolls her eyes and gives a disgusted shudder.

"Wait. What?" I'm taken aback. Violet's always known she's going to have an arranged marriage. But we all thought she was going to have more time. Graduate college first. I blink at her, a little shocked. She's only nineteen. Her twentieth birthday isn't even for a couple of months. They want to marry her off already?

She glances around, chewing on her lip as she ensures no one else is within earshot. "Katie told everyone she was pregnant last night. And it's not Finn's."

I fight to keep my expression neutral even though my eyes want to expand to the size of dinner plates. Katie is the little princess of the family. And by princess, I mean her dad runs the whole shebang. She was born and raised in Boston, though she's been out enough times that all the Wild Flowers have met her. If Katie is rebelling and "disrespecting the family," then no wonder Vi's parents are cracking down hard.

"I'm so so sorry," I pull her in for a hug.

Her fingers dig into my back as she whispers in my ear, "If I give you the high sign later, I expect a full rescue mission."

"On it," I reply.

"Thanks," Vi gives me a grateful look before stepping back, taking a deep breath, and marching off through the crowd.

I stand where I am, hoping to soak in a tiny bit of silence before I have to paste on a happy face, when a low voice behind me chuckles.

"Nipple pasties, huh?" The man's voice is like a dull knife sliding into my skin, sending a painful trickle of blood down my spine as the room seems to lose every single molecule of oxygen.

I turn only to see my nightmare in the flesh. I can't breathe as my fingers clench and I stare up into the smug brown eyes of Nick Roybal, one of the fraternity guys who turned my night out with Lily into a torture session as long and drawn out as getting pressed to death.

My knees buckle.

ANGELO

I see Rose stiffen from across the lobby, and though there is a crowd of people milling like cattle between us, at the sight of her clenching her dainty fingers into a fist, I'm off like a shot. Something's wrong. Something's terribly wrong with my girl. Instinct tells me she needs me and I heed it, not stopping to wonder what's going on or if it even makes sense.

I push aside a tall gray-haired man standing between me and her, ignoring his gruff, "Watch it!" as I surge forward. All my focus is on the stiff set of Rose's shoulder blades, clearly visible in her backless dress. They pull back toward one another unnaturally.

She turns to face a young guy behind her and goes from stiff as a board to drooping in under a second. It's almost as if an invisible hand squeezes the air from her body. Rose's legs slide out from under her and she starts to fall. To faint.

Fuck.

What happened?

My heart smashes into my ribs frantically as I extend my arms, leaning forward, reaching as far as I can, stretching and straining to get to her before she collapses and her head smacks into the hard floor.

My fingers wrap around her arm just enough to yank her toward me and her head smashes into my chest, bouncing once. I quickly wrap my other arm around her torso and pull her into me, eyes dropping down to examine her face, which looks pale.

She hasn't passed out. It's actually worse. Her eyes aren't closed, they're glazed, haunted, as empty as that night I found her in the bathroom.

Shit.

No. Lil reina.

I glance up, only to see a young guy with a basketball player's slim, tall build striding away. His back is to us and his hands are in his pockets, trying to act nonchalant when he's clearly anything but. My instincts immediately howl for me to pursue him. To rip him limb from limb, even though I don't have any idea who he is or what he just did—only that he's somehow triggered my girl.

"Rose," I whisper in her ear as I scoop her up bridal style. She weighs so little in my arms. Holding her would be perfect, a sensation I'd treasure in any other circumstance. But right now, I don't get to focus on the way her body feels so soft and pliant against mine. I'm too busy scanning her face as I carry her toward the little meeting room that we filled with pamphlets and auction materials earlier.

I nudge open the door with my foot and then kick it closed behind us. Thankfully, the space is empty.

I sit down on one of the plastic meeting tables, keeping Rose on my lap, uncaring that the table groans underneath my weight—the stupid thing was only built for laptops and handouts, not people.

I hold her close, feeling her trembling as she clutches at me, gliding those arms around my waist underneath my suit coat. Her heartbeat is frantic.

"Breathe, sweetheart. Breathe." I take slow, deep breaths, and eventually, she mimics me, burrowing in and holding me closer, as if touching me soothes her. I can't lie, a part of me absolutely loves that she's soaking up my comfort like a sweet little kitten, but the bigger part of me—the angry gorilla—wants to know who I have to kill for making her need comfort in the first place.

I pepper the top of her head with kisses as I wait for her to calm down. When I feel certain her heart rate has returned to normal, I bring a finger up underneath her chin and tilt her face toward mine.

"What happened?" I keep my voice to a whisper, knowing that if I even attempt to speak in a normal tone right now, I'm going to end up sounding angry.

Her soft green eyes study mine, flickering back and forth. Those beautiful painted red lips of hers press into a thin line and, for a second, I think she's going to deny me again. But then she grabs my hand, her small fingers threading between mine, her bones as tiny and delicate as matchsticks next to my big mitts.

"Guess you finally get to know … I went to a frat party with Lily." Her expression immediately grows rueful, regret etched across her furrowed brow.

It takes me a moment to catch up with her, to realize she's talking about the past.

She takes a deep breath before she continues, "I just wanted a break. Mom had three events in a row that week and I was just *done*. I wanted one night of not being me. So I got drunk. I hooked up with Nick." Her head nods in the direction of the door and I immediately tense because I know she's indicating that that skinny young fucker I just saw in the lobby has had his hands on her.

I want to slice off his hands. I want to turn them into a rearview mirror ornament, put a chain through them and let them swing back and forth next to the rosary already there, a visceral warning to anyone who even considers touching my lil reina. My girl.

I have to force my muscles to relax, to keep my fingers loose instead of letting them dig into her skin the way I want to in order to plaster her as close to my body as is physically possible. Part of me wants to lean down and bite her neck and then suck on her tender flesh until she bruises just so that she walks out of here wearing my claim for that fucker and all the other assholes out there to see.

But Rose's confession hasn't ended. "I went with him up to his room in the Alpha Tau house. And I said yes. I mean, at first. But once I said it … he held me down …"

I can't help the way my fingers curl into her hip then.

Her voice shakes slightly, and a single tear glides down her cheek as she continues breathily, "He called his friends in—"

RAGE.

Rage unlike anything I've ever felt in my life before glides through me like molten steel and hardens into sharp, deadly resolve.

I'm standing, gently sliding Rose down my legs and holding her upper arms until she's gotten her balance, but all of that is on autopilot because my mind has already left this room. It's out there, with that stupid fucking frat boy—mentally pounding in his nose, cracking his skull.

"He called them in?" I ask, unable to keep the growl out of my tone.

"And they … all of them … took turns …" She can't continue. She's literally unable to speak, the horror of that memory closing up her throat and making her pinch her eyes shut. Rose's fingernails claw at her thighs through her dress and I see what she's doing—my poor girl is aching for a way to release that horror scrabbling around inside her brain, to ease the pressure that has her teetering on the brink of combustion.

I pull her to me and press a rough kiss against her lips, unable to be gentle right now. But I use that kiss to wipe away her memories of those scrawny, pathetic wastes of skin. I nip and bite at her lips, suck her tongue into my mouth, and try to inhale her misery so that she won't hurt anymore.

I bleed for her. I ache inside in a way that's more painful than anything I've ever known. Even the time I got shot doesn't top this—this horrible wound on behalf of my precious girl. I pour every ounce of the desperation and affection that I feel for her into the kiss as I link our fingers. I know I've succeeded when her open-mouthed kisses become more visceral, when her tongue does just as much exploring as my own.

When I've got her gasping, her mind pulled out of that dark pit, I unlink our hands, wrap my arms around her to grip her ass, and pick her up. Now that her needs have been met, I need to deal with my own.

I carry her over to the meeting room's windows on the right side of the room, which overlook the courtyard. I shove aside a pompous, brocade curtain before setting Rose down, spinning her, and pressing my girl up against the glass.

"You stand here and watch," I order, leaning down to press one last kiss to her black curls.

She tries to turn, to glance up at me in confusion. "Angelo—"

I grab her shoulders and gently turn her back where I directed, squeezing slightly. "Stand. And. Watch." I'm barely restrained right now, about to fly off the handle. Fury jolts through me as wild and dangerous as electricity. I can't even appreciate how gorgeous Rose looks with her lips swollen from our kiss. Because I have something I need to do.

I stomp out of the meeting room, my dress shoes smacking against the floor while my eyes scan the massive lobby. Inside my chest, tension coils as my body gets ready for what's about to go down.

But the crowd that was here, milling underneath old wagon-wheel chandeliers a few minutes ago has retreated and moved on. I see people milling around the courtyard, clustering around the refreshments table. I beeline for it.

I'm certain my expression is less than friendly because more than one person takes a quick look at me and backs the fuck away. Smart fuckers have some sense of self-preservation because if anyone gets in my way right now, I might not give a shit that they're a bystander.

My eyes scan the crowd. All I've got to go on was a quick look at this cabrón, Nick, but it was enough. There aren't many young people in the crowd. Quique and his girl, Candace, are huddled over in a far corner, near the stage. They're easy to spot because of her hot pink dress. He tries to wave me over but I ignore him. I pass Rose's friends standing amongst a group of much older people and then I spot him.

He's leaving the bar, beer in hand as he walks towards the appetizer table. My gaze hones in on him like I'm sighting down a rifle, about to shoot a buck. I could wait for later. I probably should. It's reckless to proceed right now. Later, as he's leaving, the parking lot would provide a better confrontation location.

But I don't want to wait. I've already waited. I've been begging Rose to tell me who the fuck destroyed her for weeks. And now, he's here, in my grasp.

It's going to happen.

My feet glide forward slowly, methodically, carefully— contrasting the wild beast inside of me that insists I rush at him and rip his head off with my bare hands. I have to be subtle about this or I could end up in cuffs. Though I don't think that's the biggest deal, I don't want to traumatize Rose any further. I move behind a group of people chatting, standing just behind them. I pretend I'm evaluating the line for drinks as I study this motherfucker.

He's got dark brown hair and brown eyes with a smudge of a nose that looks like it's been broken before. I rule out breaking it again. I don't want him to feel familiar pain. I want him to feel something so goddamned terrifying that every time he remembers this moment, piss dribbles from his tiny dick.

He grabs a couple tiny triangle sandwiches and loads them onto a plate. Then he grabs a few crisp, thin, cracker-style breadsticks jutting up from a cup they've been packed into like stalks of wheat.

Inspiration strikes.

I advance, every muscle coiled, every breath measured, my heartbeat pumping like a bass speaker—loud in my ears. I step up beside him.

I grab a breadstick and take a quick bite as I pretend to peruse the table's offerings. "Sandwiches good?" I have to clear my throat and act like the growl in my tone was accidental. I glance around to see if anyone's eyes are on us, but Ms. Dalton is heading toward the microphone, getting ready to speak, so people are moving toward their seats.

Perfect.

"Eh, they're kind of bland," this fucker replies as he takes a bite from one of them. Nonchalant. Casual. After he just walked away from terrorizing my girl.

As soon as I see him start to swallow, I move in.

In under a second, I'm behind him, arms wrapping around Nick's waist. I shove my fists up under his rib cage and squeeze for all I'm worth as I bodily pick him up and spin him around so his torso is away from the crowd.

"Shit man! Breathe! Breathe!" I yell as I punch my combined fists as hard as I can into his solar plexus, mimicking the Heimlich, relishing the way he gasps when I steal the air from his lungs by being far rougher than necessary.

One of his hands flails back in an attempt to fight me off and he clips my jaw. Pain crackles across my skull, but it merely spurs me on. I like that this won't be easy. It makes the beast inside me yowl in perverse pleasure.

I strike again, pounding inward, and I hear a delicious cracking sound that I hope means a rib broke. My temples pulse with adrenaline lined with the sweet edge of rage as I throw him to the ground on his back. I quickly straddle him, sitting on his chest, my legs pinning down his arms to the ground as I fake a wide-eyed look to the crowd and yell, "We need a doctor!"

The crowd turns, and I can feel the energy in the room shifting as eyes fall on us. Bored expectation transforms into horrified fascination as people stare, watching my attempt to 'save' this poor fool from himself.

Still wheezing, his deep brown eyes are wide and delightfully scared as I pry open his mouth and shove my hand right down his throat. The cuff of my sleeve grows wet with spit as I push aside his writhing tongue letting my fingers scrape and scratch amongst the slimy flesh, ensuring I make it hurt as I violate this stupid fucker's throat.

"Oh my God! Someone's choking!" one woman murmurs.

"Should I call an ambulance?" a man asks.

"Yes. Call for help!" I do my best impression of distraught concern as my fingers find, pinch, and yank on his uvula.

I lean forward over him and whisper low, so no one else can hear, "I hear you like to call for your friends when you've got a woman alone."

His eyes start to water as he realizes I know.

That's right. I know what a piece of shit you are. And now, your life is in my hands.

How does that feel, little boy? How does being forced by someone bigger and stronger feel?

Panic radiates from his eyes as his hands scratch at my thighs, as his face grows redder and redder. He looks like he might burst.

The tingling, tickling awareness that I usually only experience under the light of the moon at an empty construction site as I slice into an opponent's skin surges through me. Only, this time, it's amplified to the nth degree because of the crowd, because of the fake narrative they're drinking in like margaritas, the sweet taste of my story covering the bitter, burning reality so that it's easy to swallow.

It's amplified further by the fact that I'm exacting vengeance, not for my father, not for money, but for my girl.

My queen.

I want to laugh right in this bastard's face, but I swallow the urge. I'm acting—I've never understood the appeal before, but I do now. It's so fun that I'm practically giddy. I raise a contemptuous brow at Nick before sliding on a concerned face and yelling to the crowd, "I can feel something. There's something stuck—" I shove down so far his gag reflex kicks in when I punch the back of his throat. The muscles convulse around my fist as his hands start to grow limp where my legs hold them pinned to the concrete.

I hear someone pushing through the crowd.

"I'm a doctor. Let me by."

Aww. Playtime's over.

Too bad.

But I think the point is nearly made.

I'm fairly certain Nick won't be chasing girls anytime soon.

Just to be sure … I decide to drive the point home. Literally.

I release the bit of crispy bread stick still left in my palm. It's only an inch or two, but the end is nice and jagged from where I bit it. I jam it into the roof of his mouth and drag it across the top, scratching him soundly as I lean in, pretending I need a different angle to dislodge whatever's 'choking' him.

"Stay away from my girl. And watch your back. Because if I ever find you alone …" I don't finish the sentence. I find that open threats are more impactful.

Nick is past attempting to respond via nods or even blinks. His eyelashes are fluttering like he's about to pass out.

My fingers fold the bread stick back in my palm and pull my hand roughly from his mouth. "I got it. I got it!" I quickly rise from my knees and hold the bit of soggy bread stick up as I give the crowd a false smile.

Applause and even a few cheers erupt.

Beneath my feet, Nick rolls onto his side, gagging, before he vomits across the concrete.

I ignore the pat on the back I get from the doctor before he kneels in front of his new patient. I ignore Ms. Dalton's short campaign manager as she bustles forward and starts issuing orders to people around me. I ignore Ms. Dalton's glare and Quique's nod of admiration from across the courtyard. I don't focus on the compliments from the crowd. My eyes travel past the gurgling fountain to the window of the meeting room, to Rose's wide, shocked eyes as I walk away from the scene and back toward her.

She watched the entire thing, just like I told her to.

My gaze remains trained on her as I traverse the courtyard, awaiting her verdict. Will she be appalled by what I just did? She's delicate, soft, fragile in comparison to everything else that exists around me. Her version of justice might be different than the bloody brand of vengeance that I adhere to. She might hate what I've done, be disgusted by it, or think it's beneath her. Plenty of women do.

I pause five steps from her window, heart thudding like I just ran four miles. My dick is also hard as a rock right now. Whether or not she likes it, I'm going to barge inside and kiss my woman again. I'm going to claim that gorgeous mouth of hers and tell her she doesn't get to reject me. She's mine and I'll fucking defend her as I see fit.

Those gruff thoughts don't stop my breath from catching, however, when she slowly raises her hand. My chest tightens in anticipation, wondering if she'll grab the curtain and slide it closed.

But then my girl crooks a finger, beckoning me.

ROSE

*M*y emotions are a kaleidoscope of shifting colors and shapes that morph so quickly I can't identify how I feel as blood rushes through my system. My heart is pumping crazily, as though I was part of that disguised attack. I curl my fingers into fists as I ask myself if it's disbelief thrumming inside my chest or awe. I can't believe Angelo did that. I can't believe it and yet I just witnessed it happen.

Am I horrified or thrilled? What is going on? Question after question cycles through me, swirling and spinning. The only thing I can seem to settle on is the fact that Angelo fucked up Nick because of me. For me.

Who does that?

For a second, I feel like a knockoff Borte in a Ghengis Khan karmic remake. When his first wife was kidnapped, the man who'd become known to the world as one of the most ruthless warlords of all time undertook his first raid to get her back.

God. I shouldn't have thought about that.

Khan has always been a guilty pleasure fantasy for me. The idea of a brutal warlord storming in and cutting everyone in sight down to win back his woman …

Fuck.

No. Turn it off.

Angelo didn't necessarily do it for romantic reasons. One night of flirting isn't the equivalent of marriage.

God, do I even want to know his reasons? Yes and no. I'd beckoned Angelo inside a moment ago but part of me is scared to hear any explanation from his gorgeous lips. It's intimidating because I both want to know what he's going to say and I don't know if I'm ready to hear it.

My body flushes hot for a moment then cold—simultaneously elated and terrified. What do I tell him?

I'm still trying to process this jumbled mess I've become when someone opens the door to the meeting room. I turn away from the window only to see Angelo outlined by the bright warm lights of the lobby, the warm tones gleaming off the sheen of his suit and skin like an aura.

My throat constricts at the sight of him and all the conflicting emotions within me surge up in one massive wave that nearly knocks me off my feet.

God, why does he have to walk so fast? I'm not ready.

He fills the doorway, looming, his presence seeping into the room, large and violent and utterly breathtaking.

When he closes it behind him, my lips open but then close, uncertain what to say. I lick my top lip and my fingernails drag along the sides of my legs, over the smooth fabric of my dress. *Just thank him,* I scold myself. *Wait. Thank him for hurting someone?*

When I hear the snick of the lock, my eyes dart to the door then to his back. What's he doing?

He turns, a deep fire banked in his eyes that broadcasts his intentions. An electric prickle bolts up my spine when he steps toward me. Flutters start in my stomach as he slowly prowls forward, stopping just in front of me.

In a low tone that's just shy of a whisper, I finally manage to say something. "I can't decide if you're a white knight or a criminal."

Those plush lips of his tilt up at the edges as his unsullied hand darts forward to encircle my waist. His fingers are so massive that they span across more than half of my back as he pulls me forward into him, away from the window. Our hips meet and my body eagerly soaks up his heat and luxuriates in the feel of his hard muscles as he leans down and nuzzles my ear before whispering, "What if I'm both?"

Oh. My breath catches and my hands fly up to grab at Angelo's suit jacket because my knees are dangerously close to buckling. I swoon for the first time in my life.

I hear Angelo's low chuckle, feel it rumble through his chest beneath my fingertips, just before his lips move from my ear to my mouth as he whispers, "I told you. You're mine."

His lips descend, kissing me hard as his hand on my back pulls into him so tightly it's like he's trying to meld us into one. He kisses me until I'm breathless, and even then, he doesn't relent; he keeps me close, allows me one quick gasp before he's diving back in, tongue stroking over mine. Meanwhile, his fingers drag a hot trail up and down along my bare spine, teasing at the bit of the dress that covers my ass.

The kiss in the parking lot?

It was amazing. Volcanic even.

But this is a natural disaster that's planet-ending. World-reshaping. Because that was an angry kiss about lust and betrayal. This? This is gratitude and elated astonishment on my part, mixed with a whole lot of delicious possession on his. I thought our prior kiss was the best I've ever had, but this one quickly shoves that one to second place. The kiddie corner. The lost and found.

When he finally pulls away, I'm gasping. I have to remind my legs how to work, how to hold myself upright when all I want to do is stay tucked against him.

I've only just managed it when his hand, the one that was gliding over my spine, comes up to cup my cheek.

I stare into his eyes as I wilt under his touch, ruined. Because after that kiss, I know I'll never be able to turn away.

My eyes are soft and my heart's melted into a soggy mess. I'm pretty sure I'm counting what just happened as his grand apology for spying on and attempting to blackmail me. After all, Angelo basically removed Nick's tonsils for him. How can words compare to that?

The widest smile stretches across my face at that thought. It continues when Angelo bends forward and places a series of tiny kisses over the pulse of my neck. When his tongue darts out and traces the hollow at the base of my throat, I give an involuntary sigh as my thigh muscles tighten. I have to resist the urge to press them together. Giddiness and lust are a potent combination.

Still leaving the hand that touched Nick clenched at his side, he caresses me with the other. He slides it up and down along my side gently before grabbing my hip, fingers squeezing, showing how his restraint is just as on edge as mine. I have to admit, I kind of love that.

The flutters in my stomach move lower and my hands climb up to his shaved hair, sliding over the soft velvety blackness while he sucks a tiny patch of skin near my collarbone. Inside the pasties, my nipples begin to ache. When his lower lip drags in a straight line across the base of my neck, hot breath misting over my skin, my eyelashes flutter shut and I wish that we were somewhere else. Somewhere private where we could take this moment and let it bloom into something more.

Angelo's mouth pulls away, and I give a regretful sigh as I release him from my hold.

But he doesn't step backward like I expect him to. Those sparking brown eyes locked on mine, Angelo starts to slowly hike up my skirt.

"We can't!" Urgent fear clamps down on my vocal cords and my voice comes out as a squeak as my head turns frantically toward the window, where the curtains are wide open.

"I told you I was going to check on *my thighs.*"

"Later!" I urge, not even disputing his claim to my thighs. Fuck, at this moment, I want them to be his. But my mother or one of her cronies could walk in at any moment. Or someone could turn and see us in the window. My hand moves down to cover his, which currently holds my skirt bunched in place. "We'll get caught."

Angelo doesn't respond, at least not vocally. But his hand slowly slides to the middle of my dress so that his warm palm is right in front of my panties. The heat of his body sinks through the fabric and banishes all other thoughts. My breath catches and my back arches involuntarily as my body seeks out his. Based on his smirk, he knows exactly what he's done. That cheater.

I should argue. I should. But as he stands there, staring down at me possessively—outshining every starry-eyed fantasy I've had about him—I can hardly seem to remember why this is a bad idea. Instead, I find my mouth opening and offering an alternative. "Against the wall, so no one can see."

He rewards me with a smile and a swift kiss before crowding me and walking me backward until my shoulder blades bump up against smooth, white plaster. The cold wall makes goose bumps rise on my exposed back but I hardly notice considering the fact that the rest of my body has become a tightly braided knot of lust, longing, and recklessness.

We exchange a loaded glance before Angelo yanks my dress above my ass. My hand flies up in time with his because my palm is still resting on the back of his fingers. He bunches up the skirt near my belly button, wrinkling it beyond repair. I should care. I should. It's going to be horribly obvious something happened. But when he slides his hand over and pushes the cluster of fabric to me, ordering, "Keep this up," I don't argue. I just take the bunched-up skirt. How I'm going to explain it later … is a problem for later.

"I don't care if you stay quiet or not. But if you don't want to get caught, you should probably bite your other hand or something." He slides down the front of my body as he says this, making his words lose all meaning and just become a jumble of sounds. *Angelo Walker is going down on me.*

Angelo Walker.

Angelo. Walker.

I have to swallow down the most godawful 'twelve-year-old girl at a boy band concert' squeal. He's on his knees, in a suit, godlike in his perfection. I want to remember this moment forever. I tell my brain to brand it in, to sear it to memory so that no matter what, I can always say I touched the dream. And he touched me back.

Fuck. His fingers are feather-light as he caresses my knee and stares at each of my thighs. Each tiny sensation is both tantalizing and not enough. Tension locks me up. Expectation cuffs me. I'm left completely at his mercy after just those few caresses. All that's left is for Angelo to have his way with me.

But he doesn't dive right in. His eyes scan me and I start to grow self-conscious, worried about the lines striping my thighs, the cellulite creeping around the edges. Wait. Did I misunderstand earlier? Does he really just want to check on my thighs? He's the only guy who's ever looked at them. Stared at them. Known my secret. Most guys only look long enough to spread me open and fuck me.

Horrified embarrassment and humiliated vulnerability start to drip like slime down my cheeks as I realize I might have misinterpreted what he said.

But then Angelo leans in and plants a soft kiss on one of my earliest scars, a deeper one on the front, from an era where I didn't know what I was doing. That kiss frays all the worries but then his words eviscerate them. He releases his kiss and his teeth graze over my inner thigh. He bites down lightly before licking that same spot as if to heal the wound he made. "So fucking hot."

God. Yes. I ratchet back down from embarrassment, switching over to primed and prepared for him in two point five milliseconds, giving myself emotional whiplash. All it takes is one deep breath and I'm ready for his lips on my skin again.

But he leans back, staring up at me. "Say you want it."

My eyes widen. I absolutely love dirty talk but doing it myself?

"Say you want me to suck on that cunt. Tell me you want me to lick inside you. Ask me to kiss your clit."

Oh God, those words and what they do to me. I want all of that. Every single thing he's mentioned. But saying it aloud is another thing. "Please?" I whisper, seeing if he'll let me off with begging. "Please, yes?"

His eyes harden as he stares up at me. "I'm going to need more consent than that from you, Rose. Consent to let me own your body. To throw your legs over my shoulders and use my tongue to fuck you while I finger your ass."

My pussy clenches just at his words, every one of them piling up a series of vivid mental pictures. "Yes. Please. Yes." I can already feel tingling, the slight edge of mindlessness present from his words alone. I can only imagine what it will feel like once he actually touches me. At this point, I don't care that we're in a hotel near hundreds of other people. My mother could walk in and scream at me right now. The fricking pope could come in and I wouldn't give a damn. I'm almost to the point of grabbing Angelo's face and shoving it in between my thighs.

"Say you're mine." Angelo drags a finger across the top ridge of one thigh, down to my pussy. He caresses near, but not over it.

"I'm yours." I don't even know how I spit out the words because every sense in my body has shut down in favor of touch, in favor of those sparkling nerve endings bundled together in one small spot.

Angelo's finger glides over it slowly, circling.

Yesss. I'm so elated that I don't hear his next words because he's finally there, stroking me and turning my body into an elated jumble.

But my lack of response must annoy him a bit. He must really want me to listen because he ends up tapping my thigh with his hand and growling as he repeats himself, "I said spread."

Swallowing hard, I slide my legs further apart, as far as I feel comfortable in these red heels. My face turns into a pleading pout as Angelo scoots forward slowly, trying to wedge his big shoulders close so he's in the perfect position. It's so lewd, the way my naked thighs press against his suit jacket, the feel of the fabric rubbing against my bare skin with every movement he makes. I squeeze my legs a tiny bit, just to test how he fills out the jacket and I'm rewarded with the hardness of his body just underneath. The sight alone would make me ready for more, not to mention the sensation on top of it, so I'm disappointed when he doesn't lean forward and put his mouth on me immediately.

"I could spread out more without the shoes," I blatantly offer, the shyness from a few minutes ago trickling away as desperation makes a wanton out of me.

"Keep the heels. I like them." He glances up at me with a naughty wink before diving forward. He mouths me through my silky red panties, tongue blading and gliding over my cleft, tracing a path over the fabric again and again until it's a wet mess that clings to me, and trembling pleasure rolls through me like thunder.

My hands twist the fabric of my dress into tight little bunches as I arch against the wall, presenting myself for him.

"Que bonita," he whispers.

I warm from just that tiny bit of praise, grinning and eager as his fingers walk up the outside of my leg and hook underneath the side of my panties.

"Fuck. Yes," I whisper. I can't wait to feel the direct heat of his tongue. To have his mouth on me.

Angelo drags the material down slowly, planting a kiss on each inch of exposed skin, making me wild, my pulse frantic. My entire body is racing while he's on a leisurely stroll. He ultimately leaves my panties stretched to their max, nearly at a snapping point, halfway down my spread thighs. His lips nibble and I'm surprised by how much I love it when his nose nuzzles my clit and he blows a heated breath over my smoothly shaved slit, but the feeling drives me to madness.

"Please."

"Please what, Rose?" the bastard has the gall to ask.

"Lick me," I whisper, my cheeks heating. "Lick my pussy."

"Que rico. Eres cochina," he praises me for being a dirty girl in Spanish, and hearing him talk dirty in that beautiful accent makes my cunt pulse impatiently. Was that what he was waiting for the entire time? I'm not certain but I stop wondering when he leans forward again and the flat of his tongue glides over my opening, making fire pool low in my belly. He builds up a rhythm that has my toes curling against the leather of my shoes, nails digging into them.

"Please. Please. Please," I chant, my voice nearly hoarse from need.

"Come for me, Rosie. Show me how this pretty pussy comes," Angelo pulls back and murmurs as he sticks two of his fingers in his mouth, wetting them. He then uses them to gently spread me open and spear me as his mouth locks back down on my clit.

A sound in the hall makes me tense and I freeze. Shit. We're going to get caught. Reality cuts into the delicious sensations he's creating and I decide that we need to be done. We need to get out of here before something terrible happens. I fake a whimper and tighten my thighs, pretending.

But Angelo just yanks his lips from my core and glares up at me. "Don't you lie to me. Unlike your past boyfriends, I know what a real orgasm looks like. You might not yet. But I'm going to show you."

His mouth and fingers both go back to work at a steady pace. At first, my worry overrides them, but he gradually speeds up, little by little, until all my anxiety is replaced by roiling, writhing lust.

My hips start moving of their own accord, my ass bumping rhythmically against the wall. Anyone walking by outside could hear us but I suddenly don't give a damn. Angelo's lips are sucking my clit deep inside as his fingers slam up into me, making me pant desperately.

"More. Rougher. Harder."

"Mmmm," he murmurs, his mouth still locked around my clit —delicious vibrations send me spinning off into the ether as I burst into a million rays of light.

My head falls back against the wall and my thighs grow limp. My eyes are closed and so while I hear him moving, feel him manhandling me, sliding my soaked panties back up my thighs and smacking my ass, I can't do more than mutter a vague, inattentive, blissed out, "hmm."

Angelo's chuckle revives me and somehow lends me the strength to open my eyes. I blink up at him, surprised to find him just in front of me, staring at me with a soft look that still somehow manages to be smug.

"Well, if your mother didn't hear you, I'll be disappointed," he jokes.

I punch him in the arm, though it probably hurts me far more than it does him. "Jerk. Not funny."

"Not joking, lil reina. Just like I'm not joking about the fact that I'm going to take you home later and fuck you until you pass out."

I inhale, my thighs quivering and my nipples, stiff and angry about the attention they haven't yet received, all reacting to the heat of his words. "God, I wish."

"You wish? Oh, it's going to happen."

I lean my head back against the wall and chuckle without humor. "Oh, you don't know the dark side of Ms. Dalton. After this event—after every event—there's a rage bender where she's going to rant about every single person who attended and didn't give her what she thinks she deserves."

"Well, good thing I'll get you out of it."

I shake my head at his naïveté. "There is no getting out of it. Even Quique can't get out of it and he's her precious son."

Angelo leans over me then, putting his forearm on the wall near my head, caging me in. Only, I don't feel trapped. The fire in his eyes makes me feel the exact opposite, actually—I feel exalted.

"Well, then it sounds like you're going to have to unlock your window for me so I can sneak in and ravage you in your bed."

"But—"

He leans down and destroys my protest with another of his life-altering kisses. "You're mine. Say it."

"I'm yours."

When I say those words, his grip on me tightens and his eyelids flick up as his expression morphs into pure animal lust, driving me nearly mad enough to suggest we just forego the idea of later and use the table behind him.

"You'll unlock the window?"

I nod, dazed, unable to believe what we just did, but eagerly anticipating what's going to come later. Or who.

ANGELO

*R*ose's taste still lingers on my lips an hour later. I'm thirsty, but I don't really want to wash away her flavor with my beer.

Seated at a table where I've moved around all of the name tags in order to snag the chair next to hers, I watch her mingle underneath the golden glow of outdoor string lights across the courtyard. She's the epitome of grace, all except for the wrinkles in her dress, which she's trying to hide by folding her hands in front of her waist demurely as she stands and chats. I guess it was a good thing she wore black.

Everyone is charmed by her, not a person walks away without smiling. They think that she's such a good girl.

I know better.

Yes, she's sweet enough to give you a toothache, but the way she begged me as she leaned against the wall and ground herself against my tongue was anything but the picture of innocence. She even did it with all these dipshits just outside too, which is braver than I expected her to be.

I'd been worried that seeing Nick would push her into a negative head space. Of course, it had at first, but when I'd walked back into the room after dealing with him, the look in her eyes … I've never been looked at that way.

It makes me wish I could bash in that bastard's throat all over again. Of course, her reaction could just be part of a coping mechanism to shunt her trauma aside—Rose is the kind of girl who puts on a happy face for others.

Did she do that with me?

It bothers me that I can't quite tell. I don't know if I should be worried or not. I don't want those bastards to have power over her … but is she actually okay? It's only been a few weeks. But she'd not only been willing, once we'd gotten started, she'd been an eager little kitten. And so wet.

I'll have to watch her carefully, try and rein in my dick. I'll have to let her show me she's okay because the last thing in the world that I want to do is hurt my girl.

She looks alright just now though. Not hurting, she's giggling, those breasts of hers swaying a bit and reminding me that I have yet to see them in all their glory. I grin as I watch her, wondering if her wet panties are making that pussy of hers cold in the brisk night air. I'll have to warm it back up later.

Classical music plays over the speakers, just as stiff and boring as most of the people milling about the room. The most exciting thing about tonight is the ambulance paramedics hauling that fucker Nick off.

This is not my typical scene and if it weren't for Rose, I definitely wouldn't be here. Though Dad has as much money as most of these stuffy pricks, we're more likely to let loose with a pig roast and some kegs down at Elephant Butte—though the sad little lake is really more of a sandbar these days. Dad still loves to go down there though and remember his glory days, back when he got started building vacation homes for fools like the ones swarming around me.

They think they're better than us, but I know for a fact that Johnny Sargeant over there does coke. He buys from one of the guys who works for us. Another older couple picking at the cheese cube tray is rumored to have trafficked themselves a maid from Ecuador. I don't know all of the fuckers in this room, but if I had to bet, every single one of them has hands just as dirty as mine.

A hand lands on my shoulder and squeezes. At first, I think it's in greeting but the grip gets harder and tighter, digging into a pressure point. I tilt my head up to see the Garcias, Jorge and Belleza. Instantly, I push up against Mr. Garcia's hold and force myself to my feet because there's zero chance I'm going to let my father's former partner and my family's worst enemy, hold me down.

Jorge Garcia is a portly man with leathery skin and an overgrown mustache who deserves to be taken down more than a notch or two.

"Grip's getting weaker, old man," I say, eyes spitting fireballs at him as I slide out of his grip and dust his touch off my shoulder.

"What are you doing here?" he growls.

I want to tell him it's none of his fucking business. I want to ask what he's doing here. Is he here to spend the money he embezzled from the company he owned with my dad—a feat he framed my father for?

I only hold myself back for one reason: I'm here for Rose. And she wouldn't like me starting shit.

"I don't see how that concerns you," I respond, in as calm a tone as I can manage.

"They'll let any old riffraff in here," his plastic wife tries to snub me but her injections don't really let her face move all that much.

"Clearly," I agree, gesturing at her. *Back at you, bitch.*

Ms. Dalton has obviously seen us and heads our way, winding through the crowd, a look of fear clear on her face.

"Come on, dear. I don't think this is the right place for us," Mr. Garcia intones, offering his wife his elbow and leading her away from Ms. Dalton, but more importantly, away from me. Thank fuck.

By the time Rose's mom is in front of me, they're gone, lost in the crowd.

Ms. Dalton turns blazing eyes on me, as if she intimidates me at all. In the scheme of things, she's a gnat. "What did you say to them?"

"Nothing," I tell her. It's the truth. I didn't say anything I wanted to, didn't break my beer bottle and shove it up Jorge's gut so he could feel the same shit my dad had to deal with in prison.

Ms. Dalton doesn't believe me. Her lips thin and one eye twitches slightly, but she can't rage at me in public. I give her one of Quique's patented 'well shucks' shrugs and she stomps off.

I sigh before sitting back down. It takes a few minutes for my pulse to return to normal. I use a pitcher on the table and pour myself a glass as I search for Rose.

I spot her just as one younger guy puts his dirty hand on Rose's arm. Before I can blink, I'm standing again. Rage swells my chest as I move around the table only to watch my girl deftly step back out of this guy's clutches. Her eyes immediately dart to mine—because she knows who she belongs to.

That's fucking right, Rose. You're mine.

I let my expression do the talking, but it's one hundred percent clear.

She mutters something before she weaves a few steps away from him and then she shoots me a hard look. I can read her expression perfectly. It says "stand down." But I'm definitely not going to take any orders when it comes to other men touching her so I stride over anyway.

When I reach her, the little prick has already melted into the crowd—lucky for him because I'm feeling just as wild as a bull who's seen a red flag. Rose brings out something in me that's akin to the violence I embrace when I take out someone who deserves it. She makes my heart beat just as quickly, and the same adrenaline pound through my veins.

Her back immediately stiffens at my approach and I imagine her nipples do too based on the exasperated but lusty look she's giving me—one not too dissimilar from the night of our first kiss. The air around us practically vibrates with delicious chemistry—the best I've ever experienced. I let my eyes trace over her cold-kissed cheeks, glowing pink, before smirking into her pale green eyes.

"Thought I'd check in. See if I needed to break his hand for you."

She rolls her eyes. "You overprotective gorilla."

I just thump my chest in response, earning a tiny little grin.

God, she's fucking cute.

I wish I could slide my arm around her waist right now, but I watch her stiffen and her demeanor change from my version of Rose to formal, polite, always-has-the-perfect-answer Rose as an older couple approaches us.

"Mr. and Mrs. Jimenez! It's so good to see you! How's your puppy doing?"

The older woman's eyes light up as she goes on and on about some dog she just got at the shelter Daisy volunteers for. Her husband and I both quickly check out of the conversation and he excuses himself to go grab a drink.

I don't leave, not because I'm interested in anything having to do with potty pads or puppy teething problems, but because I find myself studying the girl at my side, wondering what she'd be like if she didn't feel as if she had to suck up to all these people. Would she still be having this conversation?

Maybe. Sometimes that smile seems genuine, especially when Mrs. Jimenez pulls up a quick video on her phone of the puppy tripping over its own feet.

But then her mom will come by and it's like someone flicks on a switch. Rosie becomes stiff as a porcelain doll, her expression placid and fixed, deferring to or agreeing with her mother on every goddamned thing. It's infuriating to watch.

What's even more infuriating is how Ms. Dalton snubs me, deliberately conversing with all the other people who rotate through her circle. She doesn't make eye contact, but I can feel it, the waves of disapproval radiating from her.

That's the kind of pathetic bullshit I won't put up with.

So I don't.

I slide my arm around Rose's back only to find out she's as cold as a sheet of ice right now.

What the fuck? Why hasn't she slipped away to go warm herself up?

Smoothly, belying the anger I feel about the fact that she's not even taking care of herself, I say, "We're going to grab a drink and warm up inside."

I steer Rose away from her mother and the rest of her little group of lemmings and ignore Ms. Dalton's glare.

"What are you doing?" Rose hisses, trying to walk faster than me so that my hand won't stay planted on her back.

"You're too cold. And you looked as bored as I was."

Her eyes dart around, wondering if anyone heard me complain, worried about impressions as if she's going to know the names of any of these people in a few years. "I'm not bored at all," she lies.

I yank open the door to the lobby for her and let her proceed me into the heat. "Hmm, I suppose you wouldn't be *as* bored. You're probably still nice and *relaxed*," I say as I join her inside, letting my gaze dip slowly down to her thighs before gliding back up again.

My dirty reminder about what happened earlier sends a flurry of color to her cheeks and they grow as red as her namesake.

"Shut it."

I smirk as I take my jacket off and move to drape it around her shoulders. She tries to step away but my reach is long enough to encircle her and I press the coat down on her shoulders.

"I'm fine now that we're inside."

"You'll be fine when your spine doesn't feel like I'm touching a popsicle," I retort, placing a hand on her lower back and leading her towards the bar, where a mirrored wall and shelf upon shelf of liquor bottles serve as a backdrop for a solitary bartender in a suit. With his glasses and the set of his narrow lips, the guy looks like an engineering nerd more than a bartender, but I don't really care about the quality of his drinks right now.

"Got any Irish coffee?" I ask.

"Piñon flavored okay?"

"That'll do. Two. No whiskey for this one," I tilt my head in Rose's direction. "She's too young."

I slide some bills across the aged wooden bar top as he pours our drinks, and reflect on the fact that Rose is only twenty. Young enough to still want to please her mother even over silly things. Is she too young? Am I robbing the cradle?

I glance over at her, eyes tracing down her figure, enjoying the way only I can see it while she's draped in my coat. Maybe I should care about our age difference. Maybe I should care about Quique being her brother more. But one look at Rose and I can't muster up any sort of will to walk away. The knowledge that she's mine thrums too powerfully through my veins, a truth I can't deny.

"What's that look?" she asks, innocently.

I don't answer her as I grab our coffees and head over to a small alcove with seating. Two plush armchairs sit diagonally across from one another and we sink into them before I hand her one of the coffees.

Rose takes a big drink of hers and when her tongue darts out to lick a spare droplet off of her lip, I'm captivated.

"What?" she shifts nervously in her chair, reaching up and adjusting my jacket on her shoulders.

"Just picturing my cum on your lips later," I tease.

Her face goes white and her eyes grow as wide as saucers as she stiffens.

Fucking shit, did I trigger her by saying that?

But then her expression shifts, eyes narrowing as she bites her lip.

That's damn hot.

My mouth opens to feed her another dirty line but her scared expression returns as a hand smacks down on my shoulder and Quique's voice reaches my ears. Shit. Did he hear?

"Hey hero, hope you're not too good to talk to me now," he says with a chuckle as he comes into my line of sight. His greeting clearly implies he didn't hear my last words and I watch Rose sag with almost comical relief.

I give a casual shrug as I glance up at him and reply, "I suppose I can make an exception. Just this once."

His girl chuckles and I give her a nod of approval as he chuffs in my direction, not truly miffed at all. He hands Candace his beer and walks over to two nearby chairs, dragging them over, and inviting himself and his date to join us.

For the first time in my life, I'm slightly disappointed to sit next to my best friend. I'd much rather still be whispering naughty things to his sister, especially now that I realize she was only scared that Quique overheard and not scared by the suggestion itself.

As we talk and joke around, I wish that my arm was around Rose, that I was warming her up instead of just my jacket. The urge to publicly claim her hits me hard. We keep sneaking glances at one another in a way that makes me feel like I'm in middle school again, crushing hard on a girl and trying to see if she likes me back.

Our secret lust shines between us like a jewel but we bury it with feigned disinterest, talking to the other pair, and making conversation as if we shouldn't just be up in one of these hotel rooms right now devouring each other.

It's maddening but also an exhilarating tease at the same time. I both hate and am addicted to the way it makes me feel on edge, so much so that I lose track of the conversation for a minute. But then Enrique makes a comment that hits me across the forehead like a two-by-four.

"Two hot chicks by the bar," Quique informs me, as any good wingman would. It's a normal practice for us.

But that was before.

Rose stops talking to Candace, her eyes suddenly finding mine. "Oh, fresh meat." She arches a brow, challenging me.

This is the side of her I like. The side with that little bit of fire. "Nah, you know, I'm more interested in frozen meat than fresh. It's more tender." I wink, to ensure she gets the reference.

"You're weird," Candace remarks, giving me an odd look before sipping her wine.

Quique and Rose laugh—for different reasons. He laughs at the fact that his date just insulted me and she laughs with a little bit of naughty sparkle in her gaze that wasn't there before. I love that I put it there.

"But seriously, they're pretty hot, man."

"No. I'm here to escape work stress."

"Perfect stress reliever."

I shake my head and he leans forward, putting the back of his hand on my forehead. "You feeling okay, man?"

I shove him off, not able to deal with his games, because it makes me want to spit out the truth: I've claimed his baby sister and I'm planning to splatter my cum all over her tonight as those green eyes stare up at me. Fuck. I have to prop an ankle on my knee to hide the fact that picturing rubbing my cum into her breasts makes me hard.

It's a struggle to keep my tone neutral when I explain, "I just need a night off. No expectations. From anyone."

"Dude … seriously?"

"Yeah."

He narrows his eyes. "You never turn down girls."

"Yeah. You're a player," Rose interjects, piling on, a look on her face I don't love.

"I was. But, what can I say? I'm getting old. Time to settle down," I say jokingly, but as soon as the words roll off my tongue, they feel right. I force myself to look at Quique as I say it, not Rose, because I am definitely not going to be able to handle it if that admission freaks her out. It will only ramp up my need to claim her *now*, toss her over my shoulder and chain her up until she swears she's mine—which is absolutely the wrong thing to do with a girl who's been hurt the way she has.

She needs baby steps.

God, when did I become such a lunatic? Why she has this effect on me, I'm not quite sure—and the fact that it doesn't alarm me at all should be alarming, but it's not. It all just feels … right. She's mine. And that's that.

If I thought she was ready to embrace it, it would be one thing. But the way she'd scampered out of the meeting room earlier with an embarrassed "thanks," after the massive orgasm I gave her tells me that my lil reina still needs a little more time to come around. Not surprising, given her trauma.

I'll give her some.

Not much, because I'm not a good or patient man.

But some.

Quique clearly doesn't believe my remark about settling down because he barks out a rough laugh. "Yeah, that will be the day. Do you even know how to ask a girl on a date?" His brown eyes twinkle with mirth.

"Could probably use a demonstration," I tell him.

He turns to his date, holding out a hand. "Candace?"

The bottle blonde links her fingers with his instantly, a huge smile on her face. "Yes?"

"Ask me out and show him how it's done."

Her cheeks blush a pretty red as she stares over at him, looking a bit lost. I bite my lip in amusement because this girl is the kind of looker who's probably never had to ask a guy out in her life. She probably has to turn down dates regularly. "Umm ... want to go out with—"

"No, no, no. You have to start with a compliment. How about how my eyes are like starlight?" He bats his lashes.

"You've never complimented *my* eyes," she sasses.

"Well, they're like starlight, darling," Enrique hams it up with an exaggerated quirk of his brow and some ridiculous accent that I think is supposed to resemble a classic movie star. He's such a dipshit.

Rose snorts.

Candace rolls her starlit eyes and tugs her hand away before giving him a playful shove so that he slides across his seat. "Sure they are. I think you might need some practice of your own."

We all chuckle as Quique holds up his hands in supplication when Candace narrows her eyes at him. "Alright. Alright. One practice session coming up."

"I know," I say, as inspiration strikes. "I can practice on Rose."

If I thought I'd seen Rose stiff and awkward before, it was nothing in comparison to what she looks like now. Panic leaches the color from her face until she looks as pale as can be. She gives an infinitesimal shake of her head, but I ignore her, my gaze sliding over to Quique to gauge his reactions. Will he be pissed?

He just looks amused, thinking this is all a joke, not suspecting a thing.

I turn back to make eye contact with Rose as I set my drink on a side table and then slide out of my seat and down onto one knee in the space between our four chairs.

Candace squeals in delight and I can hear Quique's low laugh while Rose gives off a panicked squeak.

"What are you *doing?*" she hisses through her teeth at me.

"Rose, I've known you for most of your life and I've never realized how amazing you are until now. The only explanation I've got is a long-term head injury—probably one your brother gave me—"

"Damn straight," Quique cuts in. "You probably deserved it too."

I smirk as I slide forward on my knee, getting closer. I reach for Rose's hand but she tucks her free hand away and wields her coffee mug like a weapon. "I swear, I will pour this all over you. Get up off the floor." Those eyes burn into me and I've never wanted to pull her in for a kiss more than right at this moment.

Quique guffaws behind us. "God, this is the funniest thing I've ever seen."

I lean closer, unintimidated by her threats. "Ms. Dalton, I have a life-changing question to ask you."

Her cup tilts further as I say, "Will you do me the honor of …"—I let the silence draw out for a moment— "going to a football game together?"

Even she can't hold back a chuckle and I reach out, disarming her of her weapon, setting the mug gently on the side table. "Think of all the body paint we could wear."

That sets Candace off howling, while Quique interjects with a rapid-fire, "Hey, hey, hey," as brotherly instinct finally kicks in.

I link my fingers with Rose's, letting my gaze travel over that gorgeous face of hers, those defined cheekbones, those beautiful red lips, and my favorite green eyes on the planet.

"What do you say?"

"I say you're making a spectacle of yourself," Rose retorts, as her gaze sweeps the room behind me. I assume I've gathered a bit of an audience with the knee thing.

I don't glance back but quirk a crooked grin at her. "Yup. Social pressure. Will you publicly shame me?"

"You're kind of goading me into it."

"Or you could say yes," I wheedle, jutting out my lower lip. I don't miss how her eyes flash when I give her a pouty face and I store that knowledge away for later. "I'll even buy you kettle corn," I offer.

"Fine. Deal." She shakes her head as if she can't quite believe her own acceptance, but she's smiling as she does so.

I lean forward and kiss the back of her hand before I stand up. Then I strut by Quique and drop an imaginary mic. "Boom! That's how it's done."

"Cheater. You had insider info about kettle corn. You know it's her kryptonite," he accuses, far more focused on that fact than the concept that I just asked his sister out. Of course, he doesn't think I asked for real. Neither did she.

But now, I've at least set the stage. This memory will have some time to percolate before I show up with foam fingers and jerseys in hand to pick her up for the next college game —whenever it is—because a date is going to happen. Rose and I are meant to be.

Quique continues, "You'd never know that kind of thing about another girl."

He's right. But I don't need to know anything about any other girls, because the one I want is sitting right across from me.

I just shrug as I slide back into my seat. "Don't hate the player. Hate the game."

I just laugh as they all *boo* me for tossing out that overused line. But then my phone buzzes with a text that wipes the smile off my face.

I stand abruptly. "I've got to go."

I stride off without an explanation, waiting until I get outside the front of the hotel. I move from the expansive drop-off area over to the evergreen bushes lit by sporadic landscape lights.

That's when I dial the unknown number that just texted me.

"Hello?" Mint's voice answers.

"What happened?" I ask gruffly.

"Got a problem, boss. Police are sniffing around about Ambrose."

ANGELO

*L*eaving the hotel early wasn't part of the plan. I'm not even supposed to deal with the shit out in Arizona any longer, but Mint's a loyal guy—and not a total idiot. He can handle a lot. If he's texting me, then everything has hit the fan.

I leave with only a couple texts to explain myself. I send Quique one saying I had family issues. To Rose, I sent the following:

Me: Keep my jacket on tonight. I'll still be by later. Leave the window unlocked.

Her: Where are you going?

Me: Business emergency.

Her: Ok. Be safe.

I sigh, both because I love that she wants me to be safe but also because she has no clue how dangerous the life I lead can actually be. My lil reina doesn't know anything about the dark underbelly of the work I do, but if I'm going to make her a permanent fixture I don't know how I can keep it from her forever. I don't want her sullied by it, but I also don't want our relationship to be based on a lie, so I'm trapped between a rock and a hard place.

It's a problem I'll have to figure out later, I decide as I wait for a ride-share, because I need to help Mint get out of a jam right now.

Three hours later, my father and I sit in his home office. Or rather—he sits, wearing a red polo, behind a massive wooden desk while I pace across an oriental rug on the other side, tossing three used burner phones into a grocery bag so I can dispose of them later. The moon is going to wink out in an hour or two and let dawn take over; but for now, the only light is the glowing yellow sphere from his glass desk lamp. It illuminates the lines around his eyes and the massive crevices that have slowly taken over his forehead.

"Goddamn Gary. Knew I shouldn't have trusted a thief. Murderers are okay. You know where you stand with them. But thieves are liars who always think they deserve more than they've earned." Dad's hazel eyes gleam with fury as he pounds a pale fist into the desk.

I tie a knot in the grocery bag and toss it at the foot of his desk, bile singing the back of my throat. "Yeah. He's been in for years, though. He must have worked a dozen jobs with me and Mint." My lip curls as I picture the massive man. "He won't be able to hide easily."

"We won't be letting him hide at all," Dad states with a tone of finality as he opens up a desk drawer and rummages through it.

"Mint claim the kill?" I ask casually, as I slide into the seat across from my father.

"Not yet."

"If he doesn't want it, I do," I state, hands gripping the armrests hard. The fact that I worked so many jobs with that bastard makes me feel vulnerable.

I should have seen it, should have scented his disloyalty. I don't like feeling the way I am right now, snakes writhing in my stomach. Once we catch Gary, I want to make sure his death is a very painful, very drawn-out affair. It should become an urban legend among our underground network, something that strikes fear into the hearts of dark and depraved men the same way the tale of La Llorona used to grip me as a child. The story of the crying ghost woman who would drag children into the ditch and drown them always kept the kids away from the arroyos.

Gary's going to become a scary story of the same sort. Perhaps he'll be the death of a thousand nights … a man brought to the brink again and again. I'll have to be both brutal and creative, which is my favorite combination.

"He's yours," Dad states, knowing how important it is for us to seal this crack in our reputation.

I give him a firm nod to show him I'll handle it before I relax back into my seat. I settle, feeling more content and certain now that Dad and I have plotted out the course of future events. A few of our guys will help smuggle Mint out of Arizona away from the cops. He'll come to me for a bit and then I'll get him set up in one of our builds by the lake. So long as he keeps his head down, this whole thing will blow over. A 'friend' of mine will plant some evidence that Ambrose has skipped out to Mexico.

"I'm thinking fifty grand for the bounty," Dad leans back in his chair, a freshly cut cigar and a lighter in his age-spotted hands.

I hate that we have to spend a cent on finding Gary, but dangling a big carrot is the quickest way to get results. "Sounds good. I'll spread the word," I agree. "If we need, I know a guy who can create a deep fake video of Ambrose abroad too."

"It's settled then," Dad gives me a grim grin before shoving the cigar between his lips and lighting it. The orange glow and the soft scent of the tobacco fill me with a nostalgic sense of comfort and I nod.

I think we have it worked out, I really do though a tiny bit of guilt scratches at me over the fact that Mint's been fingered for the job and we've got a traitor in our midst who'll have to be rooted out. I should have noticed. But I'll fix this. And I'll ensure that Gary's screams echo for years, so that no one ever double-crosses me again.

But now that those issues have been addressed, there's one more I need to discuss with him.

My father leans back in his desk chair, crossing his pale, tattooed arms, the ink the only remaining evidence of his stint in the clink thirty-odd years ago. He and I look nothing alike. I got my mother's complexion, her eyes, and he would say, her attitude. But he and I share a ruthless streak that's as black as coal.

Dad kicks his feet up onto the side of the desk, thinking we're done and we have everything settled.

I clear my throat before broaching the topic. "I need to tell you about an unrelated complication,"

"Shit, Ang, that ain't enough for one night?" he asks, running a hand through his gray-streaked hair, wrinkles forming at the corners of his hazel eyes.

"This is good news. About a girl."

"A girl?" His expression and demeanor immediately morph into curiosity.

"*The* girl," I clarify.

He puffs on his cigar, inhaling and then exhaling a perfect smoke ring, watching it hover in the air for a second before looking back at me. "You sure?" In our world, it's dangerous to bring anyone in. If they're in, they're all in.

Rose and I have only had a few encounters since things have shifted between us.

But this feeling in my gut … it's unlike anything else.

I nod once.

"She know?" He doesn't elaborate, but his meaning is very clear. He wants to know if this girl is aware of all the things we do.

"Not exactly—"

He starts to shake his head but I cut him off because I don't want to hear him tell me to let her go and find someone who's already in our circles. I wouldn't listen, but it would piss me off to a level of lividness that I'm pretty certain would cause a rift.

"It's Rose Dalton."

"Fuck!" His curse is violent and sudden—utterly unexpected.

My hackles rise in response and I immediately go on the defensive. "Don't rule her out just because—"

"No, no, it's not that. *Dammit.* Your mother called it five years ago." He shakes his head ruefully, a slight smile crossing his face. "She said you'd be gone for that girl the moment you grew up and got your head on straight. Now, I owe her a fucking tennis bracelet."

I join his laughter—relief and joy bubbling and fizzing inside my stomach like a soda. "Don't act like you can't afford it, old man."

"Don't act like she isn't going to hold this over my head for the rest of my life," he retorts, flicking the ash from the tip of his cigar into an ashtray.

"She will. She's really good at that," I reply fondly.

He points at me with the hand holding his cigar. "If you're sure about this, and she's sure about this … you're going to have to bring her into the loop. Carefully, though." He drops his feet from the desk and leans over it, closer to me, the lamplight painting half of his face and leaving the other half eerily shadowed. "If she can't deal, son, you know what will have to happen."

My stomach bottoms out, and I suddenly wish I'd swallowed my words and kept this shit from my father, because he basically just said—without so many words—that if I let Rose in and she can't handle us, she'll have to die.

ROSE

I sit, perched on the edge of our leather couch in our formal living room, fingers digging into the seat, back uncomfortable and ramrod straight. Enrique and I sit in shadows, because the room is dark except for one lamp over in the corner that's always on a timer since Mom's events often run so late. It's casting sideways light upon us as we stare up at our prowling mother. My perspective only emphasizes the spot where Mom broke her nose when I was ten. Took a rec-league softball right to the face. She'd had it reset, but there was still a bump if you knew where to look for it.

I watch her pace aggressively like some lioness, and her demeanor makes the hairs on the back of my neck stand up. She's clearly worked up, clearly in a terrible mood that resulted in a stiff silence for the entire hour-long drive home. I don't know if I've seen her this furious and frazzled since Dad tried to get the house in the divorce.

Maybe I shouldn't have left my window unlocked for Angelo like he requested.

Maybe that was a mistake.

Maybe everything involving him is.

"Well, one look at that Walker boy and the Garcias turned tail and left," Mom says, the muscles in her neck tense, and her voice vibrating with a barely controlled edge of fury. "LEFT! Not a dime. They weren't there to bid against the Jimenez couple—tonight was a total disaster! We're at least a million short of our projections."

Mom runs an exasperated hand over her hair, though even her fingernails can't penetrate the shellac that her hairdresser put on her curls earlier.

Her brow furrows as she shakes her head. "I don't even think I can get their support back now. Not with the disastrous rumor mill saying you and Angelo are *engaged*, Rose." The full brunt of her anger turns toward me and I suck in a breath, because I work so hard never to earn that look. I hate that look and the way it makes self-loathing foam up inside my throat, clogging it.

My eyes drift down to my knees. "I'm sorry," I whisper. I don't bother saying that it was just a joke, because, in the grand scheme of things, that doesn't really matter. A joke just cost her a ton of money—money she needs for advertisements, for flyers, for signs. God. I feel like such an idiot. I normally don't let my guard down at those events. But I did tonight because of him.

Look what happened.

Quique calls out from his end of the couch, "Mom, it's not her fault. I was teasing him and we got carried away. Rosie didn't do anything!" He lifts a hand and gestures in my direction.

But his words only earn him a sharp, pointed finger. "Do not interfere. She knows better than to make a spectacle. That's all *that boy* knows how to do."

"Yeah, he's so awful. He saved some guy's life tonight and Rose's life all those years ago." Quique stands, using his height to look down on Mom. "Total bastard."

I sink back into the couch, curling my legs up, because—as much as I love that he's trying to defend Angelo, trying to physically intimidate Mom is absolutely a mistake. Dad used to do the same thing.

As I expect, Mom does not appreciate that. I can practically feel invisible spikes shooting out of her spine, as if she were a porcupine. Her brows knit and her tone becomes danger-ously low as she shoves her pointed finger into Quique's chest. "You think you know better, mijo? You don't. That *cabrón* is a murderer!"

Those words wallop me across the face as if she was holding a tire iron. They smash in my teeth and my breath leaves my body for a moment.

"What the fuck? Who told you that bullshit?!" Enrique and she get right in each other's faces, a screaming match ensuing.

But it's as if my ears have been filled with cotton. Their yells sound far away, distant, as I float to my feet and down the hall, away from them. They don't even notice—too intent on yelling themselves hoarse.

It can't be true. Can it? He's too good. Too silly. Always cutting-up with Enrique. A guy who can do those things, can't just be a killer … can he?

The way he took Nick out though, instantly and brutally, even publicly, without regard for the consequences …

No.

No, I'm overthinking. I'm applying stupid, hateful rumors and using them to overanalyze what happened. I shake my head, trying to dislodge the cotton, as I turn my knob.

I'm shocked to find my window wide open, even though I left it ajar. My dazed musing made me completely forget that he was coming.

And my mother and brother are still locked in a screaming match—over Angelo.

Shit.

I hurry to shut the door and lock it behind me as if I can hide the horrible things that are being flung by my two hot-tempered family members. Then I turn to see him.

Angelo stands in my room, still in his white dress shirt and pants, though he's lost the tie. In his hands, he holds a book he's plucked from my bookshelf. It appears as though he was reading the back of it but stopped when I entered. His profile is lit by my bedside lamp, which he has turned on, giving his skin a golden glow. My eyes are particularly drawn to the muscles of his neck when he turns to face me and swallows hard. The expression on his face is strained.

Fuck!

My stomach slides down from its place in my abdomen and tumbles to my toes. He definitely heard what Mom said. Shame lights up my cheeks at the fact that my own mother would say those things. God, I wonder how that makes him feel? How much would it hurt to have your second family say that kind of terrible crap about you?

I cringe.

I've known Angelo for years and I'd never—not in my wildest dreams—have come up with a rumor even half as cruel as the one she's in there spreading … If I heard people talking about me that way, I'd burst into tears. And it's his best friend's family, no less.

Quickly, I cross the room, needing to touch him, to soothe him, to smooth this over. Trepidation vibrates the tone of my voice as I half-whisper, "She doesn't mean it. She's stressed. Trying to blame you for the fact that her fundraiser did awful. I'm sorry. I'm so, so sorry." I clutch his arms, running my fingers over his sleeves in soothing circles as I try to distinguish what the look on his face means. His lips are pressed together and his eyes are distant for a moment before he focuses back on me.

Something in his face looks desperate. Longing. It draws me in like a moth to the flame and I step even closer, planting my feet between his thighs as I gently pluck my copy of *Outlander* from his grip and toss it onto the desk next to my bookshelf.

It looks like he needs me to show him just how much I don't believe those wild, hare-brained lies.

"I'm sorry. She's crazy," I say, leaning up on tiptoe and pressing a soft kiss to his cheek, then another to his dream-worthy lips. "I don't believe her." I let the words ghost across his mouth before kissing him harder, and when he hesitates —as if he's unsure that I actually mean what I say, I wrap my hands around the back of his neck and pull him in closer, deepening the kiss.

I remain the aggressor for a moment, rubbing my hands along the back of his neck and shoulders, nipping at his lips, delving my tongue into his mouth.

But finally, a switch flips and he starts to trust me and my words over the spiteful acid my mother spewed. His hands come up to knead my ass and I spread my legs wider, hopeful that his fingers will knead me everywhere. I rub against him, loving the press of our chests, appreciating the bulge inside his suit pants, and feeling a heady sense of naughty pride that I turn him on. I bring my hands from around his neck down to his shirt collar, popping the first button.

He breaks the kiss to stare at me but doesn't stop me as I undo every single button on his shirt. He's still as a statue while I remove his cuff links. Meanwhile, I'm amazed at the fact that I even find his wrists attractive. There isn't an inch of this man I don't adore and I plan to show him just that.

He moans in delight when I glide my hands up over his undershirt and circle the dark shapes of his nipples through the fabric before bringing my hands back out and shoving the collared shirt down over his arms, pulling it off one arm and then the other.

"Shh," I grin at the fact I have to remind him to be quiet. He's already forgotten that my brother and Mom are still in the house. I haven't. If anything, I feel far more aware of everything because of it. Normally, I'd never even dream of doing something like this—or I'd dream about it but never actually do it. But something about tonight, about the way he stood up for me, about the way Mom is showing her true colors, something's making me wild and reckless. I'm throwing caution to the wind.

Mom can hate him all she wants, but she's wrong about him. Quique knows it and so do I. The fact that I'm going to do unspeakable things to him under her roof is nothing less than the disrespect she deserves.

My senses heighten with every touch Angelo and I share. My skin is not only aware of his fingertips but of the cool air drifting in from my window and wasting all the heat billowing up from the vent near my bed. The contrasting temperatures mix around our bodies and make goosebumps rise on my skin.

My hearing is also enhanced—the piercing chirps of every cricket outside and every tiny groan of pleasure Angelo makes coursing through my nervous system. My family's shouting ended a while ago, and the front door slams at one point—which means Quique's going back out. Mom has most likely retreated to her home office—it's where she spends the majority of her time—so she's on the other side of the house. Near but not near enough to hear, so long as we remember to stay quiet.

Angelo doesn't look like he's going to be any use remembering things right now, however. His jaw is clenched as his eyes rake down my body.

"Get naked before I rip that dress off of you," he growls.

God, he's such a bossy bastard. But I kind of love it. I grow wet at his order, biting my lip as I lift my black skirt and yank it up over my head. The dress is relatively easy to shed, and once it's off, Angelo immediately steps forward, his hands coming to cup my breasts.

"Fuck. You are never allowed to wear these again," he murmurs, thumbs gliding over the pasties that hide my nipples and sending a delicious sensation spiraling through me. "I want to see those nipples hard for me at all times, you hear?"

"Mmm," is the best response I can give him because I'm not thinking about later. I just want him to keep touching me. I love his big, calloused hands and the way they contrast my soft skin. I love how my breasts almost fit in his palms.

His fingers grip one side of a pastie and start to pull. The sticky tape stings like a yanking off a Bandaid, only one that's stuck to some of the most sensitive skin on my body, and I hiss, involuntarily shoving his hand away. "Ow!" I whisper-shout, batting him away and folding my arms protectively across my breasts.

"Think about how I feel," he retorts. "I can't get to those pretty tits. That hurts worse."

Bastard.

I smack him but he just laughs and pulls me across the room toward my desk chair, which has his suit coat hung carefully over the back of it. He turns the chair so it faces me before he sits down. "Straddle me," he orders. "I'm going to lick and suck you until those damned things fall off."

Oh. God. "Don't threaten me with a good time." I scold.

"I can and will."

"Then I want you shirtless," I counter, simply because his giving orders riles me up, even if I like them.

His undershirt is off and on the ground in a millisecond leaving me to gape at his washboard abs. All of his delicious tattoos—a crow, a cross, and a rose, all jump out at me as my eyes travel over his body, which is unreal. I'm hypnotized as I climb up on him, half tempted to tell him to lose his pants.

But I'm not naked yet either, and I don't want tonight to be quick. I want our first time to be a slow pleasure that I can brand into my brain and remember forever. So I straddle him, still wearing my red panties and matching heels.

When I settle down on his bulge, I can't help but grind against him, fingers digging into the hard-earned muscles of his shoulders.

God, he feels so good.

His hands wrap around my lower back and pull me up as he dips his head. Then Angelo's lips wrap around my nipple, through the pastie.

Fuck, I've always fantasized about this boy's lips and now I know exactly why. They aren't just a work of art, they are scientific perfection. These are the lips that every lip in history has aspired to be. The pinnacle of evolution.

He sucks on my right breast, even with a barrier, lapping, nipping, laving me—and I'm driven completely out of my mind.

By the time he's finished, my pastie is soaked. When he slowly peels it off, it no longer hurts, other than from the ache of wanting him, from my nerve endings craving direct contact after being teased for so long. "Yes," he whispers, as his mouth dives down and wraps around me, sucking on my sensitive bud without any barrier this time.

I end up shamelessly grinding against him, nearly over-whelmed by sensation. Moaning a soft complaint when he pulls away, my hands dive into my panties. I need some relief and when my fingers glide down either side of my clit, jagged pleasure shoots through me and I nearly come.

When his mouth moves to the other pastie, I rub myself in slow circles as my hips swivel over him, the rub of his bulge and the heat of him making me tighten in anticipation. I move my hand more quickly when he finally starts to use his teeth to pull the tiny covering off my nipple. I pinch my clit then, the intensity fracturing me into pieces so that I'm shuddering as he frees my nipple. I'm moaning desperately when his lips finally close around it and tug gently, that final touch from him sending me spinning. As he suckles, the torrent inside me goes from a rainstorm to a dark sky pierced by a lightning bolt.

I collapse against Angelo with a contented sigh and he wraps his arms around my back, standing and shuffling forward. I'm still in the haze of my afterglow when he lays me on the bed and then crawls up over me, leaning on his elbows.

That's when it hits me.

I'm bracketed by him. Pinned down by the hips.

Panic makes my throat cave in.

Angelo's face suddenly flashes out of existence and *that night* erupts from nowhere, from the recesses of my memory. Three shadowy figures loom over me, holding me down on the bed. My entire body clenches up and my lungs halt mid-breath.

"What is it?" Angelo immediately freezes. "Rose?"

His voice calls me back into the present so that my eyes can see him, see his chiseled face above me and not the disgusting drunken leers of those fuckers, but my body is still in a limbic, panicked response. I can't uncurl my hands or unlock my knees, only stare up at him with a terrified expression.

His face softens for a moment, and I watch him shut his eyes as he swallows hard—either shoving back lust or anger, I'm not sure which. But he quickly moves off of me, climbing from the bed and backing away toward my bookshelf, arms held up in a pacifying manner. "We don't have to …"

The fact that he's gone, out of my space, lets me breathe again, albeit slowly. My lungs restart and I gasp as I take in air, gulping as if I've just been drowning. My mind races a mile a minute to process what just happened. I try to calm my pulse and reconnect with my reality by rubbing my fingertips up and down over my comforter, the familiar texture of the soft threads reminding me that I'm home. I'm here. Not there. I'm safe. It's okay.

My eyes travel across the shadows of my bedroom, trying to convince my limbs that I'm truly secure when I see him turn. The reality that Angelo's facing my window, ready to leave, smashes into me like a fist. Fuck. What have I done? I've just ruined this blooming, budding, explosively brilliant thing between us.

"No. Wait." I force my stiff limbs to sit up, fighting their stiffness as I push up off the comforter. When I shove my hair back from my cheek, I realize my face is wet. A tear has escaped. I swipe it away angrily, annoyed at myself. Guilty. Horrified. Embarrassed.

"I'm sorry," I whisper as I knot my fingers in my lap. I'm apologizing because those bastards intruded on our moment. I'm agonized by the fact that it happened because I never even thought it would or I wouldn't have unlocked the window for him.

I've done so well. I've shoved them and that night aside and I've been putting one foot in front of the other since then. I haven't cut myself either. I … I was proud of how I was coping. I thought it was all over and done. Apparently, I was wrong.

They've been waiting. Those nightmares have been waiting for the right moment to pounce so they could destroy me a second time.

Fuck them.

That's not fair.

I sniff a little as I murmur, "I don't want those fuckers to own me. To break this. Us. I'm sorry. I'm sorry." My words don't even make a lot of sense, but my mouth isn't able to keep up with my thoughts, which are pulsing with fury and self-loathing.

They don't deserve a single additional millisecond of my time or attention. And they definitely don't deserve to have the power to steal away my happiness. But here they are, fucking me up at the worst possible time in the worst way. Here I am, letting them.

Pathetic.

"Hey, shhhh, none of that," Angelo croons softly, taking a solitary step toward me, careful not to come too close.

Because I'm a freak show.

Because he doesn't know what set me off and he's worried he might do it again.

Fuck.

Fuck.

Fuck.

I bury my face in my hands and let out a sob.

There's a creaking noise that has me peeking up, certain he's slipping out my window, but I find him sitting down in my desk chair, holding his arms out toward me. "Do you want—"

He doesn't finish his question before I'm striding over to him. Without an ounce of hesitation, I climb onto his lap and wrap my arms around him before burying my face in the crook of his neck. Slowly, gradually, his touch reaches my back. It's feather-light until I drop one of my own hands down and wrap his grip more firmly around myself, showing him I won't break. "I'm sorry," I repeat, gazing at his face through glimmering eyes.

"Rose, I want to kill them, only death isn't good enough."

"You're right." I give a broken laugh. "Maybe we should use all the worst torture methods in history on them instead. Like the goat's tongue."

"Goat's tongue. What's that?" Angelo's voice is curious as his hand finally dares to dart up and caress my cheek.

I lean into his slow touch as I explain, "Romans used to dip someone's feet in a salt solution. Then they'd tie that person up and tie a goat nearby. The goat would lick their feet. It would initially feel like tickling, but the goat wouldn't stop licking until the skin was all gone."

Angelo stares up at me, his mouth dropping open, and I worry that I've scared him. Not everyone wants to know about the bloodthirsty horrors of the past and even though Daisy constantly indulges me, I know I can be a bit over-the-top about it.

But when he speaks, his voice is soft and awed, and the fingers gliding over my cheek stop to cup it. "History," he murmurs.

"What?"

"You want to major in history."

My stomach clenches and even though I'm wearing nearly nothing, Angelo's words make me feel naked.

Vulnerable.

Seen.

"The books on your shelves. That little comment. You want to major in history don't you?"

"It's a useless degree—"

"No. You have a plan for it."

I lick my lips and realize how hard it is to make my mouth shape the words of my most secret wish. It's like slitting open an envelope that's lain dormant inside a trunk tucked into an attic for a century, the thoughts etched on the paper inside faded until they're more fancy than reality.

"I want to write historical fiction," I admit softly.

"Then you will." His umber eyes are sure, not even encouraging, just utterly confident in a way I could never hope to be. As if something will happen solely because I want it to. As if he really believes that's how the world works.

I blink at him and somehow want to cry all over again. I'm not exactly sure why, only that he's made something lodge in my throat precariously, and something else lodge inside my ribs. Both somethings are sharp and painful, piercing right through me.

Two deep breaths—and innumerable heartbeats because my pulse has shot sky high—later, I attack him with my lips, pulling him in for a punishing kiss. Frantically, I scratch at his back and thrash my tongue against his as soon as he allows me access to his mouth.

His fingers dig into my hips and try to keep me still, but I fight against his hold, kissing him harder and rocking against him, letting my nipples drag up and down over his chest as I rub myself against him like a cat in heat.

Finally, he engages and starts to kiss me back. Each kiss unravels a knot that was tied tightly inside of me until I'm a thousand unfurled strings stretching in a million different directions. My thoughts and feelings are all so scattered, except for one. There's one thing I'm sure about.

I pull back and climb unceremoniously off Angelo's lap to yank my panties off. "Get naked," I order.

"Rose—"

"I'm going to fuck the living daylights out of you," I threaten as I kick aside my panties but leave on the red heels he loves. I'll probably need the leverage.

"But—"

"As long as we stay off the bed, I'll be fine," I promise, though I have no idea if that's true. I'll make it true. It has to be true. Because I'm not giving up the one fucking person in the world who actually *sees* me.

Angelo reluctantly reaches for his pants, but he's not fast enough. "Let me help you." Impatiently, I kneel to pull his pants off and then his boxer briefs to reveal his length. His dick is long and dark, dark hair trimmed neatly at the base, with a bulbous head that's slightly narrower than the rest of him. It's perfect. Leaning forward, I wrap my fingers around the base and slowly lick up his length before making eye contact.

His hands are gripping the sides of my desk chair as if he's about ready to rip them off. Chest unmoving, I'm pretty certain he's holding his breath in an effort to stay in control of himself. The fact that I have that sort of power over him makes me grin just before I take the head of his dick into my mouth.

I slide up and down, getting a slow rhythm going as I listen to his breathing for cues about what he likes. It's only when he whispers, "Shit," a little too loudly that I even remember there are other people in the house.

I pull off him and lean back on my heels, putting a playful finger to my lips. "Quiet. You don't want to get caught." My eyes glance toward my bedroom door, which is locked. But after his gaze follows and our glances reconnect, I can tell that the possibility has energized both of us.

When my tongue goes back to lap at the underside of his cock, Angelo finally puts a hand on my head, threading his fingers through my curls and taking some control.

"Suck me."

I take him into my mouth and his thighs tense. The dirty talk he spouted earlier at the party resurfaces as he says, "I thought about your mouth all night. I want you to leave lipstick stains on the base of my cock so I can see it tomorrow."

Fuck.

The idea of him playing with himself in the shower and looking at the red marks left by my lips spurs me on to suck him in deeper, trying to push past my gag reflex. Even so, I can't get my mouth all the way down on him—it's impossible.

I pull back up, coughing and sputtering, but he grabs my arm and hauls me to my feet, kissing me hard and muttering, "Good girl. You're such a naughty little cocksucker."

I reach over into my desk and grab a condom packet out of the top drawer, ripping it open with my teeth and then carefully rolling it down his length before I straddle him again, this time sliding my legs through the gaps beneath the armrests so that my heels touch the ground.

We start another vicious makeout session, and this time he's a whole-hearted participant. His hands come up and cup my breasts, circling my nipples, pinching them lightly. Tendrils of pleasure unfurl in my veins and heat gathers between my thighs. I grind against his length until I feel my own arousal coating it, my body crying out for more.

I break our kiss, rising up onto my feet a bit and reaching down between our bodies to line us up.

"It's okay to not be okay," he whispers. "At any time. We can stop and it will be okay."

My throat nearly closes and I'm barely able to restrain another emotional avalanche.

No. No. I'm done with those. I've had enough for one evening. I just want the mindless bliss of an orgasm. I cope with Angelo's sweet words by moving the hand not on his dick up to his neck. I wrap it firmly around his throat, as far as I can reach, squeezing lightly as I slowly sink down on him. "Shut. The. Fuck. Up."

I don't know if my words or my hand silence him, or if it's the fact that he stretches me so fully. I don't really care. He feels so right and perfect inside of me, that it's all I can think about.

I start to ride him, embracing the heat of him inside of me, relishing the glide of his cock when I change angles and he presses against my G-spot. God. Yes. That's what I need.

Mindless.

Fucking.

Bliss.

"I mean it. We can stop," Angelo's words are choppy as he disregards my threat. Or maybe he likes being choked. I bring another hand up to his neck and complete a circle around it, collaring him, feeling the way his pulse flutters underneath my touch.

"You don't get to talk like that," I rasp out slowly, between thrusts that are stealing my breath.

"Why not?"

He only grins when I contract my fingers around his throat and start to ride him more savagely, my hips smashing down into his as a climax as violent as the way I'm throttling him approaches.

I don't mean to answer. I really don't. But the words spill from my lips as I reach the crest. "Because you'll make me fall in love with you, estupido."

That does it. That breaks the dam of his self-control. Any illusion that I was in charge, or that my hands did a damn thing around his monster throat, collapses as his hands come up to grasp my hips and he slams up into me. Red stars flash and fade behind my eyes, flares warning me of looming disaster.

I embrace the crash.

Angelo doesn't stop, forcing me over the edge of my orgasm and roughly through it, a finger coming down to strum at my clit when I start to sag onto him, pushing me into a second orgasm as he groans, leaning down and biting at the juncture of my neck and shoulder as he finds his own release.

I crumple, falling limp onto him, having already forgotten our conversation. But he clearly hasn't. His arms wrap loosely around my back and hold me on his lap as he whispers, "Good. Because that's my diabolical plan. To make you fall so in love with me that you never want to leave."

ROSE

*A*ngelo—in typical over-the-top Angelo fashion—
goes overboard with the whole no-bed thing.

The next morning, I've hardly woken up, barely stretched
and yawned beneath my covers before I get a text from him.

Boyfriend: I've made a list of every place we can have sex
that's not a bed.

Me: Good morning to you, too.

Boyfriend: Are you sore? Morning.

He tacks that last bit on as an afterthought and I can't help
but chuckle as I sit up in bed and rub the sleep from my eyes.
What a typical man.

Me: No.

I'm deliciously aware of everything we did last night as I
press my thighs together beneath the sheets. While my
nipples are a little sensitive, that might just be from the
pasties, and it's not at all an unpleasant sensation. It brings

up vivid memories of what we did together and has me leaning back against the headboard savoring them.

Another text dings and I glance down to read it.

Boyfriend: :(Then I didn't do enough. Don't worry. We'll make up for it today.

I bite my lip as my heart leaps up and does a giddy little dance. He wants to see me again? Already?

***

THAT AFTERNOON

I STARE up at the chandelier sparkling above me as we defile the dining table. I bite down on my forearm as I attempt to hold in a scream that threatens to convince the neighbors there's a murder taking place.

My hips roughly jut up into Angelo's mouth as he sits in a chair and tongue fucks me. I'm beyond thinking as I grab his head and hold his face to my core with absolutely zero regard for his safety as I come undone, bucking and panting as pleasure cartwheels up my spine.

The bastard is smug as he leans back a minute later and wipes his cheeks with his abandoned t-shirt.

Meanwhile, my ass plops back down onto the wood and I realize that I'm never going to be able to sit through Mom's Thanksgiving dinner again without thinking about how Angelo spread me open and devoured me.

Worth it.

Monday

SHOWER SEX … hot as fuck. But what's even hotter is when Angelo carries me out of the shower and bends me over the countertop. I'm naked, dripping wet, breasts dangling as he reaches forward and wipes the steam from the mirror, making eye contact with me in the reflection before ordering, "Watch me own this pussy."

And I do. I watch every frantic thrust.

Wednesday

I'M NOT sure there's a main room left in my mother's house that we haven't used. The couches have been christened. The floors. The walls. I've been obsessively opening windows and lighting juniper candles so no one can smell all the sex. I can try to cover up the scent, but it's harder to hide the grins that keep popping up, randomly curving my cheeks. I don't have an explanation for those, other than, "I just had a really good day." Yeah, a really good day and four orgasms.

Thursday

I SKIPPED a rally meeting for Mom to meet with Angelo. We were supposed to go to his apartment, but we didn't make it farther than the cab of his truck, which is surprisingly spacious.

I only kicked the horn once as he fucked me roughly, both of us still mostly clothed. I've discovered I love the tight feel of my panties around my thighs restraining me as I spread against them. There's something deliciously wicked about the fact that we can't even wait to get our clothes off.

I also discovered yesterday that nothing makes Angelo hotter than me telling him that I belong to him. So I carefully reach down my side, hand curving beneath my ass, fingers searching. I cup his balls as he rams into me with all the power of a freight train and whisper, "I'm yours."

He comes with a roar that I'm certain the entire parking lot hears.

FRIDAY

HE CAN'T SEE me today. He says a friend has come in from out of town and he has to take care of some things he's been neglecting.

Even though that's practical, I can't help the fact that my throat grows tight at the thought that I won't see him.

That is, until I get a text.

Boyfriend: By the way, I licked your vibrator. Think about that the next time you use it.

I do.

And I've never come so hard or so fast solo.

SATURDAY, SUNDAY, & MONDAY

I THINK Angelo might be trying to kill me.

I'm pretty sure he's invented the sex equivalent of the board game Clue and is acting it out with me.

In the hot tub, doggie style, with a vibrator.

On the balcony, against the railing, wearing a buttplug.

On top of the piano, feet on the keys, my hands cinched with a rope.

TUESDAY

WE AGREE to meet up somewhere since our last attempt to drive together in his truck was a disaster.

We go for ice cream at a cute little cafe called *Donna's* that backs to a park. It's mid-afternoon when we get there, and I'm dressed more conservatively than I have been around him. I wear a knee-length puffy jacket over a long-sleeved black shirt and black yoga pants.

I get the mint chocolate chip and he gets butter pecan and we decide to stroll through the park since it's a rare, semi-warm winter day.

It's not very scenic, without leaves on the trees and everything brown and barren, but it's quiet. There's a neighborhood surrounding the little ice cream shop so the entire area is pretty much abandoned by people working or schooling or just getting out. We're the only ones there.

I'm just about to ask Angelo what his favorite movie is—to broach some kind of first date topic—when something wet and cold hits my nose.

For a horrifying second, I think a bird's shit on me.

Then the wet substance drips onto my lips and I hear Angelo laughing. I turn to see him licking his fingers.

Suspicion rolls through me.

I let my tongue dart out to lick the speck on my lips. That bastard threw ice cream at me! Swiping a hand over my nose, I hiss from between my teeth. "Oh, it's like that, cabrón?" I launch myself at him, my cone raised like a weapon.

With a laugh and a whoop, he darts off through the grass. The bastard has legs that are twice as long as mine and I chase him around the entire perimeter of the park, huffing and screaming, leaving a trail of green drips behind me. I only end up catching him near the slide because he lets me.

When he comes to a dead stop in front of a child's ladder leading up to the colorful playset and puts his hands—one still holding his cone—up in surrender, I narrow my eyes, untrusting.

"Truce. We need a truce or our ice cream is going to melt."

I grit my teeth but grudgingly agree. "Fine. But you're still a bastard." Anyone else would get a fake smile, but Angelo—I don't have to pretend with him. I don't have to be nice. And it's so damn refreshing.

I stick my tongue out at him before I go to lick my ice cream and I find myself getting spun around a second later, captive in his arms, my back to his front. Holding me in place and pinning my arms down with one hand across my chest, he attacks me again, gliding his frigid ice cream cone over my neck.

Pure ice sears my senses. "You bastar—"

I stop cursing the moment his tongue drags over my pulse, lapping up the ice cream. The warm, wet heat makes me nearly go limp in his arms and my desire to win this battle starts to retreat.

He shifts the hand pinning me to him and then drags his cone across my shirt, the chill seeping right through to my skin. I hiss through my teeth, but one second later, he's in front of me, mouth over one of my breasts, sucking until my shirt is soaked, the wet patch sinking all the way down to my nipple, which has hardened under the chill and his ministrations.

He yanks up my shirt and draws a thick line of ice cream across my low belly before kneeling on the ground. He laps at my stomach, until I whimper, "But someone could see."

"No one's here," he counters.

A quick glance around proves him right. It's midwinter and midweek and a few crows hopping through the dead grass are the only creatures nearby. My stomach is fluttering with nerves, but also with a naughty, flickering heat.

Angelo snakes my yoga pants down an inch, drawing another line of ice cream. His eyes flash up to mine for a second, before his tongue snakes out and he licks a slow, warm path across my skin. The warmth of his mouth is nothing compared to the burst of fire between my thighs.

My yoga pants are tugged down another inch, panties with them. At this point, I'm panting. My own ice cream drops to the ground, forgotten, when he draws a sticky new line to lick.

And when he commands, "Reach up and hold the ladder rungs," that's exactly what I do.

WEDNESDAY

WE TAKE A VERY, very needed day off, one that I regret by the time eight o'clock rolls around. People say meth is addictive? They haven't tried Angelo's orgasms. I think my brain might be permanently rewired to desire his touch.

I text him.

And the raunchiest FaceTime phone sex conversation ensues until Quique gets home and pounds on my door.

"What the hell are you watching in there? Porn?"

My brother chuckles at his own joke as my hands slide out of my panties, orgasm completely ruined. My heart thumps painfully against my ribs as I stare at my phone, giving his best friend panicked eyes.

What are we doing?

What if Quique had opened the door? What if we'd gotten caught?

FRIDAY

AFTER OUR SCARE ON WEDNESDAY, and because I have a paper due, we really do take Thursday off.

But now? Now he's on his way over.

And we're going to go out.

Or try to.

I grab my purse, trying to ignore the fact that my hands are clammy, and my heart is racing. My body does this every time I'm about to see Angelo, some strange amalgamation of excitement and nervousness spiking and making me quake. I would have thought I'd have gotten used to it by now—it's been almost two weeks—but I'm not. I adjust my emerald sweater dress and the knee-high boots that I'm wearing before checking my lipstick in a mirror in the entryway.

Too nervous to stand inside, I lock the front door and make my way out to the driveway just as I see his black truck turn the corner. Is it pathetic how my heart jumps up just at the sight of him?

Maybe.

A tiny part of me twists in guilt that we still haven't told Quique anything. But I don't know how he'll take it—if he'll get territorial about me stealing his best friend, or worse, hurt. And if he finds out, then Mom will end up finding out and she's still off the deep end. Her campaign has lost some momentum and she still—unreasonably—blames Angelo.

The Wild Flowers know ... kind of. They know we've been hooking up, but I haven't told anyone the way that Angelo makes me feel like I've discovered fire or invented the world's first plane. He changes the darkness from an enemy into something conquerable; he transforms the sky from the place of dreams to the place where I can soar and see the world in an entirely new light.

I think Daisy might know, based on the looks she gives me, but I haven't said anything aloud. Not yet.

Because it's precious and personal.

But also because it's uncertain.

Other than that first night, when my mouth slipped and he responded possessively, the "L" word hasn't slid out again.

Obviously, it shouldn't.

It's too soon.

But we haven't really been out on a date either. I don't count ice cream because it turned into … well, what we always end up doing. We couldn't even finish our cones off without him finishing *me* off.

I don't know if that's a bad sign or a good one. If we're serious or not.

The uncertainty of us—of what we are and where we stand is making me feel a little seasick.

My knees are still wobbly from the ambivalence when I climb up into the passenger seat of the truck and give him a smile.

"Ready?" he asks as soon as I click the seatbelt into place.

I nod.

Angelo drives me to the construction site he's working at, intending to show me around. I start off full of bubbly expectation about meeting some of his employees. But the way his hand clamps around my thigh and his gaze keeps flickering over to me on the drive has me breathing shallowly. My nipples pebble from those glances and he very clearly notices, because I'm not wearing a bra—just the way he prefers.

His fingers start to stroke my inner thigh as he makes a final turn into the lot, weaving around a still and silent bulldozer. A knot of guys in highlighter-yellow vests are working together in the fading light of the last hour of sunshine, but with the way he's touching me, I doubt I'll meet any of them.

I'm absolutely right. He parks and comes around the car, helping me up out of it, wearing his fuck-me eyes, this dark, intense look he gets that I now am quite familiar with. That look alone has the Pavlovian ability to soak my panties.

Part of me wishes this would turn into a real date, but another, far more prominent part of me is ready for all the ways I know he's going to own my body.

Angelo leads me straight to his office in a portable building. His office is nondescript, with typical industrial carpet, and a box full of safety gear—hard hats and safety glasses and vests —in the corner. The faint scent of sawdust fills the air, not unpleasantly.

His desk is a mess. There's no computer screen. He's already told me that he uses a laptop so he can move from site to site. But there are a ton of disorganized papers scattered across the surface. I stare at them as he locks the door behind me, wondering if his apartment is this messy—wondering why I haven't seen it yet.

"God, I missed you yesterday," he admits, striding forward and wrapping his arms around my waist as my hands come up to glide over his neck.

"Same," I murmur softly, eyes tracing the planes of his face as if we've been apart a year instead of a day or two, depending on how we count phone sex. I think I might be developing an unhealthy obsession. But at least it appears to be a two-way street on the physical front. On the emotional front? Who knows …

He walks me back toward his desk until my ass bumps the edge of it. "Play my dirty secretary and suck me off."

He doesn't ask it as a question, he never does, the bossy bastard, but he leans down to kiss me roughly in a way that I've come to see as both dominating and pleading and just plain hot.

"Mr. Walker, I couldn't …" I playfully push him away, staring demurely at the floor.

"Rose, you want to keep this job, don't you?"

I gasp, letting my eyes grow wide, glancing up to meet his lust-filled gaze and luxuriating in the way the drag of his eyes over my figure feels like a physical caress. I've become a lot less shy about our dirty talk in the past week, though this is the first time he's wanted to act something out. Instead of being scandalized by it, I find myself intrigued. Maybe even a little turned on.

He raises a solitary brow as he steps away from me and strides around the desk. I turn to watch. He's only wearing a deep blue polo and jeans, but he has an air of authority and confidence that would make him the perfect boss. I'm more than a little turned on.

If I was his secretary, I really would fuck him. Daily. I'd probably have to reprint every report I ever walked inside to hand to him because they'd get dropped and scattered, bent and folded, crumpled in my clutching fingers as he railed me against this desk that's now annoyingly between us.

I like this boss fantasy far more than I thought I would.

He pulls out his chair and sits down in it, legs spread wide so that I can see his hardness outlined through his pants. I lick my lips, breath catching in my chest.

"If you want to keep your job, prove it."

My acting skills falter as I make my way over to him. I forget
to be a shy, reticent secretary and just think about the fact
that I'm going to get to take Angelo's cock in my mouth. I
never used to like blowjobs; they used to be a necessary evil
to get a guy off so he'd leave me alone. But now, they're a
precursor to everything I've ever dreamed about. I take the
edge off for Angelo and then he eats me out for half an hour
until he's hard and ready to fuck.

One blowjob for him equals three or four orgasms for me.
Plus whatever I get during sex. It's a win-win-win again
proposition that's made me absolutely love taking him
between my lips.

I kneel down on the cheap carpet and edge forward on my
knees as I reach for his zipper. He lifts his hips and I slide
down his pants and boxers just enough to reveal his hardness. The drive over must have really been hard for him
because I can see a tiny drop of precum already there. I lean
forward and drag my tongue over it, savoring his moan.

"Yes. Rose. Fuck." It only takes a few minutes of deep-
throating before Angelo's grabbing my hair and whispering
naughty Spanish words as I drink him down. I sit back on
my heels, trying to swallow some of my smugness and
continue living out his fantasy.

"Was that okay, sir?" I try to weave a tremble into my voice.

"Passing," he murmurs, really getting into his role as a
bastard boss. "You'll have to hope your pussy is more satis-
fying than your mouth." He stands, yanking up his pants.
"Get on the desk—"

"But, sir," I bat my eyes before flashing a look at the door.

His hand is on my wrist. "You're testing my patience."

Why do I find it so fucking hot when he growls angrily? Why is it such a turn-on? I never want anyone to be angry with me, but with him—I step right up, pressing my chest against his, eyes flashing. "You're a monster."

We stare at one another, the air between us as wild and energized as a hurricane. He breaks character first. "God, Rose. Fuck."

He grabs my ass roughly and picks me up, setting me down on his desk. His kiss is hard and eager as he changes his grip, sliding his hands around my body and underneath the hem of my dress. "So perfect," he mutters in between punishing nips at my lower lip. "Fucking hot."

Instead of going straight for my pussy, this time his fingers slip back further. I yelp into his mouth as he traces around my back entrance through the fabric of my panties. But he doesn't stop. He just keeps teasing, circling slowly as his lips and tongue maul my mouth, until the sensation moves from alarming to delightful, until I'm begging him for more.

"Angelo. Angelo," I murmur.

"Say you're mine," he growls against my lips.

"I'm yours," I whimper.

His hand slides up my slit to pinch my swollen clit through the silk. He tugs at it quickly.

I writhe against him, small whimpers of "Yes, yes, yes," spilling from my lips.

His grin is merciless as he sends me over the edge with these words, "That's right. I own you. I'm going to conquer all of you, Rose. Tonight, your body. Tomorrow, your soul. I'm taking it all."

He always says just the right things. He's got the perfect phrases down pat. But as he puts on a condom and pulls my panties aside, I worry that they're only words.

ANGELO

A lot of families have family dinners. But my mother has always been more of a breakfast person, so Sunday brunch is her thing. She always cooks up a lavish feast and insists we talk about our lives, even when one week is just the same as the last. Of course, this past week—this past two weeks—hasn't been exactly the same for me. And she knows why. That doesn't stop her from harassing me about Rose.

This morning, I'm the first one to sit down at the round table in my parents' eat-in kitchen. My mom bustles over, wearing a broom skirt and a patterned blouse, shushing her parakeet as it squawks at its mirror from its cage in the corner. Her new tennis bracelet glitters on her wrist as she places a plate with a huge steaming burrito leaking red chili from its folds in front of me before wrapping me in a tight hug. It smells like heaven rolled into a tortilla.

Of course, she offsets the delicious food with a nagging little question after she kisses my cheek. "Mijo, when do I get to meet this girl of yours?"

"You've already met her." I try this tactic again, even though it didn't work last week.

"Not since you've been dating," my mother clicks her tongue. "Are you ashamed of us?" She goes right for the guilt barb.

I roll my eyes even as I drag her plump form in for a hug to thank her for the food. "Mom, I've already told you she's shy—"

"He's also too chickenshit to fight her brother over it." Tatiana wanders in, her hair still a giant fuzzball from sleep, a fuzzy blue robe tied over her pajamas, her big cheekbones stretching in a yawn. She takes after Dad more than I do, in her coloring at least. She could pass for white instead of mixed with those freckles and her brown hair.

"Fuck off," I tell Tati, ignoring my mother's smack across the back of my head.

"Language!" Mom scolds, as if that ever does any good. I simply glare and my sister and she reflects the same stubborn contempt right back.

"She's not ready for that." I turn back to my burrito, annoyed that I have to defend myself.

"What is she ready for? When will she be ready for that?"

"Hush, Tati. He's romancing her right now." Mom suddenly switches sides, jumping to my defense even as she moves to the coffee pot and starts pouring out cups for all of us.

Tatiana snorts derisively and her hands fly to her hips. "Romancing? Really? Are you buying her flowers and writing her poetry?"

I curl my lip in disgust at the idea of any of that sappy, sobby shit. That isn't the kind of connection Rose and I have. The fire between is more likely to result in angry banter and curse words which lead to biting kisses. I love that she's so utterly soft and fragile, except when it comes to me. With me, she's a tigress.

"Yeah, thought as much." Tati shakes her head as she grabs her coffee mug from Mom and adds a gallon of milk to it. "You're not doing a damn romantic thing at all. You're going to mess this up because she's going to feel like your dirty little secret."

My burrito drops to my plate and the burning sensation at the back of my throat is no longer from the heat of the chile. I glance between my sister and mother, who are both staring down at me with harsh, judgmental eyes. Fuck. Could they be right?

Does Rose want romance?

I FEEL LIKE A PRICK, like an idiot. My neck is too damn hot as I stride through the mall. I keep my back ramrod straight and my eyes up, faking a confidence I don't feel as I search for Rose through the congestion of people.

Teens wearing all-black clothing stride around. Some of them scan the crowd, looking to connect, while others have their noses buried in their phones. Harried parents drag their kids by, arms loaded down with bags of clothing. A few older couples stroll leisurely, not out to buy anything, just out for a walk in the February cold.

Rose said she was meeting her friends here for lunch and shopping. But where are they?

A family bustles past with a jumping toddler and I have to lift the single red rose in my hand up high, out of reach of the sticky-fingered little terror.

This was a terrible idea.

I should have waited to see her later. I should have met up with her after she was done. But the thing is, I see her and my rational side just clicks off. Some baser instinct takes over, my brain stem dominates, and the need to claim her overrides anything else.

I need the crowd.

I need to be in public so that I won't be tempted to strip her bare and have her ride my cock until she's falling apart. The crowd is essential because the very idea of someone else getting to see her body makes rage stab down my spine like a row of spikes. It makes me want to throw something through the nearest display window. She's mine and mine alone.

I make my way to the food court with its bizarre combination of smells: pizza and Chinese mingling with Greek food.

Rose is immediately visible the second I step into the space between two tables. I pick her out instantly, even though she's in the middle of the line for pretzels and four other people stand between us. Her dark curls and signature ruby-red lips instantly draw my eyes.

I stalk closer. She doesn't have the same innate radar, apparently, because she stands beside her friend Violet, chatting and unaware of me while I approach.

Rose is wearing skintight jeans that hug her ass in a way I love but hate that everyone else can see. And her pink sweater is tighter than should be allowed. Fuck. The downside of seeing her in public is the fact that I can tell the bastards sitting two tables to my left are staring at her, and knowing that kind of makes me want to yank out my pocket knife and shove it in their jugulars.

I'm unreasonable.

Insane.

Some might say I'm unhealthily obsessed, but to me, it feels like just the right amount of devotion. It doesn't feel unreasonable to think that I should lock Rose up and fuck her five hours a day and let her stay home writing her historical books the rest of the time.

That would be perfect.

But it's only a possibility if I can get her to accept me.

If I can convince her this shit between us is real.

And apparently, that means flowers and crap.

I walk closer and unintentionally overhear part of their conversation.

"All I'm saying is I think Lily's having a really hard time," Violet spins some of her stick-straight blonde hair around her finger. "She even slept at my house last night. I swear, every little noise is making her jump right now."

Rose chews her lip thoughtfully, but the very motion makes me want to reach out and peel her teeth away from that precious lip so I can suck on it. "Has anything actually happened? You know, since he's gotten out?"

Violet sighs and shakes her head. "No. It's all paranoia right now. Which, don't get me wrong, I get it. Having a stalker would be really scary, but—"

"Maybe it depends on the stalker," I cut in, deciding that's my cue. They were about to dive into some heavy territory and it didn't feel right to listen in.

Both girls turn and look surprised to see me, Violet in a shocked way but Rose … her face glows with a warmth that lights me up.

"Hey." Her tone is soft and shy, far too reminiscent of the people-pleasing Rose that other people get to see.

That's not going to work for me. My girlfriend is going to give me a far more enthusiastic greeting than that.

I take a step forward, wrapping my arm around her shoulders and curling her into me. Then I lean down and place a chaste but very firm kiss on her lips so that she—and everyone else in this fucking place—knows who she belongs to. When I release her from the kiss, I smile down at her, loving the quick rise and fall of her breasts as she pants. "What's your opinion on stalkers?" I ask.

Those green eyes of hers immediately flash fire in my direction. "My experience has varied. Some days he's annoying. Others—he's irresistible." There's her fire. My little Rosie is showing her thorns and I love them.

"Hope today's an irresistible day then," I say, holding out the flower.

Rose freezes as she stares down at it.

I'm vaguely aware of Violet muttering something and excusing herself. But whatever she actually says fades into the chatter around us because suddenly, my heart is thumping hard and quick, and my pulse feels as loud as a compressor in my ears.

Why doesn't she look happy? Why's the blood draining from her face?

"You don't date," she whispers, still staring. "This morning, at breakfast, Quique was saying—"

"I love your brother but he's an idiot. Don't listen to anything he says." He's lucky he's not here right now, or so help me, I'd clock him in the jaw without a second thought or an ounce of regret.

Why the fuck is this going so badly?

God. Did I already mess this up?

I drop my hand from Rose's shoulder to grab her arm and lift it. I physically wrap her palm around the flower and force it into her hand.

Tears fill her eyes and her voice cracks. "But you're not a flower guy."

"That's right. Now take the damn flower." I close her fingers around the stem and lean down to whisper in her ear, "I'm not a flower guy. But if you're a flower girl, then I am. I'm not a poet. But if that's what you want, then I'll fucking write a sonnet. I'm not into candlelit dinners but I'll fill a whole damn room with candles, Rose. For you—I'll do those things."

Her lips press together in a hard line and her eyes brim with unshed tears. My entire body vibrates with adrenaline, sweat pouring down my spine as I stare down and fucking wish that she was inside my head. That she could see what I see and feel how I feel. Then she'd understand that I'm all in. Then she'd have to believe me.

Rose reaches out with her free hand (the one not clutching my flower) and wraps her fingers around my wrist. I almost shout in relief. But when she turns and tugs me out of the pretzel line, confusion furrows my brow. When she starts to run, pulling me along as she zigs and zags through the crowd and I have to quicken my steps to keep up with her, I start to wonder what she's thinking.

She darts into the nearest department store, past a perfume counter that has me scraping the dense scent off my tongue with my teeth, and weaves through the racks of women's clothing so quickly that some of the items smack my arms as I try to keep up. I open my mouth to ask what she's doing when she abruptly drops my wrist and grabs a hideous left-over ugly Christmas sweater—one of those printed with a man's beer gut and Christmas lights strung over his chest.

She then looks back and jerks her head for me to follow her as she turns right.

That's when I spot the changing rooms. And my confusion morphs into anticipation when she casts one more sultry glance over her shoulder.

Oh, fuck yes.

The rooms are unattended, thank God, and I follow her adorable ass down the hall to the largest one at the end. She slides inside and I'm there a second later, banging the door closed behind me and sliding the measly little bolt shut.

The Christmas sweater falls to the ground as Rose leaps onto me, her arms wrapping around my neck, legs encircling my waist. I ignore the fact that she nearly knocks the breath from my lungs as I slide my hands underneath her ass to keep her from falling. Her eagerness has me twice as excited as usual. Apparently, this romance crap pays dividends. Well, then, I can officially say I'm a fan. I walk her to the wall, pressing her back up against it as I kiss her. Claim her.

A random thorn from the flower clutched in my girl's hand pokes into the back of my neck, scratching my skin. I don't bother telling her about that minor irritation. I'm too busy with all the other sensations she's giving me. With the feel of her supple body against mine, the frantic bite of her kisses, the softness of her skin as I peel that pink sweater up and over her head.

I toss it on top of the ugly sweater, before ridding Rose of the flimsy bra she's wearing today. Her skin is so silky smooth beneath my touch. Freeing those gorgeous tits from their lace prison, I lean down to suck one of her nipples into my mouth. God, I love every inch of her body.

But she has to know, it's not just her body. I let her nipple slide out of my mouth and straighten back up. "Just to be clear, you know this means something big to me. That it's not just sex?"

"Just to be clear, you know I'm expecting a sonnet, now, right?" she chirps back before assaulting my lower lip with her teeth. Little minx.

Keeping one hand on her ass, I reach up and play with her breasts as she bruises my lips in a way I will definitely not regret tomorrow.

I let her wind herself up until her hips are rolling against me in an effort to find some relief. That's when I gently lower her to the ground and take a step back.

I love the outraged look on her face, as if I'm depriving her of her just dues. Smirking, I sit down on the corner bench and command, "Get naked. And then get up here and sit on your throne, lil reina."

When I point to my lips, her eyes flash wide for a moment, scandalized, before something heavier enters her gaze. Then she eagerly bends down and strips off those skintight jeans. God, I could watch her body every damn day and never get tired of it. She's the manifestation of every wet dream I've ever had.

I love that she doesn't let go of her rose, even when she's naked. She has a death grip on that stem as if it's precious. She's precious.

She scrambles onto my lap, bracing her feet on the edges of the bench I'm sitting on before she slides up my body and leans into the corner above me, bracing her hands on either wall. I give myself a moment to inhale the naughty scent of her arousal, to glance over at the dressing room mirror and see her ass poised and waiting, back arched.

The sight is so hot that I reach down and stroke my dick through my pants.

So is the sight of her smooth slit, lips pouting and ready for me. I keep touching myself as I lean forward and lick slowly over her opening, priming and teasing her. I alternate soft swipes of my tongue with warm bellows of breath against her until she's whimpering, begging me, using that phrase I can't get enough of. "I'm yours." Damn straight—she's all mine.

I keep a slow and steady pace even when one of her hands lowers to the back of my head, trying to force me deeper. When her hips begin to cant upward temptingly, I let my tongue snap out against her clit, tapping it until she's moaning, her fingernails loudly scratching down the side of the dressing room. All my thoughts go up in smoke as my goddess finds her release on my mouth and I kiss her clit as she smashes my head back into the corner. I keep on kissing until she's shuddering and pulling away.

A little rush of pride fills me as I carefully lower her to the ground, well aware that her limbs can't hold her up right now and of the fact that I was able to melt her mind. She gives me a lust-drunk grin that I can't help but return because that look on her face squeezes my heart in a grip tighter than I've ever known before.

After she regains her balance, I move to shuck my pants and boxers.

And that's when we hear someone enter the dressing room.

I pause with a condom packet from my pocket in hand as Rose's entire body stiffens like a startled deer.

Fuck that bitch who just walked in here, I think bitterly, eyes falling to where my girl's tempting pussy is shining so pretty and pink, primed and ready for me.

When Rose turns toward me and grabs the condom packet from my hand, I take it as my signal that playtime's over. But when she uses her teeth to rip it open, and kneels in front of me to roll it down slowly and silently with her mouth—fuck, it takes everything I have not to bust my nut right then and there.

My girl is being naughty.

Her eyes are sparkling with mischief as she slowly stands and moves to straddle me. When she sinks down onto my shaft, the tight, hot squeeze of her makes my breath catch. But we can't be loud.

Fuck. We've done it with people nearby before. But never at this level. Right now the chance of getting caught is very, very real. Somehow, that makes my blood rush faster, adrenaline weaving together with lust.

The sounds of a woman changing in a stall nearby, the thud of her shoes hitting the floor as she kicks them off, travel clearly through the fitting rooms.

Rose and I share a long, desperate look. So close. We're so close. Can we get away with it?

We're about to find out.

Since we can't be loud, we'll have to be slow. Deliberate. My hands glide up and down Rose's sides, memorizing the shape of her, cupping her breasts, gently squeezing as I make my dick flex slightly inside of her, tapping that special little spot up front.

Her look of astonishment and accompanying little gasp are worth it, especially when I get to give her a scolding look and put a finger to my lips.

That pisses my girl off and she grinds against me in retaliation. The urge to clamp my fingers down on her hips and fuck up into her is so strong that I have to drop my hands from her breasts and squeeze the bench I'm sitting on so that I don't give in.

The next ten minutes become a solid test of our patience and will as each of us constantly tests the other's mettle, daring them to be the first to give us away—all while some innocent woman hums and tries on sweaters nearby.

I lap at Rose's nipples until she gasps. She gets back at me by leaning to one side so she can gently cup my balls, rubbing the center just the way she knows I like. The stripes of pleasure she creates make me thrust up a few times, until I come to my senses and realize the wet sound of sex is going to be overheard.

So I yank her hand away only to reach up and grab onto her hair, wrapping some of those dark curls around my wrist and tugging. I double the ante by leaning forward to suck on her sensitive neck, a move that leaves her moaning and then swatting at me.

When she starts to ride me slow and steady, I swear the sight of my dick sliding in and out of her nearly does it.

God, how long does it take to fucking try on some clothes? Go away, already, bitch! I want to fuck my woman.

Rose and I start to sloppily make out, both of us impatient, the tease having gone on long enough.

The sound of a fitting room door smashing carelessly open, and the retreating hum of the unknown shopper is like the green flag at the start of a race.

Thank fuck!

As soon as the footsteps have faded, I grab Rose's ass and turn, shoving her against the wall and pound into her until my balls are boiling, my spine is quivering, and pleasure shoots through us both. I feel her clench down on me a second before a star explodes behind my eyes as I come deep inside my girl.

My one.

My only.

The girl who's accepted the softer side of me, one I've never offered up to anyone before. But the question remains, can she handle the darker side as well?

ROSE

*a*nother week of near bliss passes—well, near bliss if you don't count my mother's rampages about the volunteer shifts I've been late for. I didn't even miss them, I just arrived a little bit later than expected after Angelo and I … took a little longer than expected.

But, for the first time in my life, her anger doesn't cow me. I'm not scraping my eyes across the floor each time her nostrils flare in disapproval.

Quique teases me about it one afternoon while we stuff envelopes asking for campaign contributions in a poorly lit basement room that's giving off serial killer lair vibes. "Looks like Rosie finally found her big girl finger." And then he raises his middle finger. Of course he does, because my brother doesn't take anything seriously. "Fuck off, Mom!" he mouths. "I was wondering when those rebellious years would hit. Welcome to puberty."

I throw a flurry of pre-stamped envelopes at him but he just guffaws, thinking he's the cleverest man alive.

We'll see if he's still laughing when Angelo and I go public. We've talked about telling my family but he really wants to keep our perfect little honeymoon bubble a little bit longer. I can't say I blame him.

A long time ago, Quique made a public declaration to his friends that I was off-limits. I'm not certain he remembers, but I do. I'd been fifteen, and desperately nervous—so much so that I probably constantly reeked of sweat when his friends were over—which was always, because my brother was a king in high school. He has the kind of honeyed personality that draws everyone in with his sweetness. And then his humor makes him sticky. He's actually a great guy. I glance over at him, stuffing envelopes, wondering why he's here. Why his job consists of night shifts at a warehouse instead of something more substantial. He notices.

"What?" Quique asks.

"What do you want to do?" I ask.

His brows shoot up because we never ever talk about real things.

He grabs a pamphlet and slides it smoothly into an envelope as he considers his answer. "You sound like Mom."

"I'm sorry." Immediately, I apologize and drop my eyes because that is probably one of the worst insults Quique and I could lob at each other. The only one worse would be if he compared me to Dad. I take a careful breath as I focus on my envelopes, trying not to let my hands shake or my thoughts spiral down at that comparison. While my mom has good qualities Quique is most definitely referring to her snobbery which has gotten far worse with this campaign.

Quique sighs. "I didn't mean that. Sorry. She's always asking and I get defensive. You know? I care less about what I do and more about who I get to be all day. An office? Stuffy-ass quiet computer shit? That sounds like hell. At the warehouse, the guys and I joke and cut-up all night long. It's fun. I don't love it but I don't dread it. You know?"

I stare at my brother with a little bit of awe as I press my lips together. What he says makes so much sense. So, so much sense.

"What do you want to do?" He throws my question back at me and immediately, my stomach curdles like cottage cheese and his defensive answer makes sense.

I glance around, neck prickling, ensuring Mom is not in the room before I turn back to him. I open my mouth to say it aloud, but unlike with Angelo, where my deepest secrets just seem to unwrap themselves and lay me bare at his feet, the words don't come spilling out. Instead, I find myself saying, "Well, I don't want to be a doctor."

Quique's eyes flash with some sort of emotion—I'm not sure whether his expression is full of pride or surprise. But he nods after a second as if it makes sense. He -seals another envelope before he says, "You know her love is supposed to be unconditional, right?"

I snort. "Yeah, if only that were true." I mean for the words to come out lighter than they do, but the bitterness about always being rigidly perfect—always jumping through her hoops, even when it feels like I'm in the middle of a circus and the hoop is on fire—seeps through.

His gaze cuts right through me as he tilts his head, like he's noticing the real me, the person underneath Mom's required happy facade for the first time. "Well, mine is. You do you, Rosie Dosie."

There, in one of the creepiest rooms I could ever dream up, surrounded by some of the most boring work I can imagine doing, my brother gives me a gift I didn't know I needed. As soon as he says those words, my chest clenches and releases —as if I've been holding my breath for years and can only now let it out. I swallow hard and turn back to my envelopes, slightly overwhelmed.

Does he really mean that?

In the context of work and careers, sure ...

But what about if I tell him that I'm falling for his best friend? What if I tell him that we've been dating behind his back? What about if I tell him it's already so serious that if Angelo breaks up with me ... I'm not sure I'll recover?

People like to throw around the term unconditional love a lot—but they very rarely mean it.

I'm not even sure unconditional love is possible.

There's always going to be some sort of line, isn't there? Cheating. Drinking.

Something.

Of course, we don't always know what our lines are until someone crosses them. Mom didn't know that substance abuse was a hard limit until Dad was out of control ...

I wonder what my hard limits are?

I hope I'll never have to find out.

ANGELO and I cocoon ourselves in bliss a little bit longer.

Mom ends up getting a big, shiny new donation from some company no one's ever heard of the week after I stuff envelopes. After that cash injection, she's too busy planning commercials to worry about her wayward daughter.

So I get to slink off and enjoy my personal slice of heaven.

Especially when Angelo makes an appearance to play video games with Quique one night after work—because my brother has been bemoaning the fact that Angelo has all but disappeared.

It almost becomes a game for Angelo and me to appear disinterested in one another when Quique is looking and shoot salacious looks across the room when he's not. I've gotten particularly fond of trailing my fingers over my body and cupping my breasts through my shirt whenever Quique is facing Angelo. My boyfriend gets this twisted look of near pain when he has to restrain himself. And then I know I'll be in for a good, hard fuck against the wall after—him whispering in my ear what a naughty girl I am.

I've discovered that I like being naughty. I've been 'good-girl Rose' for so many years—but naughty me is so much more fun. I'm more relaxed. I smile more. Joke more. Even Daisy has commented on it.

"I think he's good for you."

And … I haven't told anyone this, but that gnawing urge to release tension, to draw a little red line on my skin to let the pain escape, has receded. It's not gone completely, but the tension that used to feel like it was boiling underneath my skin has lessened.

Life is more perfect than it's ever been. Even if my Math T.A. is the worst teacher on the planet. When he finishes his unintelligible lecture about factors and the bell rings, I sigh in relief.

"I think he's getting even more boring," I tell Lily as I pack away my books. On either side of us, Violet and Daisy do the same. This is the one class all four of us have together. Of course, it has to end up being the only one on the planet that could compare with watching golf on television.

Lily didn't even take notes, so she's already packed up. She waits for the three of us who want to actually pass the class by scrolling through her phone. "Not possible. Hey, did you see the signs around campus for a modeling gig?" She holds up someone's online picture about it.

"Ugh, don't trust those, they're a scam," Violet groans as she slings her backpack onto her back and then pulls her blonde hair out from behind it. Her blue eyes take on a lecturing, motherly look as she explains, "They just want to get you to pay for modeling classes and then headshots. Melinda did it. Don't waste your money."

Lil pushes her lips together like she wants to argue, but she doesn't.

We spill out of the building and soak up the bright morning sunshine. Today it's warmer than usual and part of me wishes I could strip off my coat and let the sun just dance along my skin as I walk, but there's no time for that. I have a laundry list of things to do before Lily comes over tonight.

She's been switching between sleeping in one of our guest rooms or over at Violet's—not wanting to be alone. She tried Daisy's house one night but said the sex noises over there were just too much for her to take.

Cringe.

I haven't admitted to her that Angelo sneaks over nearly every night—but in my defense, at least we know how to be quiet about it.

I don't know how long Lily's going to keep this nomad routine up. I know she's scared about Montoya getting out. But no one has seen hide nor hair of him since. Part of me wonders if Lily just does things for attention sometimes. I feel cruel even thinking that, but it has crossed my mind.

Lily's sweet. But she's also kind of thoughtless, completely unaware of how she affects other people

It kind of reminds me of our disastrous attempt at sharing a dorm room last semester. We'd tried, but she's so much of a slob—clothes literally littering every available surface—that I ultimately had to back away, even if that meant living with Mom and Quique again. She moved into an apartment after that. But now, maybe she's just finding out living alone doesn't suit her.

Or … maybe she needs to talk to someone. Maybe can't file away her trauma and lock it in a steel box with reinforced sides like I do. Glancing over, I note dark circles under her eyes before she slides down the sunglasses that were planted in her hair. I part my lips to ask how she's doing but then I hear my name.

"Rose!" Angelo's voice booms across the courtyard. I glance around but don't see him.

Daisy taps my shoulder and points to our left, where he's standing on a grassy knoll underneath some pine trees. "Boyfriend's calling you." Her gray eyes shine with mischievous delight at getting to use that term.

I just roll my eyes and jab back at her. "Don't you need to be texting Daddy?"

Her cheeks color but my ability to shock her with teasing has faded over the month or so she and Gunnar have been together. "Actually, I do. Otherwise I'll get spanked." She winks when my jaw drops.

Dammit. She's clearly won this round.

Waving goodbye to her and the other girls, who walked on ahead of us and are already in deep conversation about Vi's failed date last night, I leave them behind. I figure I'll talk to Lily later.

Striding over to Angelo, a wide smile stretches across my face. "Hey, stranger. What are you doing here?"

He pulls me into a hug immediately, wrapping his burly arms around my back. I sink into his warmth gratefully, nestling against his broad chest, realizing with a little bit of shock, just how comfortable I am with his public displays of affection—especially considering how I've been with past boyfriends. It always felt awkward. But with him, everything just feels right.

He clears his throat before he broaches a topic that's clearly brought him all the way out here to the campus. "I made us an appointment."

"Appointment?" My brow furrows and immediately, the alarm bells go off. "Doctor's appointment?" Does he have STDs? Oh, God. Has he been sleeping with someone else? We've seen each other almost daily—so I just don't know where he'd find the time but …

"No. No."

Relief nearly makes me sag into him as all the worry drips right out of my system. When I see he's serious and actually somewhat disturbed by the idea of going to a doctor, I'm finally able to joke about it. "You sure you're not pregnant?" I tease.

He chuckles and pinches the side of my stomach in a spot he knows is highly ticklish. I squeal and grasp him tighter.

"Brat," he murmurs in my ear as he leads me off on a sidewalk to our right, acting as if he knows exactly where he's going. Of course he does.

When we stop walking in front of a familiar two-story, stucco building, I freeze and glance over at him.

"What is this?" I ask, with the smallest hint of trepidation, releasing the hold I'd had on his waist and grabbing onto my backpack straps as if they can support me. I try not to let my mouth gape open in shock but this is literally the last place I expected him to take me.

"I made you an appointment with the Chair of the History Department," he responds calmly.

I glance between him and the building and back again. Disbelief and shock hold my feet in place as certainly as a glue trap. I feel a little like a creature caught in one, too—my heart races with anxiety … but also, maybe, possibly, with the tiniest hint of excitement.

Do I want to do this?

Do I want to go up there and hear what a stupid idea I've got, what a terrible life plan it is to want to become a writer?

Or worse … do I want to be given hope?

What if the Chair is sweet and grandfatherly? What if he's supportive? What if he tells me he knows someone I can talk to who's walked that same path?

I sway a tiny bit on my feet.

If I go up those steps and into that meeting, it will stop being just a dream.

If it's not just a dream but a possible future, with a path and steps all laid out—just like the one my mother's built for me … what will I do?

Angelo moves to watch me and positions himself in front of me, waiting patiently as I stand as still and silent as the grave. Inside, I'm anything but.

His hands come to cup my cheeks, as if he can hear the voice inside my head. "It's your life, Rose. Your life. And to be honest, I don't give a damn if you want to go to clown school and terrorize children for the rest of your life—I just want you to come home happy. To me."

Then his hands drop and he holds one out, palm up, offering to hold my hand.

Reacting unthinkingly, I take it.

And suddenly, I have the strength to take a step.

"YOU WANT TO EXPLAIN THIS?" Mom bursts into my room, the completed paperwork for my major clutched in her hand.

I turn off the classical violin music I was listening to while I outlined a paper for my English class and pull the earbuds from my ears. Night has fallen and my room glows bright and cheery, the windows reflecting everything inside—including her furious face.

I turn in my desk chair to see her in a navy skirt suit, hair done for a commercial or a meeting—I haven't kept up with her schedule in weeks. Slowly, somehow, her life and mine have become less entwined.

I gnash my teeth together as I stare down at the paper she holds. In a passive-aggressive move that my churning stomach now regrets, I'd pinned it to the fridge with a magnet, just like I used to do whenever I got an A on a test.

Only, this time, the paper heading read: Major: History/Creative Writing.

Maybe I shouldn't have done it this way. Perhaps I should have sat her down and had an adult conversation, but I'm just finding my courage—and it still fails me sometimes. And, in my defense, I don't think she sees me as an adult.

Mom's eyes are hard, her jaw is clenched, and she's brimming with fury. "You're throwing your life away!" she shouts.

I have to force myself to take a deep breath and relax the fingers twitching on my lap. *I will not look at the floor. Keep eye contact.* Two more calming breaths have to go through my system before I'm able to find my voice. "No. I'm choosing it. I'm just not choosing what you want me to."

"Madre de Dios! This! This! History?! *Writing*?! What are you gonna do with that? Huh? How are you going to eat?"

I take a slow deep breath and look away from her face, which looks like it's about to catch fire. Instead, I train my gaze across the room at the photo of Enrique, Angelo, and me.

"I'm going to be fine." I stand, forcing myself to stare right at her. I'm surprised by the fact that my hands don't tremble, given how my heart is racing right now. But they are steady, as if they truly believe what I just said. And I realize, with a start, that I do. I honestly think that I'll be okay.

Because I have him.

But also because he's changed me.

I don't really know how or why, only that I'm not the wilting little Rose I was before. I stiffen my spine and take a deep breath. "I'm going to write historical fiction. I'm not going to be a doctor."

For a few brief, insane seconds her jaw drops and I think I might have gotten through to her. But then she ruins it. "What has gotten into you? Are you taking drugs?"

"No, Mom." I want to add "I'm high on life," but I don't think she'll appreciate sarcasm at this moment and my bravery is still a very tenuous thing. My inner child is still urging me to scramble underneath the bed where she can't reach me.

She makes some wild hand gestures that look like she's trying to strangle the very air in front of her before ripping the paper in half.

"No. I won't allow it."

Those words cut right through the last of the threads binding me to her. My anxiety floats away while anger that's as hard and heavy as a stone, drops in my gut and settles my stomach.

"You don't get to allow me things any more."

She takes a step closer, a vein in her forehead throbbing in a way that looks painful. "I won't pay for it."

She doesn't care what I want. Doesn't care about my dreams. Won't support me even though I've supported her through all of this stupid campaign bullshit—running around to every tiny town in the state, dinner after dinner, meeting after meeting … I know what it's like to be Tolstoy's wife. She once compared herself to furniture—something useful to him, nothing more.

I'm just an object to her.

I turn back to my desk slowly, not used to anger as hot as lava coursing through my veins. Unused to the light-headedness of pure rage. With deliberate movements, I pull open my desk drawer and take out a small black memory box. I open it—ignoring my mother's words behind me.

She's shouting, but she might as well be a dirt devil raging outside, while I'm tucked away behind the walls of my anger.

I turn back to her and hand her the flash drive—the one I kept meaning to destroy but didn't. Because it was my first glimpse of who she truly is.

"This is for you," I say, walking up to her and pressing it into her hand.

She tries to grab at me, as though she can shake some sense into me, but I dodge around her and head for my door, scooping up my purse and keys on the way.

"ROSALINDA!" she shouts at the top of her lungs.

I turn back and give her a tiny smile, before adding one more log to the fire. "By the way, I'm also dating Angelo Walker."

ANGELO

Quique and I stand almost shoulder to shoulder in my tiny-ass apartment. The shouts of neighbors down the hall and the sound of evening traffic seep under my front door, though I tune them out automatically. Behind us, two beers sit on my Formica countertop, which is backlit by 1980s kitchen box lights. My friend leans against the edge of the counter, arms crossed and eyes narrowed as he gives me a faux glare.

"Do your worst," he challenges.

"Oh, I will. Have your Kleenex ready because you're going to be crying like a baby," I quip, lining up my feet and squaring off against the dartboard hung on the far side of my living room, which is at most, twelve feet away.

I'll never get back my deposit on this place because the cream wall behind the board is riddled with missed shots, but I don't give a fuck. This one-bedroom hole-in-the-wall has only ever been a waypoint while I decided on my next move.

Now, I know what that's going to be.

It's all centered on that pretty girl who's the subject of every other thought I have.

I pinch the dart carefully and exhale. Just as I get ready to lob it, Quique calls out, "Dick cheese!"

I was expecting his outburst though, so I follow through smoothly, and the dart lodges firmly into the board, just missing the target I was aiming for. Crap. "You're so predictable," I tell him, shaking my head scoldingly as he straightens up and gets ready for his own throw, grabbing his blue-tipped dart from the counter.

"I'm not predictable. I'm a damn enigma," he jokes, turning to face me and lobbing his dart over his shoulder. "Betcha you weren't expecting that, huh?" His throw goes wide of the board and lodges in the wall.

"Great aim, Enigma," I troll.

"You know, the board's overrated anyway."

I chuckle and grab my beer as his phone buzzes in his pocket and he snatches it up. Taking a sip, I don't notice he's frozen until afterward. That's when I realize my best friend's face has hardened, his cheeks are paler than normal, eyes glued to his phone.

"Everything okay?" I ask, my gut immediately knotting, wondering if something's happened to his family. To Rose. Disasters flick through my mind, one after the next—car crash, fire, shooting—

"You bastard!"

Before I can blink, Quique's fist smashes into my cheek, and beer splatters from my mouth. Pain smears across my face in one fell swoop, my entire jaw screaming. The bottle drops from my hand and spills foaming suds everywhere as it rolls across the counter and clatters to the floor.

"My sister!"

I swivel my face back to look at him and realize I've never seen my best friend's eyes this wide, his teeth clamped together so hard they look like they might crack.

Shit.

Fuck.

"You fucking touched Rose!" He's livid. That's why, even though I see the second punch coming, I don't back away. I'm no stranger to pain. And he deserves this. It's no less than I'd do for Tatiana.

The second blow glances across my nose, leaving a new throbbing ache there and ensuring I'll need to ice my face. Even my gums pulse, the pain spreading down into them and taking root. But still, I just straighten and look at him. Letting him get it out.

"That was for keeping it from me. And this—" He rears back, a right hook getting ready to swing through the air.

I don't step back, don't lift my hands to defend myself. But I do say, "She's the one."

I don't apologize, because I'll never apologize for anything associated with my Rose, even the fact that I lied to my best friend about it. I've loved every damn second of stalking her and making her mine. And I kept things from him knowingly —with the full understanding that this might be the final outcome. He's my best friend, my brother. But she's my soul.

Quique pauses with his fist in midair before he clenches his jaw and squeezes his eyes shut. I watch him swallow hard, almost as if he's swallowing down his fury, before he drops his hand, shaking it out. "Pinche cabrón. Fucker, I don't know whether I should strangle you right now or … " He trails off, uncertain what to say.

"I'm gonna go with or," I reply wryly as I gingerly touch my jaw and give it an experimental swivel.

That draws an unwilling chuckle from his lips. "I hate you."

"I'm a hate-able guy."

He sighs and walks around me, stepping over the puddle made by my beer and opening the freezer door on my fridge. He grabs a bag of frozen corn and lays it over his hand. "What the fuck is your jaw made of, granite?"

"Same as your hand," I say, reaching for a dish towel and dropping it onto the ground. I swirl it around with my boot to sop up most of the mess. I didn't bother changing after I got home from work today, since Quique had wanted to come over and hang. Following him into the tight space between countertops, I grab my own bag of frozen carrots and thump it onto my face before asking, "Who texted?"

Of course, the moment I ask the question, I've already figured it out. Rose wouldn't have messaged him, not after we decided to wait to tell our families. Someone else must have seen us or figured it out.

When Quique says, "My mom." though, I'm thrown for a loop, because I definitely did not think that self-involved woman had a clue about her daughter's life. Maybe I've been wrong about her. Did she notice the sparks at her fundraiser?

"She hates you, you know, so enjoy that complication." Quique raises his beer as if to toast me before taking a long pull.

I give a shrug that somehow makes my jaw twinge even more. "Is it even a real relationship if your in-laws like you?"

He snorts before what I said really sinks in. "It's that serious?"

I start to nod, but given the fact that my face is currently swelling to twice its normal size and my neck aches, I go with a simple, "Yes." *As long as your sister can accept a side of me that even you don't know about.*

That thought makes my heart sink a little because last night, Dad asked me again where Rose and I stood on that front. I'd told him I was working on it, but I haven't been. In fact, I've been putting it off, trying not to ponder what I'm going to do to convince my sweet, innocent Rose that someone as ruthless and corrupt as me deserves her. Because I don't and I know it. But I'm smart enough to know when I've caught hold of a handful of happiness and selfish enough to keep it. Someone's going to have to pry her out of my cold, dead fingers because that's the only way I'm letting go.

A second later, my phone vibrates and I pick it up. 'Lil Reina' flashes across the screen. I swipe to answer, sliding my frozen bag of carrots to the other side of my jaw, giving it some attention as I realize that Rosie might not be able to ride my face for a day or two. That knowledge is worse than the pain, because then I won't get to hear her wild moans. "Hey."

I move out of the kitchen and into the living room, to give myself and my girl a little privacy, because I'm going to have to break the news to her that one of her friends must have spilled the details about us.

She doesn't give me a chance, though. As soon as I've greeted her, words spill through the phone speaker. "Ohmygod. I think I might have just gotten myself kicked out of my mom's house. And cut out of her will. And I can'tbelieveI-didthis but I gave her the flash drive! *The* flash drive!" Her speech is so frantic and fast that it takes me a few seconds to string her words together into something that makes sense.

"Wait …"

"I told her about my major. And needless to say, it didn't go well. Everything kind of just—exploded. So … I'm kind of going to be couch surfing at Lily's for a bit—"

"No, you're not." Possessive heat comes over me at the fact Rose is even considering going to someone else. She's mine. If she has an issue, she comes to me. I try to keep the blistering fury out of my tone but my words scrape roughly against my vocal cords as I growl, "You're coming here."

"But—"

"There is no but. You're coming here. You're staying with me." I almost say home, but I can't call this shithole that word. It's nothing more than a place to sleep and shower. "I'll send you the address." I belatedly realize I haven't had her here yet. Probably because I semi-hate this cardboard box and the neighbor next door who yells at the news programs twenty-four-seven.

But after I hang up and text her, I glance around and see the space with new eyes—not just dislike but disgust. I have a decent leather couch and TV and my bed's fine, but the rest of this place looks like it was scraped up off the bottom of someone's shoe. It's definitely not good enough for my Rose.

"What's that face?" Quique asks and I realize I've pursed my lips even though it makes my face ache.

"Your mom just kicked Rose out," I reply.

He lets out a wolf-whistle and shakes his head. "About damn time."

I glare in his direction.

"Rose has needed to find her backbone for a long time coming, man. So, if that has anything to do with you, I'm all for it." He holds up his phone and waggles it back and forth. "I'm guessing it does since Mom was the one who texted me about the two of you."

My eyebrows shoot up in surprise. Well, shit. If Rose told Ms. Dalton during their argument, then my sweet girl might really have stood up for herself. I have to swallow a lump of pride that gets lodged in my throat at that prospect.

"She's on the way.""Good. I'll get to punch her too," Quique smirks.

"The fuck you will." Immediately, my hackles rise—instinctively—even though I know that Quique would never in his life hit a girl. Rationality fades in light of my protective instincts and I take a step toward him.

"Joking. Joking." He holds up his hands to pacify me, though it takes a full minute of deep breathing before I can slow my racing heart and calm the hell down. "Geez, you've got it bad."

"You have no idea."

"I want to have *no idea*. There is no way I want to think about Rose getting romantic—ever. I still remember the days when she picked her boogers and ate them!" he shudders.

I cock a brow at him and grimace at the resulting loop of pain that tightens over my cheek. Discomfort doesn't hinder my sarcasm, however. "You still do that."

"Well, they're salty and delicious, and when there's no tortilla chips around …" He gives a casual shrug and a lopsided grin before finishing his beer. "I'm going to head out. It seems like you and Rose have a lot to talk about." He shakes his head slowly as if he does not envy me. But then he adds, "Including how you're going to make it up to me. I prefer gift cards, but I'll also accept apology balloon arrangements so long as they are giant arches that are so obnoxiously colored that they draw the attention of the neighbors."

"Get out of here."

He gives me a nod as he digs out his keys. "Tell her I said I'm glad I'm not the only disappointment to Mom anymore."

"Fuck off." I yank open the front door and glare at him as he saunters outside onto the second-floor landing. As if I'm going to tell Rose anything that might upset her in this volatile state. Of course, Quique doesn't know how fragile his sister really is.

Only I know—because she's mine.

I'm going to take care of her and coddle her and make sure that tonight—the first night she stays with me—is so good that she never wants to leave.

❁

FUCK ME.

When Rose knocks on my door fifteen minutes later, I shove a lighter into my pocket and glance around the room.

I dug out some camping candles and just lit them, setting them on the coffee table. My bed's made, there's bleach sloshed in the toilet, and I have instant chocolate chip cookies baking because I keep an entire tub of that stuff in the fridge at all times for late-night snacks—but that's about as good as it gets. I can't do anything about the speedbag or the dartboard holes that declare this a bachelor pad. It grinds me up that I'm not ushering her into something nicer, a place I'm proud of.

We'll have to build that place together.

I head over to the door, my chest suddenly swarming with bees like I'm a preteen. Ridiculous. Exhaling slowly, I twist the knob and pull it towards me.

Rose rushes in, not even glancing around, just smashing into my chest and wrapping her arms around me, squeezing as if she's trying to leach out my strength. I push the door closed behind her and enfold my girl in a hug slowly, tension easing out of me. No matter what this place is like, she's where she belongs—in my arms.

We spend the next two hours on the sofa, her ranting, me listening and encouraging her—eating cookies and then Chinese food that I get delivered. I let her repeat herself at least ten times, a number Tatiana declares is essential for a ranting woman to "get it all out."

Finally, Rose seems to run out of words. She grows silent and stares at me with those huge Bambi-like eyes of hers, blinking and yawning. I think she's exhausted herself—and tomorrow, she has class and I have work.

"Let's get ready for bed," I say, standing and holding out a hand, leaving the takeout containers scattered across the coffee table.

She leans over and blows out the candles, gathering up the containers and ignoring my order to "Just leave it."

"I prefer not to have cockroaches, thanks," she sasses, tempting me to smack her cute ass when she bends over the table and stacks the cardboard.

I resist, only because I don't think she's ready to get frisky tonight—she's too overwhelmed. After she's gotten everything stuffed into a stack that she balances precariously in one hand, she links her other fingers with mine and we detour to the kitchen trash can so she can get rid of it all.

Then I lead her to my room.

The second we step inside and she sees the bed, she inhales sharply. Her fingers squash mine as she stares at my comforter.

Shit.

I turn and immediately lead her back out to the living room, unsure what just triggered her, other than the bed itself, but certain she needs to be out of that space. "Hey. Hey, we can sleep out here," I try to calm her, pull her back to the present and out of the nightmare that's clearly playing out inside her head.

She's put her free hand on her chest and is counting her breaths, trying to fight the tremble that sinks down her spine despite her best efforts. Finally, she's able to get words out. "It's the blue bedspread."

Fuck.

Anger blotches my thoughts and the corners of my vision but I tamp it down with concern because Rose is sinking onto the couch and rocking herself slowly back and forth.

"I'll throw it out, I'll burn it—" I tell her, unlocking our fingers and moving towards the offending room.

Her words make me stop short.

"I just want to be normal." Tears fill her eyes and she glances away from me, staring at the floor. I can practically feel the shame leaking from her—hot and horrid.

Her pain is mine. Her grief sinks sharp teeth into my chest and bites down. My poor, sweet Rose. Those bastards are dead men.

Carefully, so that I don't startle her, I move back to the couch. I sit down next to her and wrap my arm around her shoulders before slowly dragging her soft form into my lap. I kiss her hair, the crown of her head, her forehead. "Hey. Hey. Hey. We'll get there. We don't have to rush. We have plenty of time. We'll get there."

We have forever.

And I'll be damned certain she gets whatever she needs.

My words set her off and she bawls against my shoulder, her tears warm and wet against my sleeve. I pet her hair and smooth my hand over her back gently until she's cried herself out. I have to breathe slowly and steadily to keep myself calm while she cries because each tear feels like a knife wound to the gut. Guilt rips at me and the gorilla inside wants to rage and rant at the universe for making me figure things out after she was hurt and not before. If I'd realized what she means to me two weeks earlier then I'd have been around to protect her. Two weeks earlier and it never would have happened. She wouldn't have been at that party. Those fuckers would never have laid their hands on her.

As it is, all I can offer her is revenge.

But that thought right there is a turning point for me … because maybe revenge is what she needs. And maybe it's how I can introduce her to the pitch-black side of myself without sending her running for the hills. Maybe … Maybe …

I squeeze her when she sniffs and whispers, "I don't want to be broken."

Cleaved in two. I'm ripped apart by her own impression of herself because she's not fucking broken—she's just hurting —but I have to hold myself together because she needs strength. She needs someone to pull her up and out of this. And I know a way to do it, even if my way might tarnish some of my beautiful girl's pure soul.

"Lil reina, I have an idea and you might hate it. And that's okay. This doesn't have to be your thing. But you know what we can do?" I say softly, carefully. I have to wet my lips after I speak because they're suddenly dry. I'm second-guessing whether or not I should tell her. But time isn't the only healer out there. And I do know that the smooth satisfaction of violence burns like vodka for a second before it warms your belly and makes you giddy in a way that can't be described to someone who's never taken a shot.

"Hmm?" Rose asks, somewhat distracted, still caught up inside her own head.

I'm not certain she's really listening, and this is important. I need to know whether she really wants to consider this or not. Actually, given the conversation with my father, I need her to do more than consider it. So I gently cup her cheeks and smear the tears from them, waiting until her eyes are firmly on me before saying, "We can hurt them back. Just like I did with the first guy. There are two more, Rose. We can hunt them down. Make sure they jump at their own shadows from now on."

Her lips part for a second as she stares up at me, thunderstruck.

The need to explain struggles against my desire to stay silent and let her think. This proposal might seem out of the blue to her. She knows me as the guy who tackled her at a construction site, who parties with her brother. Yeah, she thinks I blackmailed her, or hit a guy at a party, but that's the tip of the iceberg. She doesn't really know this other side of me, the part that's eager to stomp those stupid fucks into the ground.

Her eyes race with a thousand thoughts that I can see in passing—like comets flying by—but I can't get a read on her and what she wants.

I'm going to have to peel the onion back a little, explain more. "Rose, I *need* to hurt them. I need it. What they did to you? Fuck—they deserve it. I know you want to heal and move on, but what if we don't do *just* that? What if we do that *and more?*"

I take a deep breath before adding, "The rumors about my family are true." I wait for a moment as her eyes widen, giving her the opportunity to pull away, blood rushing through my veins at the possibility that she might, my dad's threats to destroy her pinching my throat and making it hard to breathe.

Don't run away, Rose. Don't run from me. I stare at her, jaw clenched, willing her to obey my very thoughts.

She doesn't pull back.

Despite what I've said, her cheeks remain between my palms, those green eyes surrounded by thick black lashes blinking slowly up at me.

"They're true?" she asks, her tone barely above a whisper.

I nod. "Let me show you how sweet revenge can be."

Her head tilts and she stares, but doesn't say anything.

God, what's going through her head?

I have no clue, but the need to convince her, to seduce her with all the darkness I can offer, overtakes me.

I lay it out for her more clearly, just in case she's trying to explain away my confession, wrap it up in a tidy explanation that's clean and neat and excuses me of any wrongdoing. My fingers stroke her silky soft cheeks as I say, "In my world, people cheat and lie and steal. But there is no God in the sky doling out punishments. There's only me. And those fuckers who touched you deserve to be punished."

Her slow blinks are the most agonizing thing in the world as I wait for her decision. She licks her chapped lips once and I hold my breath. But she doesn't speak. She fucking doesn't speak, lighting a torch of panic inside my belly. Did I say too much? I might have left her so shell-shocked that she's not even able to think clearly.

Eager to reignite our connection, worried that my girl is floating away from me, that I overwhelmed her—that I've fucked up—I drop one hand from her cheek and interweave our fingers. I bring her knuckles to my lips one by one and kiss them before staring back up at her and asking, "What do you say, Rose? Be my partner in crime?"

ROSE

What is a bad guy, really? Every story has two sides. So does every war. Every hero's also a villain to someone. But Angelo is on my side. So to me, he's Captain-fucking-America. He's my own personal Ghengis Khan and I'm his Borte.

Equal parts nervously excited to the point of being sick and scared out of my mind, I follow Angelo through a parking lot as the sun sets. He holds open the door to a fifties-style diner and as we step inside, my nose is immediately assaulted by delicious scents: French fries, hamburgers, green chile.

His hand slides to my lower back possessively, in a way that sends a little thrill up my spine, as we wind around red and chrome tables. Chit-chat and music fill the air along with the sizzle of the grill from the open kitchen.

Everyone else is here for a casual evening out, except for us.

We're here to plan revenge.

I might need to scream just to get out the energy dancing through my veins right now.

We slowly make our way to a booth in the back corner where a huge, middle-aged bald man sits. He looks like he belongs on the WWE or some kind of wrestling show—his muscles are massive and intimidating, but they don't appear to be just for show like a bodybuilder's. He looks like he knows how to use them. The man lowers a menu and smiles at us, revealing a gold tooth. "Hey there," he greets us, friendly enough, though there's something about him that's intimidating. If I weren't with my boyfriend, I'd definitely turn and walk in the other direction.

"Mint, meet Rose. Rose, meet Mint." Angelo's introductions are brief as he nudges me to slide into the booth and then sits next to me.

A waitress comes over to take our orders and Angelo orders for me. Somehow, he knows I like strawberry shakes—a fact I'll have to grill him about later because despite the years we've known each other, I seriously doubted he paid that much attention to me. The idea that he did shoots little sparkles right down to my toes.

He doesn't let me order for him, of course, but I knew he'd get onion rings and a chocolate shake with his burger before the words even spilled from his lips.

Mint asks for some homemade green chile stew and tots. Then we reach the awkward silence phase of this dinner.

How do you ask a guy you don't know to conduct illegal surveillance for you?

I have no frickin' clue and so my eyes slide automatically over to the man next to me, who doesn't seem anxious about this evening at all. If anything, he looks energized and excited.

Is excitement catching? Is that why I'm excited? Or am I really just a twisted sort of evil?I am—unbelievably, shockingly—excited to punish those nameless Alpha Tau frat boys who hurt me.

It's been three nights since I've essentially moved in with Angelo, and I haven't been able to sleep on his bed for any of them. I'm over the trembling that overtakes me whenever the sun sets and I stare at his mattress, willing myself to be over this already. Even though he's changed the comforter and bought something floral just for me, I still can't force my limbs to climb into that bed. I'm ready to end the fear, tired of waking up on a fucking couch with a crick in my neck— and I can only imagine how Angelo feels sleeping on the couch with me curled up on top of his chest every night.

Instead of launching right into our proposal, Angelo says, "Hey, Mint. My girl here likes to read."

Immediately, the older man's eyes light up and his entire face softens as he turns toward me, an almost childlike expression of delight on his face. All the intimidation I felt emanating from him dissolves when he asks, "Yeah? What's your favorite?"

Three days later

We're back in the exact same corner booth with Mint, this time, joking and laughing through our meal. After we ate, and Mint and I debated whether or not *Pillars of the Earth* is indeed the best book of all time—spoiler alert: it is—he pulls out a manila envelope from his jacket and slides it onto the table.

I immediately stop reaching for my shake, hand freezing in midair.

When Angelo opens the envelope and pulls out a stack of candid photos of Alpha Taus going and coming from their frat house, an edgy, twitchy feeling hits me as everything solidifies. Reality hits. We're actually doing this.

I search my chest for regret but can't find a single ounce of it. I only sense eagerness and anticipation. With Angelo at my side, my anxiety has lessened, and I feel like an entirely new person, a woman who gives as good as she gets instead of just a coward who turns the other cheek and hopes not to get hit as hard the second time.

Angelo's deep brown eyes sparkle with anticipation as he stares down at me and I give him a tentative smile in return. I feel crazy thinking it, but I love that we're doing this together.

He wraps an arm around me and slides me across the bench seat until I'm tucked up against his side. Then he carefully sets down the stack of photos. "Show us," he commands.

Flipping through the photos causes a physical reaction I don't expect. Heat crawls up my neck until tiny beads of sweat drip down underneath my dark curls. Each flick of my wrist, each new face, causes my stomach to tighten painfully. Will I even remember what they look like? It was dark. I only heard one of their names and only barely remember it— panic took an eraser to entire portions of that evening. Mike or Mick … something like that.

But when I spot the first guy, it feels as if I've been doused in ice water. There's no question. No hesitation. I slide his photo out from the pile and set it in the middle of the table.

Angelo plants a soft kiss in my hair before whispering, "Good job, lil reina. You don't have to keep going. We can figure out the other one another time."

I shake my head, despite the slight tremor in my fingers, because I don't want to stop now. I want to finish this.

I only have to flip three more times before I see the second guy's face. He's paler than the other two. Skinnier. Shiftier looking. I yank his picture out and slide it out. "Him." I'm surprised by the vitriol I manage to fit into that singular word.

Mint picks up the two photos and studies them. Then he slides the pictures into a pocket in his worn blue button-down shirt. "Want me to take care of them?"

"Nah, just collect them," Angelo says as he slides out of the booth and then grabs onto my hand to help me follow him. "We're going to take care of them ourselves. We have a plan."

Two days later

I'm BOUNCING on the tips of my toes tonight. I expected to be nauseous and ready to puke tonight, but apparently, the thought of revenge on those motherfuckers—the idea of stealing their breath from them and sucking the very life from their souls the way they did to me—appeals to me on a visceral level.

Some people would say that's wrong and call me evil.

Fuck them.

I've been pondering this a lot the past few days, staring off during classes or zoning out while I watch TV, and I've come to the following conclusion: Sometimes justice isn't shiny handcuffs and metal bars. Sometimes it's a fist to the face.

Angelo has been annoyingly calm throughout this whole process, not pacing and muttering aloud like me. He went to work this morning, even though I wanted to ditch class and get him to call in sick so we could work out all of my hyper-activity in a horizontal position.

"Alibis are important," he'd told me. "Acting normal. Routine. We can't do anything out of the ordinary."

He's right, of course, though an immature part of me doesn't like it. Part of me wants to pregame before the main event. Fuck me for even calling it that, but it's what it feels like. Tonight is the big showdown and my nails are a wreck from all the chewing I've done. But, I know, deep down, that Angelo's giving me good advice. After years of being under-neath my mother's thumb, I've learned the importance of appearances. The only difference is, this time, the appearance is for my benefit instead of hers.

So I went to class this morning. I smiled at the Wild Flowers. I pretended I had a headache when they asked me questions so that I wouldn't have to answer when I couldn't follow the flow of the conversation. And I've made dinner, though I did burn the meat a bit in my distraction. I'm almost done pretending—and I'm practically salivating for what comes next. Just a teeny, tiny bit longer and we're done. We just have to set up the alibi for the evening.

Our alibi is that I'm organizing some of Angelo's files tonight —something I've been doing this week anyway to help him out and not feel as though I've moved in just to be a burden. I've been cooking too, hence tonight's dinner. We just finished off some semi-edible spaghetti. Standing in the tiny apartment kitchen, I deftly pack the leftovers into plastic containers and slide them into the fridge before heading back out into the living room, stomach coiling into Celtic knots while my fingers try to do the same.

It's time.

I pace as I watch Angelo finish packing a duffel bag with the gear we need and zip it closed—the sound unnaturally loud in my ears. He's dressed all in black, though his clothes would look casual enough to a random observer—he's not wearing a black turtleneck or a catsuit. No one would guess what we're up to.

I'm wearing black yoga pants and a green t-shirt to look even less suspicious, but there's a big, black raincoat slung across the back of the couch that I'll slide on later to hide my figure.

When Angelo turns to look at me, I catch my breath at the intensity of his stare. In the low lamplight, I can almost imagine that we're a war party hundreds of years ago, standing by the fire just before an attack. My nerves dance when he brings a finger to trace the contours of my cheek.

"You sure?" he asks, for the millionth time.

I narrow my eyes and glare at him. "Angelo Walker, if you want to keep that finger, you'd better not ask me that again."

His chuckle is so full and loud that I imagine I can feel its vibrations. "Love those thorns."

Then he lowers his hand expectantly, waiting silently until I slide my palm over his. He squeezes my hand possessively, and our connection at this moment isn't just physical but something far more potent.

He lifts the duffel and I reach around him to grab my coat. And then we're off to commit our first crime together.

How romantic, my brain remarks sarcastically, but my heart is swooning at the fact that this man will do anything for me. Anything.

The ride to the construction site is silent because I don't really know what to say but also because I worry that if I start speaking, I won't be able to stop, words will just flood out of me due to this excess of energy that's built up in my system.

When Angelo parks, he turns toward me, his profile lit by the angular light of the setting sun.

"My dad's here. He's going to vouch for us."

My throat hollows out like the inside of a dry, dead tree and horror fills me for the first time tonight. "Great way to officially meet him as your girlfriend," I squeak.

It's not as if I've never met the Walkers. I've seen them once or twice, his father more than the rest of the family because they often had jobs that coincided with Mom's back when she worked with the mayor. But that was different. I was a kid. A kid sister. Meeting Mr. Walker as his son's girlfriend? That's another matter. "God, what is he going to think of me?"

Angelo gives a soft laugh. "You'd be surprised. He's actually quite impressed by you. Mom hasn't gone out with him on anything like this since they had kids."

That comment gives me something to ponder, a bit more insight into the Walker family. Should I care about the fact that they're criminals? Maybe. But I know Angelo—deep in my bones I know who he is—and he's good. Good for me at least. That's all that matters.

I make that decision and lock in my answer as he slides out of his seat first and comes around the side of the car to open the door for me, a move he's been very insistent on every time he drives me. I haven't argued, because I love the feel of his thick fingers around my waist and the way he slides me down the front of his body each time he sets me down.

Tonight, he doesn't just set me down and let go. Once my feet hit the dirt, he stares, mesmerized. I'm certain the sunset is doing odd things to my features because it's blazing across his, striping him with fierce orange lines and making him look bloodthirsty, wild in a way that sets my body off. His eyes drop to my lips telling me what's coming the second before he dips his head.

This kiss isn't just sweet and isn't just possessive. There's a desperate, dark, and feral taste to it that makes me as light-headed as taking a shot of whiskey.

When he pulls back, I'm breathing hard, all thoughts erased save one: I crave this man in a way that's completely unnatural. Maybe even unstable.

He leaves me standing, still unsteady on my feet after that kiss, and turns and grabs our things before slamming the door of his truck shut. Slinging an arm around my shoulders, he walks me toward his portable office building, raising a hand to greet a few of his guys who are standing by their cars, pulling off their vests to go home for the night. We've made a habit of evening filing so they don't even give us a second glance when I give them a quick wave and a smile. Suddenly, before I'm quite ready, he's swinging the office door open.

Angelo's father sits inside at his son's desk, wearing a button-up shirt much like his son's. Style-wise, they seem similar. But their appearances couldn't be more different. His dad is pale and with his gray hair and black shirt, could almost look like a black-and-white film character. But when he stands and smiles, holding out his arms to both of us, he emanates a warmth that's more genuine than I've ever felt from my mother.

"Hey kids. Rose, it's a delight to meet you. I can see my son is definitely the lucky one."

"I am." Angelo's husky response makes me light up as I try not to trip over my feet and make a fool of myself as I step forward to shake his father's hand.

I'm pulled into a hug instead, a hard fast hug followed by a quick peck to the cheek before Mr. Walker steps back with a mischievous smile. He gives Angelo a full hug too before clapping him on the shoulder and saying, "Enjoy tonight. And remember, the couple who flays together stays together."

"Dad. Don't," Angelo threatens.

Mr. Walker just gives a big grin, almost as if this whole thing has him giddy. "Car's out back. Go on. Have a great date night."

I giggle and swallow the manic laugh that wants to erupt afterward. *Calm down,* I scold myself, trying to focus on my breathing.

Angelo just shakes his head and glares as he puts his arm back around me and leads me to a door on the opposite side of the portable. We walk down a ramp to a beat-up old four-door sedan that's missing a license plate.

"Jacket on," he instructs, tossing it to me, before grabbing a set of gloves out of the duffel. Tossing the bag in the back seat, he slides on the black gloves before opening the door for me. "Your chariot."

"Thank you, kind sir." He winks before hustling around the front of the car and getting in on the driver's side.

"I think it goes without saying, but don't touch anything." He motions to the dash, which is so old it still has a tape deck in the radio section.

"Got it." I want to say his Dad is funny. I want to tell him about how I've got butterflies in my stomach over this whole thing, and how strange that is because you're only supposed to get butterflies for good things. But Angelo's face is set in concentration as he navigates us through back roads without street cameras and drives us out of town. So, instead of talking, I play with the lining of my jacket, wiggle my toes inside my shoes, and try not to bounce my leg annoyingly.

I sink into my own body and try not to let thoughts of the future or the past overtake me, to just live in this moment. And, before I know it, an hour has passed and he's pulling onto a road in the middle of nowhere, parking, and helping me out so we can walk the last leg of our journey.

"Here goes nothing," I finally whisper, under my breath as we walk hand-in-hand and I drink in our surroundings.

The desert air is unusually warm tonight, as if Hell is fully aware of what we're doing and its flames are seeping up around us in support. I regret the jacket, but it's a minor regret in the scheme of things. I still don't feel regret for what we're about to do, which makes me wonder if I'm an undiagnosed psychopath.

Meanwhile, the moon is nearly full and it's easy to see we're traveling along a walking path worn between scrub brush and low pines. A coyote calls in the distance. But otherwise, we're so alone out in this vast wilderness that I can see all the stars. The light pollution of the city smudges the horizon but doesn't encroach over the mesa we passed on our drive. Out here, there's nothing but calm.

For now.

We come around a low, squat pine tree and a dilapidated, abandoned gas station greets my eyes. The single-story cinder block building has peeling white paint and orange slogans interrupted by wooden panels covering the windows. "Get your kicks … " and "Ice Cold … " are pale relics of once-vibrant paint. The gas pumps out front are covered in rust, though two are missing. *Who would want to take a gas pump?* I wonder as we traipse around the side of the building.

A junky, old, white van is parked at the rear—it's ugly enough to fit in with its surroundings and looks like it was abandoned the same year as the station—but Mint sits behind the wheel, chewing on a toothpick.

The sight of him makes everything more real.

When he spots us, he swings open the front door and the hinges creak loudly, though the pulse pounding in my ears is just as harsh. This is actually happening. No turning back. I'm part of a crime now. He kidnapped those boys and I'm here. I've crossed the line.

God, I should be terrified. But whatever shattered inside of me that night must have also tipped over my ethics and made that fragile value system smash to pieces. Those butterflies in my stomach flutter their wings.

Mint slams his door shut and the moon slides blue light over his bald head as he gives Angelo and me a single downward nod of respect before saying, "They're inside." He pockets his toothpick and I realize that it's probably so he doesn't leave any DNA evidence here at the scene.

"Good. Give you any trouble?" Angelo asks.

"One kicks like a mule," he replies as my boyfriend sets down his duffel.

We all watch as he unzips it, still addressing his acquaintance. "They see you?"

Mint snorts derisively. "This isn't my first rodeo."

Angelo gives him a smirk before passing out balaclavas. "Well, just in case."

We slide on the headgear and immediately, the heat rises to a stifling level. My fingers flex as they come down from the hood, needing something to do, to hold, to mangle to expel this extra energy flowing through my veins. A second later, a small black voice modulator is handed to me and I take out my stress on it, squeezing the little square speaker over and over.

"Test," Angelo's voice comes through his speaker—warped by the machine so that it's low and mechanical.

"Testing," Mint replies, his voice altered the same way so that the two of them are nearly indistinguishable.

"Test," I reply, speaking into the miniature microphone attached to the speaker. My voice doesn't pitch quite as low as theirs and the difference is noticeable. "I'll try not to talk," I offer.

"It's fine, just stay back so they can't hear your real voice instead of the speaker," Angelo warns me as he lifts the duffel.

I nod. Stay back is my rule for the night. I'm allowed to be here. I'm allowed to watch. I was allowed to help him plan every detail of this event, but Angelo doesn't want me to get close enough to touch.

"I don't want their fingertips staining your skin," he'd murmured last night before kissing my neck and securing my promise to adhere to his rules. I don't ever want those fuckers touching me again, so I had no qualms about agreeing.

Mint breaks our circle first and heads over to a beat-up old door at the rear of the station. I only notice the gloves he's wearing when he opens it for us like a bouncer and gestures for us to enter. *Tonight's exclusive club is only open for special guests.* My giddy mind makes terrible, cringeworthy jokes that I swallow down as I peer inside.

A construction light on a tripod is the only thing breaking up the darkness. It shines like a spotlight on two men, torsos wrapped in rope, who dangle from massive pulleys set into the ceiling. Heads covered in hoods so they can't see us, I hear one of them cursing quietly. The second one's shoulders are jerking, as if he's trying to free himself from his bindings.

Angelo's voice comes as a shock when it cuts through the darkness, robotic and harsh. "I wouldn't do that."

"Fuck you," one of the hooded men shouts. So they aren't gagged.

We'd discussed it, but Angelo said it would be better to measure their terror by their screams. Then we'd know how effective part one of the plan was.

I belong in a mental institution for being okay with this.

Angelo drops the duffel, the sound immediately making both men stiffen. "You've dishonored the brothers of Alpha Tau. Tonight you'll pay for your crimes."

Both guys immediately start spluttering out excuses, polluting the air with nonsense and making me roll my eyes.

They seriously believe their fraternity brothers would kidnap and bind them and drive them out of town? Fucking fools. But fine. All the better for us if they actually buy this bullshit.

I ignore their idiotic outbursts, following Angelo's lead. He pays them no mind as he pulls a bat from his bag before he glances over at Mint and gives him a nod.

The big, bald man shuffles over to the light and turns it slightly to the right, revealing a fifty-pound animal feed bag strung up on a rope about ten feet to the side of the frat boys. Then he walks across the room and I see him grab the rope strung through the pulley holding up the bag. Turning his modulator to another setting, he gives a thumbs up to Angelo, who speaks.

"I'm going to number you. And then one of your brothers is going to pick a number. You'd better hope it's not yours." Using the end of the bat, he roughly punches the guy closest to me in the gut. "One." The guy gives out a horrid, ragged gasp as his diaphragm contracts and he swings through the air like a limp puppet.

My boyfriend takes a step over and punches the second guy the same way, calling out, "Two." The guy flops like a fish and ends up landing a wild kick to Angelo's face.

I suck in a worried breath and take a step forward but Angelo and Mint both hold up their hands to keep me back, so I stop, frozen, but concerned.

Acting as if nothing happened and like the kick doesn't even hurt, Angelo moves over to the feed bag. He shoves the bat into it, calling out, "Three!"

After that, Angelo turns to me expectantly, the lines we practiced the last few nights dancing like sugarplums in my addled, frenzied brain. Adrenaline has me staring at him, hardly able to hear as he asks the question I'm already expecting. "Brother, what number do you choose?"

"Three," I tuck my chin in and speak carefully into the voice changer.

"Three." Angelo slowly repeats my words, letting it sink into the guys that they haven't been picked, waiting for their limbs to go limp in relief. As soon as they've calmed, he states, "Let's find out if you have candy inside when I break you open." Then he steps back, takes up a batting position, and whacks the feedbag with all his strength as if it's a piñata.

Mint—voice still altered by the voice-changer but not mechanical sounding anymore—gives a screech that makes the hair on the back of my neck stand up.

"Fuck, man. That's too much. Whatever we did—that's too much. You're gonna kill him!" Frat boy number one calls out, his tone a panicked, nasal whine.

"You don't even know why you're here? You haven't figured it out?" Angelo queries before he swings the bat again and gives the bag a solid thunk, making it swing through the air. Mint sucks in a gasping breath and gives off a pathetic moan as he expertly maneuvers the rope so that the feed bag doesn't accidentally hit guy number two.

"None of you? No guesses as to what could ruin our frat's reputation? Get us kicked off campus? Our name splashed all over the news?" He waits, letting the silence grow heavy and thick with expectation as the two guys try to think through the haze of their panic.

Minutes pass.

"That girl," Number two says quietly. Finally.

My blood boils at the fact that I'm just *that girl* to them. Someone nameless. Passing. I'm furious that it took them so long to figure out which crime was so horrific that it deserves this sort of punishment, that I'm not seared into their brains the way they are in mine. I should haunt their thoughts. I should be branded into their skulls. They should have trouble sleeping on a bed with someone they love. They should *suffer* … they should suffer all of that and more for what they did.

All my life, I've held in hatred. I've turned loathing inward. Blamed myself for things that others did. But now, staring at them, it's as if a dam inside of me has burst and all those years of hatred come flooding out.

I wish I hadn't promised to stay back. I wish the bat was in my hands.

Fuck it.

265

I break my promise and quickly stride over to Angelo, holding out my hand. He stares at me for a long second, before relinquishing the bat and taking a step back.

"When you treat people like objects, you're going to get the same done to you," Angelo warns.

I hardly hear him. The hatred inside is so intense, it can't be contained. It bursts out when I hit the bag for the first time, awareness zinging up my arms all the way to my clenched jaw. But the hit feels good, and the terrified pleading of the fuckers beside me feels even better.

I swing again. And again. Hitting with all of my strength, not counting my strokes, not listening to Mint's fake screams, but relishing the sounds of the two suspended men begging me to stop while I ignore them, just like they ignored me.

I am fury made flesh.

I hit until my arms burn and my fingers ache where they grip the bat. I hit until I realize my jaw is starting to lock up and my hip hurts from twisting. I hit until the anger pouring out of me lessens to a trickle.

I'm breathing hard when I stop, the bat falling limp in my hand.

Angelo dashes forward to scoop me into his arms and pull me away from the swinging feed bag and carefully pries the bat from my fingers. Mint lets the bag fall to the ground with a thump, as though a body is hitting the floor.

I watch in grim satisfaction over Angelo's shoulders as the dangling boys curl inward as much as their bindings will allow. Their shoulders rise nearly to their ears as they anticipate what's coming next.

They think the same is going to happen to them.

Good.

Bastardos.

I want this night to be a horror for them. I want them to second-guess themselves for years to come. I hope they can never walk into a bar showing a baseball game ever again. I hope they can't throw a ball to their future sons—if they have any. I hope their triggers are everywhere and they have to walk quickly, eyes cast down, so they aren't chased by their personal demons.

I draw in a slow, deep breath and realize that fear has a scent. It's urine mixed with a strange sour sweat that's worse than a male locker room. It's got a darker undertone, I'm discovering—with a warped sort of pleasure.

I smile up at Angelo, though I'm certain he can't see my expression in the dark with my balaclava on. But his gloved hand comes up to cup my covered cheek and I know he knows—the same way I know he's smiling back down at me.

We share a moment until I take a step back and nod, signaling for him to proceed, because this night isn't over yet.

"Your turn," Angelo's mechanical voice comments.

"Look man, Nick already had her in there—" Number one starts making excuses for himself.

"Save it. Unless you want the same treatment *he* just got." That makes Number one seal his stupid lips.

"Let them down," Angelo instructs Mint before he walks over to the duffel.

As Mint turns back on his voice-changer and then lowers the two men carefully, so that just their tiptoes touch the ground, Angelo digs through the bag and retrieves three objects, objects he had me carefully select earlier this week.

I watch him as I try to catch my breath and slow my racing heart.

He's so calm and collected and sexily sure of himself as he says, "You're going to get to choose an item. You won't know what it's for until after you've chosen. Choose wisely."

My heart hammers at my chest as Mint unfurls some of the rope surrounding Number one's hands. Angelo snatches the guy's right hand and drags each item across his palm: sandpaper, a cheese grater, and garden shears. "Choose. Item one, two, or three," he orders.

"One," Number one's choice is exactly what we predicted it would be and I have to bite down on the chuckle that threatens to spill from my lips. Like rats in a maze, turning exactly where we want them to go.

Angelo turns and stares at me and it's as if I can hear what he's thinking, our connection a strong vibration through the air. *Pathetically predictable, aren't they?*

I nod, because they are. They've done exactly as Angelo suspected they would this entire time. I'm not saying he's an evil genius … but I'm not saying he's not either.

Angelo hands over the sandpaper and steps back, ordering, "Hands up and stay still unless you want us to take the bat to you."

Number one freezes instantly, clutching the sandpaper tight —he might even be holding his breath. It's fascinating what terror will do to a person.

Mint's hands reach around Number one's waist and quickly yank down his pants.

"Ten strokes with item one on your dick," Angelo orders.

The blubbering cries that come from underneath the hood are music to my ears. A wide smile stretches across my face as I become someone I never knew I could be but relish having become—a vengeful bitch.

Guy two is already trembling when Mint unties his hands. "What did you do to him?" the second frat boy demands.

"Shut up!" Angelo barks—the mechanics hiding his tone but not the volume of his words, which seem to bounce off the walls. "Choose an item."

Of course, Number two chooses the cheese grater over the garden shears, thinking it's the lesser evil. When Mint strips his pants off, he shrieks.

Angelo then calmly lays out the rules. "Ten strokes on your ass. Each one better shave skin or it doesn't count. When you both have finished your strokes, you get to go home."

Then my boyfriend walks back to me and we link hands as we watch my rapists defile their own bodies.

Afterward, we step back out into the night with Mint, who'll clean up and drop the bastards back on the campus.

The moon is bright and pretty overhead and the night has cooled down quite a bit—either that or the relief from pulling off my balaclava makes the air feel refreshing.

When I turn, I gasp because Angelo's just pulled off his own face covering. He's got a bruise forming on his cheek where that fucker kicked him and his lip is split open. I quickly stride over and cup the side of his cheek, gazing up at him in concern. "Are you okay?"

"Are you?" His brow furrows in concern, eyes studying me.

I nod.

I'm perfect.

"Then I'm great," he murmurs before leaning down to give me a peck on the lips that makes my heart shine brighter than all the stars in the sky.

When he pulls back, he swipes his knuckles across his bleeding lip. Violence has never looked so beautiful.

ROSE

Two Weeks Later

We stand in the tall foyer of a southwestern-style house with archways leading off in three different directions. Some floral plug-in scent fills the space, which is decorated with all of the knick-knacks and accoutrements of a typical grandma's house. Still, though, afternoon light pours in through the windows and the place is beautiful.

I can't believe we're looking at houses together—Angelo and me.

I mean, I agreed to it. I'm here. But still, most days I feel like I'm floating in a dream.

I glance over at him, at his dark hair and the tattoos curling up his neck, at those lips that I can't get enough of. Even in just a t-shirt and jeans, he's so delicious I can hardly stand it. *God, I adore this man.*

He glances down at me and smirks as the realtor's heels click on the tile floor in front of us, completely unaware of the eye fucking going on right behind her.

"This house is an estate sale, so I think you can get a good deal if you like it. It has two bedrooms and two bathrooms, along with—"

"Can you give us a minute?" Angelo asks her.

She turns quickly. She's a new-to-us agent and this is our first showing with her. Worry crosses her features as she spends a second wondering if this house was a mistake before she blinks her false lashes rapidly.

"Of course." Her smile is as fake as my mother's.

"We'd like to feel out the space ourselves first," he declares, gaze not on the space, but burning into me, running down my skin like lava.

Oh, yes.

I like this idea.

As she pulls open the front door, he leans down and whispers to me, "I'm going to give you to the count of three—"

I'm off like a shot, giggling as I race haphazardly into the first room. It's a dining room with a Mission-style table and chair set. I could try to hold him off here, racing in circles around the table but he's leaped the dining table to get to me before. That's how we scandalized and lost our last agent. So I keep running. I go past a kitchen that has a stove with coil burners that I don't think anyone's used since the Cold War.

Angelo's heavy stomps sound behind me. He never starts off running. He likes to build up the anticipation. And, oh, does he. This is our third house tour. The third space we've violated by fucking hard and quick up against a wall, over someone else's dining table ... this new game is quickly becoming a new obsession for both of us.

Where should I let him catch me today?

A quick flash and I'm past a lime green bathroom. I bypass a bedroom and hurry down the hall. But when I come to the master bedroom, I stop short. The room is absolutely gorgeous. One wall has old adobe bricks along it while the other walls are smooth plaster. The bed faces a set of French doors that look out onto a patio where a small fountain with fluttering birds carved in it sits. The bed itself is an old-fashioned four-poster bed, a colorful quilt carefully laid on top. It's beautiful and something about it just tugs at my heart. I can instantly imagine a cushy chair on one side of the French doors, myself curled up on it, a book in my hand, listening to that fountain as I read.

Angelo nearly bowls me over, grabbing onto my shoulders as he stops himself. Once his feet are planted, he turns me to face him.

I've never stopped running before.

"Rose ... ?" he trails off as his umber eyes study me, trying to interpret the tears filling my gaze.

I'm still trying to interpret them myself ... until I realize, this is it.

Our home.

Our room.

Our bed.

The start of our life together.

Overwhelmed by a billowing sense of rightness, I reach up and slide my fingers around the back of his neck. And then I kiss him. Slow and soft, with all the hero worship and gratitude I have for him pouring out through my lips.

When I pull away, his expression is so soft and adoring that something inside of me unlocks. Some part of me that I didn't even realize was closed off unfurls, opens like a bloom.

I stare up at him for a second before lowering my arms from his neck and taking a step back. Releasing a breath, I slowly pull down the straps of my flower-print maxi dress. I let the top slide down to my waist before I push it down the rest of the way and kick it aside. I'm not wearing a bra today, just the way he likes.

His eyes immediately dilate, but he doesn't move toward me. Always, always so conscious of my needs. Instead, I step toward him and brush my pebbled nipples over his shirt as I reach up and steal another soft kiss.

"I want to try," I tell him. "But can I be on top?"

"Anything you want. Always," he intones.

Slowly, I drag his shirt up over his washboard abs, his pecs, his head. I pull it off and give myself a moment to trace his tattoos as I mentally check to ensure that I'm okay. But I don't feel panic corkscrewing through my belly. There's only a needy anticipation and a gentle sort of peace.

I've got my person. And now I've found my place.

I undo his pants and slide them down, letting my lips ghost over his hardness as I undress him.

When I straighten and point to the pillows, he instantly goes, laying in the middle of the comforter. I let myself study him then, from the bottoms of his feet to the top of his head, where his hair has started to grow out a bit, getting shaggy and easier to tug on. The perfect, sculpted body is beautiful, but these days—I see so much more than that.

And today, for a split-second, I glimpse something when I stare at him ringed in afternoon light.

Not something real. Something ephemeral and fantastic.

Maybe heaven doesn't exist and Angelo's right about that.

But that doesn't mean angels don't walk among us.

I know I've found mine.

And he's not some sweet, harp-stringing golden-haired romantic.

He's a warrior.

He's my guardian.

My everything.

Emotion drags thankful tears from my eyes as I slide down my panties and climb onto the bed. Straddling Angelo, who reaches to brush away my tears, I smile.

"You're crying. We can—"

"Happy tears," I correct him, smiling while I try to internally reconcile this revelation with everything else I'm feeling, every shade of adoration, every color of lust. It's too much to process, too much to feel all at once. I can't think through it. I just have to release it. And so I pour all of my desire into each kiss and touch I give him. I focus on that and nothing else.

Brushing over his body with my own, I tease his lips with mine until he's moaning against my mouth. Then I sit back and reach behind me to stroke his hardness as his lips follow me up and he latches onto my breast.

The sensation makes me pant until greed takes over and I use my free hand to direct him to the other side while I grind against his stomach. He gladly switches, flicking his tongue with a motion he knows drives me mad as his fingers come up between my spread thighs and trace over my opening.

I end up grinding sideways to get to his finger, squeezing his length hard to punish him when he tries to slide those hands away. He relents and I rock against him until sparkles start to form behind my eyes.

Right as I'm about to combust, I wrench back from his hand and guide him into me. The hard heat of his length makes me shudder and I writhe against him, grinding down and getting him deeper as I use his body to shamelessly plunge over that edge into bliss.

I fall forward onto him, panting, my cheek just below his neck, listening to his racing heart.

A minute later, when the limpness has left my limbs, I push up onto his chest and stare down at him. "I did it," I find my throat tight as I say the words aloud. "We're in a bed."

A tear slips from one of his own eyes as he nods silently.

I lean forward and swipe it away with one of my fingers, hating that my pain is his pain but loving that my triumph is also his triumph. "Hey. No crying. It's your turn now."

He shakes his head. "No. No. Fuck that." He quickly slides out from under me and stands up, glancing around for his clothes.

Confusion furrows my brow as I stare up at him. "Did you seriously just say no to an orgasm?"

"I'm not doing anything that's going to ruin your progress. We can go fuck in the bathroom or outside with you bent over that fountain," he replies as he quickly tosses everything back on at warp speed. "You stay there and see if you can make yourself come," he orders, pointing at me. "I'm going to go tell the realtor that we're making a cash offer, no inspection, fifty grand over asking, but they have to give us that ugly-ass goddamned abuela bed."

And as my soulmate walks out the door of our new bedroom, I burst into full-fledged happy sobs.

ONE WEEK LATER

MOVING IN TOGETHER WAS DECEIVINGLY, blissfully easy, though the kitchen renovations have been annoying as hell. Who wants to wash dishes in a bathtub because there is no sink? First-world problems.

Other than bending over the tub and having dishwashing turn into a doggie-style session that makes my knees ache because my boyfriend can't stand seeing me bent over without getting naughty, my life has no real complaints.

I'm going to work as Angelo's secretary over the summer and save up some money for tuition. So long as I keep my grades up, I'll be able to qualify for the in-state scholarship and I should be able to keep going to school and majoring in what I want.

Quique just got our massive, obnoxious, penis-shaped apology balloon arch delivered yesterday. We'd had the delivery people set it up over the front door so he'd see it first thing when he got home. He'd texted us tons of photos of himself posing in front of it as my mother hurried around in the background, wielding a pair of scissors and popping all the phallic balloons before the neighbors saw.

Needless to say, the prank means we've been forgiven.

Mom will probably take a few more decades, but it is what it is. If she can't handle having a daughter instead of a puppet, she doesn't deserve one. That's what I keep telling myself.

Otherwise, everything is absolutely perfect. Well, except for the fact that I'm not quite the same anymore. I always used to think of myself as a good girl, a rule follower, a kind person. I know that's not true anymore. I've awakened a streak of cruelty within myself. And I have absolutely zero clue what to do about it.

I've tried going to one of those rage rooms, the places where you rent a sledgehammer and pay to smash random stuff to smithereens? I dragged Daisy there with me two days ago.

But it hasn't curbed the itch inside of me. And so, I decide I need to talk about it, particularly after I wake up from a nap full of fighting dreams where I punch and kick an unknown assailant. My eyes open to find Angelo sitting next to me on top of the covers, casually scrolling through his tablet. I stretch, realizing I fell asleep fully clothed, phone still in my pocket, before I nuzzle into him, shoving back my bedhead as I ask, "Can I tell you a secret?"

Those huge lips of his purse before he sets aside his tablet, deciding this conversation must be serious. "You can tell me anything."

"I'm a little bit sad ... for the stupidest reason ever." I shake my head, embarrassed to even admit it. But Angelo puts an index finger underneath my chin and raises my gaze to his.

"What is it?" he asks softly, those eyes of his as irresistible as chocolate.

"I'm sad that the Alpha Tau guys—that it's over, I guess." My face burns even admitting that much, though it shouldn't. This is Angelo. He knows every inch of my body and every inch of my soul.

"You want me to punish them more?" his tone immediately gets aggressive.

"No! Not really. They got what they deserved. I heard Nick dropped out of school and the other two left the frat, or that's what Mint said, at least." I shrug, because that was what the last text from the giant bald man had told me, right before he recommended I read *On a Night of a Thousand Stars*. "I guess ... I just ... God, I feel like a terrible person," I whimper, sitting up in bed and wringing my hands.

"What are you trying to say, Rose?"

I have to close my eyes, and out of habit, my face tilts toward the covers. I feel like I'm kneeling in a confessional as I whisper, "I keep dreaming about more. Thinking about more ... violence."

Shameful.

Insane.

I'm horrible.

These are the thoughts of a crazy person, aren't they?

But a second later, Angelo's arms are around me and he's dragging me out of the bed, where he still refuses to be intimate if I don't initiate. He carries me across the room and pins me against the cold wall with his hips. And then he's kissing me, brutally. Savagely.

When he breaks the kiss, he ghosts those amazing lips over my chin before whispering, "God, you're perfect."

"What?" I laugh brokenly as his lips slip to my racing pulse. I'm the opposite of perfect, I'm messed up. Either I lash out at myself or I want to lash out at someone else. And now, I don't even need a reason, apparently.

But Angelo's lips leave my neck and he straightens as his hands come to the wall on either side of my shoulders. "In my world, Rosie, there's always someone who needs to be punished. I love your innocence. But if you crave more darkness, then just say the word."

I suck in a breath and I'm terrified to acknowledge how my nipples tighten at his words. "Really?"

His head tilts and he gives a single nod. "You remember Mint?"

"Of course."

"Someone framed him for murder."

I suck in a breath. "They did?"

He bobbles his head from side to side as he clarifies, "Don't get me wrong. He's not innocent. But they helped him do it and then set him up to take the fall." His finger comes up to trace the side of my face, gently swooping over my cheekbone. "And guess what? My father just had the fucker dragged back up from Mexico."

My eyebrows waggle with a silliness that's completely inappropriate for the situation—but one I feel nonetheless. "Does he need help?"

Angelo groans as he presses his hardness against me. Once, twice, three times. "I'll make sure it happens," he promises.

I'm about to kiss him again when my phone buzzes in my pocket. I grab it, planning to toss it over onto the bed but I see that Violet is calling.

We always text; we never call first, unless it's an emergency. *Crap.* I swipe to answer immediately. "Hello?"

"Have you heard from Lily?" Violet asks. "I haven't been able to get ahold of her for the past three days."

"No," I say, immediately holding up a hand to pause Angelo from bending to kiss my neck. "She didn't stay with me this week. I thought she was staying with you?"

Violet sniffles, obviously crying. "She didn't stay with anyone. I already talked to Daisy. Last time I talked to her, Lily said she just wanted to be home. Said she was over being silly and paranoid over nothing."

My hand flies to my mouth and covers a gasp as my pulse hammers. I'm almost too scared to ask my next question. "Have you checked her apartment?"

"Yeah. I'm here right now. She's not. But her place is all messed up." Violet's voice grows thick. "And not the way she leaves it. It's not just messy. It looks ransacked."

My stomach drops out as I hesitantly ask, "Do you think she was right? Do you think … *her stalker's back?*"

Violet's voice is as as sharp and painful as an icepick when she says, "Yeah. I think he took her."

AFTERWORD

Lily's story will be next in the series. Join my email list or Facebook group for updates about that book and all my others!

I hope I made your day just a little bit naughtier and more exciting. Thank you from the bottom of my heart for supporting my dream of corrupting minds like yours with book boyfriends who are better than reality.

If you need more dark romance, check out my Feral Princess series. It is an omegaverse shifter story with dub-con and tons of heat.

Please consider reviewing this lil read before you go. I'd really appreciate it!

Kisses,

Ann

ACKNOWLEDGMENTS

To the hubby who inspires me and helps me format every single one of these suckers, thank you. I'd never have written without your support.

Thanks to RK and Ivy for being the best friends ever and being my safe space for my chaos. Thank you to Tati for letting me borrow your name and your eyes to make sure I got this one right. Thank you Lori for word-smithing me up to sound better than before. Thanks to Sylvia at Book Brander Boutique for the beautiful cover.

And thank you to all my readers who trust me to give you a good experience even when I genre hop. You're an amazing group and I'm so happy to have found you.

ALSO BY ANN DENTON

Choose from books on the following pages based on your current reading mood.

The standalone or the first book in each series are listed by mood. The darkest reads appear first and grow progressively more light-hearted so it makes it easy to find just what you're looking for next. I also tried to add some basic mood info at the bottom of each series page for you.

FERAL PRINCESS SERIES
(Completed Trilogy)

A hot, dark shifter omegaverse with dub con, a steamy alpha, a loving beta, and a sassy omega who thought she was going to be an alpha female. She was sooo wrong, but when she's claimed by the pack alpha, make no mistake, she has something to say about it.

Defiant - Book 1

Mood - #DARK #DIRTY #ALPHA

TANGLED CROWNS SERIES
(Completed Trilogy and spinoff in progress)

A medium-burn, medieval fantasy romance with a reluctant princess, the knights she jilted at the alter, and an enemies to lovers story that weaves laughter and tears together along with a plot to save the kingdom. (Reverse Harem)

Knightfall - Book 1

Mood - #BANTER #REDEMPTION
#WHAATJUSTHAPPENED

Pinnacle Series
(Completed Duet)

A medium-burn paranormal romance about a girl who gets herself sent to a reform academy on purpose, so she can recruit criminally-minded guys to pull off the magical heist of the century. (Reverse Harem)

Magical Academy for Delinquents #MAD - Book 1

Mood - #BADASS #FUN #SEXY GAMES

Lotto Love Series
(Completed Duet)

A medium-burn, contemporary romantic comedy reverse harem about winning the lotto and doing whatever the hell you want with it, even if that means holding a Bachelorette-style competition for an entire harem of hotties.

Lotto Men - Book 1

Mood- #LOL #BLUSHING #NO WAY

RUBY - JEWELS CAFE SERIES
(Standalone)

A medium-burn, fated mates reverse harem with an angel on her last strike, some nerds and a tech demon determined to help her, and Christmas miracles.

Ruby

Mood - #SWEET #AWWW #GIGGLES

DARK TEMPTATIONS SERIES
(Incomplete)

A fast-burn monster reverse harem in an alternate reality
where monsters rule the earth. A human woman is captured
and auctioned off to the Four Terrors who will haunt her
nightmares and her dreams alike.
Cowrite with Katie May.

Ravaged by Monsters - Book 1

Mood - #DARK #FATED LOVE
#WILD SEXY TIMES

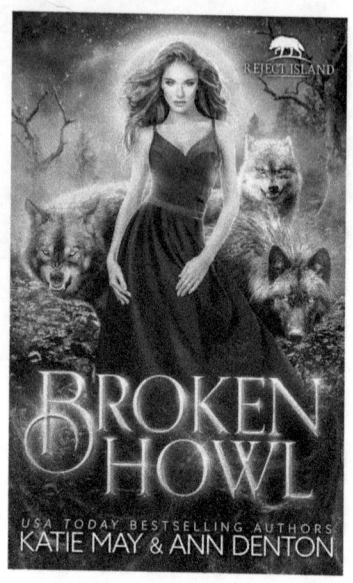

BROKEN HOWL
(Standalone)

A female omega rejects her mates so she can escape her abuser. She's sent to an island for rejects but her mates refuse to let her go...
Cowrite with Katie May.

Broken Howl

Mood - #CRYING #HEALING #FIGHTING

DARKEST QUEEN SERIES
(Incomplete)

The devil is a woman. And this is the story about she fell from Heaven only to rise as God's greatest enemy… (A reverse harem spinoff of the Darkest Flames series) Cowrite with Katie May.

For Whom the Bell Tolls - Book 1

Mood - #FURY #SOUL-DEEP CONNECTIONS #BATTLE OF WILLS

DARKEST FLAMES SERIES
(Completed Trilogy with a novella)

A medium-burn paranormal romance about a girl who tries a love spell on the hot guy at school and accidentally summons demons instead. It contains psychotic, alpha males, and student/teacher relationships. (Reverse Harem) Cowrite with Katie May.

Demon Kissed - Book 1

Mood - #OOPS #NAUGHTY LAUGHTER #FORBIDDEN HEAT

DEMON'S JOY
(Standalone)

Santa's daughter has to save Christmas from demons! And all she's got to help her are five funny reindeer. (A reverse harem spinoff of the Darkest Flames series)
Cowrite with Katie May.

Demon's Joy

Mood - #SILLY #HOLIDAY CHEER #YUM

MAGE SHIFTER WAR SERIES
(Completed Duet)

A medium-burn paranormal mafia romance. A fae princess is taken captive by three shifter criminals. (Reverse Harem) Cowritten with Elle Middaugh.

Fae Captive - Book 1

Mood - #BONNIE&CLYDE #BADASS #HOT

HAMMER TIME
(Standalone)

A medium-burn paranormal comedy featuring Thor's daughter and a quest to save demigods from prison. Expect lots of ancient deities and potty humor. (Reverse Harem) Cowritten with M.J. Marstens.

Hammer Time

Mood- #PUNTASTIC #NOYOUDIDN'T #SNORT

CONNECT AND GET SNEAK PEEKS

Do you want to read exclusive point of views from different characters, make predictions and claim your book boyfriends with other readers, see my inspiration for these books, and hang with fellow romance lovers? Then join my Facebook Reader Group! I promise you'll love it!

Join Ann Denton's Reader Group

Facebook.com/groups/AnnDentonReaderGroup

ABOUT ME

I'm a shy lady who has always been obsessed with reading, travel, and live theater. I've lived in five states and currently reside in Maryland.

I have two of the world's cutest children, a crazy dog who licks the fridge obsessively, and an amazing husband who is my total opposite, meaning he actually loves talking to people in real life.